What people are saying

Leav

"Kate Lloyd explores familial bonds in this warm and moving novel. She deftly captures the complicated relationships between mothers and daughters, exploring both expectations and disappointments. This talented and capable writer will leave you wanting more."

Suzanne Woods Fisher, author of the best-selling Lancaster County Secrets series

"A lovingly written tale of family, forgiveness, and redemption. Readers of Amish fiction will love every moment."

Hillary Manton Lodge, author of the Carol Award–finalist *Plain Jayne*

"In *Leaving Lancaster,* Kate Lloyd gives us a fascinating glimpse into a tightly knit Amish community—and the terrible impact a daughter's thoughtless rebellion has had on three generations of women. This novel is well crafted and compelling!"

Serena B. Miller, author of *Love Finds You in Sugarcreek, Ohio*

"In *Leaving Lancaster,* Kate Lloyd has penned an inspirational novel about a long-kept secret that threatens to destroy an entire

family. While the truth seems painful at first, Kate's beautiful story demonstrates how forgiveness can heal even the deepest of wounds."

Melanie Dobson, award-winning author of *Love Finds You in Amana, Iowa* and *The Silent Order*

Leaving Lancaster

Leaving Lancaster

~

A NOVEL

KATE LLOYD

David C Cook®
transforming lives together

LEAVING LANCASTER
Published by David C Cook
4050 Lee Vance View
Colorado Springs, CO 80918 U.S.A.

David C Cook Distribution Canada
55 Woodslee Avenue, Paris, Ontario, Canada N3L 3E5

David C Cook U.K., Kingsway Communications
Eastbourne, East Sussex BN23 6NT, England

The graphic circle C logo is a registered trademark of David C Cook.

The website addresses recommended throughout this book are offered as a
resource to you. These websites are not intended in any way to be or imply an
endorsement on the part of David C Cook, nor do we vouch for their content.

This story is a work of fiction. All characters and events are the product of the author's
imagination. Any resemblance to any person, living or dead, is coincidental.

With the exception of Ephesians 4, Genesis 2, and Philippians 4, Scripture
quotations are taken from the King James Version of the Bible. (Public Domain.)

Ephesians 4, Genesis 2, and Philippians 4 Scripture quotations are
taken from the New King James Version. Copyright © 1982 by
Thomas Nelson, Inc. Used by permission. All rights reserved.

LCCN 2011938728
ISBN 978-0-7814-0508-9
eISBN 978-1-4347-0472-6

© 2012 Kate Lloyd
The author is represented by MacGregor Literary.

"Great Is Thy Faithfulness" lyrics in chapter thirty-four written by Thomas
Chisholm in 1923, published in *The Complete Book of Hymns: Inspiring Stories
about 600 Hymns and Praise Songs* © 2006 William J. Petersen and Ardythe
Petersen, published by Tyndale House, ISBN 978-1-4143-0933-0

The Team: Don Pape, Jamie Chavez, Nick Lee, Renada Arens, Karen Athen
Cover Design: Amy Konyndyk
Cover Photo: Steve Gardner, Pixelworks Studios

Printed in the United States of America
First Edition 2012

4 5 6 7 8 9 10

121813

For my husband, Noel

Note to Readers

Thank you for adventuring with my fictional characters to Lancaster County, Pennsylvania, a glorious location near to my heart. Any resemblance to real members of the Amish or Mennonite communities is unintended. I ask your forgiveness for any inaccuracies.

To every thing there is a season, and a time
to every purpose under the heaven:
A time to be born, and a time to die; a time to plant,
and a time to pluck up that which is planted;
A time to kill, and a time to heal; a time to
break down, and a time to build up;
A time to weep, and a time to laugh; a time
to mourn, and a time to dance;
A time to cast away stones, and a time to gather stones together;
a time to embrace, and a time to refrain from embracing;
A time to get, and a time to lose; a time to
keep, and a time to cast away;
A time to rend, and a time to sew; a time to
keep silence, and a time to speak;
A time to love, and a time to hate; a time
of war, and a time of peace.

—Ecclesiastes 3:1–8

PROLOGUE

Anna Gingerich stood in the barnyard waving good-bye to four of her five sons as her neighbor Beth's minivan pulled away, transporting the men to the Lancaster railway station.

"Ach, why Montana?" Anna voiced her complaint aloud, though no one but the orange tabby and the Lord could hear her grumblings.

She shuffled around the side of the house for one last wave, but the van had already sped from view, leaving an empty hollow in its wake.

The oak trees across the way snagged Anna's attention. Clusters of leaves lay scattered on the ground, decomposing and mingling with the aroma of dew upon the greenest grass on earth. Did grass even grow in Montana? How would she walk barefoot during the summer? Were all of Montana's trees evergreens? How would she mark the changing seasons if the trees never shed their foliage?

Quit your griping, Anna admonished herself, and tried to be grateful for the help of her Mennonite neighbor, Beth. Though a gulf as wide as the Susquehanna River ran between the two women spiritually, over the last thirty years Beth had felt more like a daughter to Anna than Esther—her own flesh and blood she'd probably never set eyes on again.

Anna stuffed her hands in her apron pockets. Like a spinning wheel rewinding, she recalled her and her daughter Esther's final argument—more like a screaming match.

"I'm leavin' and you can't stop me," Esther had said, her nutmeg-brown hair out of its prayer cap—all *schtruwwlich,* streaming down her back in defiance. Esther stomped her foot. "It's my running around time—*Rumspringa.* I'm goin' ta see the world."

"*Nee!*" Anna had barred the doorway. "You're scarin' me. Wait 'til your dat gets home." No matter, though. Levi's meeting hadn't disbanded for hours, and by then Esther had slipped out of the house.

If only Anna had listened patiently instead of lashing out, Esther and her beau, Samuel Fisher, might not have severed their family roots that threaded deep into the Pennsylvania soil. They might have returned home, eventually become baptized, and gotten married instead of …

A rustling breeze lifted the hem of Anna's skirt.

Today, according to her sporadic letters, Esther lived an *Englisch* life and belonged to what she labeled a nondenominational church in Seattle.

"Meanin' what?" Anna said, and glanced around to make sure she was still alone. For sure, her daughter's church ignored the Ordnung and the ways of the People.

She watched her youngest son, Isaac, stride toward the barn, hours of work ahead of him. He'd already milked their two dozen Holsteins, but corn demanded harvesting, a fence in the back field was sagging, and a buggy wheel needed repairing. And the veterinarian would stop by later to evaluate Cookie's fetlock. The old mare's deterioration—Isaac called Cookie a nag—reminded Anna of herself.

Now that Anna was standing still, a vague dizziness visited her, spun her off-kilter. She leaned against a fence post for support. Over the last few years, she'd sought the opinion of several doctors, but had left their offices feeling brushed aside, discounted—because she was almost eighty. None was able to solve the mystery of her afflictions and forgetfulness other than citing her declining age. With dismissive words, they'd offered pain medication and antidepressants, but she'd refused.

She returned from the barnyard to mount the stairs leading to the kitchen. Had she remembered to put in the bread? Or even turn on the oven?

Her toe caught on the second step and she stumbled forward, landing on her knees and palms. Again, she was grateful for solitude; no one had seen her clumsiness.

She'd planned to put up tomatoes for most of the day. By herself. She was in no mood for chitchat. But how would Anna get the lids on tightly enough to seal them, let alone stand for hours on end in the kitchen? Her hands and shoulders ached as though they'd spent the night in the icebox. She might as well go back to bed.

It was moments like this she missed Levi the most. But he lived in heaven, at the feet of the Lord, she hoped. At rest. In peace. She'd come to accept his passing as God's will—what the bishop had suggested at his funeral.

Not that she didn't miss Esther, too. Every day.

Anna believed Esther's leaving had set her husband's death in motion. His buggy wouldn't have been on the road that night weeks later if word hadn't circulated throughout the community that Esther and Samuel were camped out in an *Englischer's* basement in New Holland, north of their farm. Her husband would have been home sitting in front of the fire recounting his day, and Anna would have been quilting.

In fact, the night he died, Esther and Samuel were clear across the country. Esther hadn't attended her father's funeral.

Anna knew she harbored resentment, for which she rebuked herself. God demanded forgiveness. Stewing over the past only bogged a person down. She prayed she'd truly risen above her bitterness and regret, and wished Samuel's mother felt the same way.

Anna entered the house, but instead of checking her bread, she sat at her writing desk to contact Esther one last time. Anna would spill the beans, tell her daughter the truth, admit how ill she was, and beg Esther to come home before the men sold the farm. But she knew Esther wouldn't.

If only Anna's elusive illness would consume her in one swoop this very afternoon and spare her the agony of leaving Lancaster County.

CHAPTER ONE

"Holly Samantha Fisher," Mom called from down in the shop. "Come talk to me."

When she summoned me by my whole name, it spelled trouble, so I grabbed my half-empty coffee mug and trotted down to the first floor like a good little girl, when in truth I was thirty-seven years old.

Clad in my bathrobe over pj's, my feet snuggled in suede moccasins, I stepped across the wooden floor into my mother's pride and joy, the Amish Shoppe. I found her in the living room—used as a showroom—on the easy chair, her knitting basket and handbag at her feet.

"Hey," I said. "Where've you been? When I got up, the house was empty."

"On an errand." She wore a charcoal-colored cardigan over a matching calf-length skirt that didn't flatter her figure. Three inches taller than me, she was plumpish in all the right places.

I perched on the straight-back bench near the gas fireplace and glanced out the front window to the buggy—minus the horse—glistening on the porch from a recent shower. Mom's customers' kids loved playing in the covered box-shaped carriage pulled by a make-believe spirited mare, as I had many times as a girl. If I closed my eyes, I could still imagine the clip-clopping sound.

The clock on the mantel chimed eight times. "I'd better get showered," I said, wishing I could tunnel back into bed. "I need to be out the door in thirty minutes."

Mom let out a breathy sigh. "First, we need to talk."

I didn't bite into her dangling carrot like I usually did, but let the words drift around the showroom. Every square inch of the house's first floor, except the kitchen, was crammed with handmade Amish products from Indiana and Ohio, all for sale: chairs and tables displaying jars of jams, apple butter, the best pickled beets, and chowchow. The walls were adorned with men's straw hats and women's bonnets of the plainest sort, aprons, and several patchwork quilts Mom had sewn herself.

The scent of baking raisins and molasses beckoned me to the kitchen. "Something smells yummy. You cooking bran muffins?"

"Yes, but they're not done."

I held up my mug. "I'll get us coffee."

"Hold still, girl of mine." Mom's mousy hair, graying at the temples, was tucked into its usual bun, but flyaway strands wisped loosely around her ears. "I need to tell you—I've got big trouble."

"To do with money?" I felt a throb at the bottom of my throat. "I apologize, I haven't chipped in enough on groceries and owe you three months' rent." Last year, I'd given up my apartment and was now camping out in my childhood room. "If only the stock market would turn around and our clients flock back." I felt like a botched NASA rocket launch, toppled on its side. Five, four, three, two, one—"I've been putting off telling you. Last week my boss gave me notice."

"I'm so very sorry, dear heart."

"After all the work I've put into building a new career, I could scream."

Her lips clamped together like clothespins. She looked pale. Washed out.

"Mom, did I miss something? You're in some kind of trouble?" My spine straightened. "Are you going out of business? Is the bank repossessing the house?"

"I wish it were that simple." Her hand wrapped the back of her neck. "There's an illness in the family."

"What family?" Then it hit me; she was describing herself. "Are you all right? Please tell me it's not cancer."

"My health is perfect."

"Are you sure you're okay?"

"I'm fine, darling."

"Is it Aunt Dori?" I was referring to Dorothy Mowan. Mom's best friend and her husband, Jim, were the closest we had to family.

Mom picked up her knitting needles and struggled with the olive-green yarn that echoed her eyes. "No, someone else. A blood relative."

"What are you talking about?"

With shaking hands, she yanked out several stitches—it wasn't like her to make a mistake. "My mother wrote me a letter."

"Grandma Anna?" I coughed a laugh, because Mom had to be pulling my leg. This early in the morning I didn't find her humor entertaining. "Did I hear you right? Grandma Anna's back from the grave?" I tilted my head and expected my mother to smile. But her stony expression remained fixed.

Her words sounded strangled. "I, I—don't know where to begin. You're going to hate me."

"Why would I do that? But I need to hustle. I'm running late for work."

"Promise to forgive me if I tell the truth?" Mom was big on the word *forgiveness,* even when the neighbor kid dented my car's fender and refused to pay for the damage.

"Yes, okay, I promise." I set my mug on a coaster on a side table. "I won't get mad."

Mom's eyes turned glassy, like she was holding back tears. I'd rarely seen her cry, only when she was chopping onions.

"I let you believe my mother passed on," she said. "I know it was wrong."

"You're kidding me, right?" Before I could demand more information, I saw a UPS truck swerve to a halt at the curb and a man jump out. Moments later, his knuckles rapped on the front door, then he jabbed the bell and turned the knob, but Mom didn't let the deliveryman in, nor did I rush upstairs to get dressed. My mother and I sat frozen in this surreal scene as we listened to his footsteps descend to the street and the truck depart.

"I should have told you years ago," she said. "My mother still lives on the family farm."

"I don't understand." My mind was doing somersaults. Nothing made sense.

As I scrutinized Mom's face—she never wore makeup—she lifted her chin and read the framed needlepoint of Romans 12:2

hanging on the wall, words cautioning believers not to conform to the world. Black thread on a white background, surrounded by a black frame. Black and white, like Mom. No cloudy areas, I'd always thought. Until now.

"Let me get this straight." I stroked my jawline as my mind explored the convoluted avenues. "The woman who gave birth to you—Grandma Anna Gingerich—is alive. But you told me she was dead, even though you knew I always wanted a grandmother?"

"Yes."

"Why on earth?"

"I was so young, I didn't know what to do. I thought it best."

"Well, neither of us is young anymore." My lungs gasped for air, as if I were sinking chin-deep in quicksand. Was our whole life a sham? If Grandma Anna were living, that meant my mother—the righteous woman who'd hammered the importance of integrity into me—was a liar. And she'd deprived me of what I wanted most in life: family.

A startling thought bombarded me. "How about my dad?" My voice turned shrill. "Is he still alive too?"

"No, darling. Samuel lost his life in Vietnam."

"If you have to be mixed up about something, couldn't it be about my father? I've secretly prayed he was a prisoner of war with amnesia who'll someday wander out of the jungle." A dream I'd never admitted before, even to Mom, because I was embarrassed to harbor such naive fantasies.

"I've had the same thought." She bundled her knitting project and tossed it into the basket like a dishrag. "But you know as well as I do, the army and Veterans Affairs swear there are no more POWs."

A familiar cloak of sadness as heavy as a lead apron draped itself across my narrow shoulders, making them slump forward, right when I should be marching off to work, even if my lofty dreams of becoming a financial advisor were crumbling.

With all the strength I could muster, I scuffled into the kitchen and poured myself fresh coffee. The muffins were in the oven and the clicking timer read five minutes. My appetite had vanished anyway. Who cared about food at a time like this? I'd always longed for siblings—a humongous family—but my father had died before I was born and my mother never remarried, so Mom and I were a twosome. All those years I'd asked about her parents—she could have told me the truth.

Returning to sit near her, I put my mug on the coaster. My stomach gurgled with a mixture of longing and confusion, like oil and water boiling on a stove top.

"How do you know Grandma Anna's alive?" I asked. There had to be a logical answer.

"She's contacted me many times."

"This is crazy. What are you talking about?" My hand swung out, colliding with my mug, splashing brown liquid onto the floor. I grabbed a Kleenex from my pocket to mop up the puddle, then decided to leave it. The mess was the least of my worries. "Mom, what are you trying to say? That your mother put you up for adoption and now she's tracked you down and wants to see you?"

"I wish it were that simple." Mom placed her handbag in her lap and opened it.

CHAPTER TWO

With trembling hands, Esther exhumed the envelope from her purse. Last night, Dori had called to tell her a letter had arrived. "Thanks, I'll come by first thing in the morning," Esther had said. No further discussion was necessary. Only Esther's mother, Anna, sent Esther's mail to Dori's address, where Esther had first lived after moving to Seattle. Dori and her husband never asked questions; they could probably tell by the feminine cursive writing and the postmark that the correspondence came from a woman in Lancaster County, Pennsylvania.

Under a drizzling sky, Esther had risen early to catch the Metro bus up the hill to Phinney Ridge. She'd found Dori lounging in a jogging suit, her short salt-and-pepper hair in need of a perm. Dori had invited Esther into her Victorian-style house, but on letter days—three or four times a year—Esther always refused.

Tucking the white envelope into her purse, Esther had wanted to savor the shape and texture of the paper before reading its contents. It was mid-October—too early for a Christmas card. And Esther's birthday was six months away.

Now, sitting in the living room, she told Holly, "This arrived from your grandmother yesterday." Esther had rehearsed the conversation with Holly for over thirty years, but the words came out clumsily, like peanut butter clogging her throat, her tongue swollen.

Holly gave her a quizzical look. Her petite frame barely filled her terry bathrobe; the legs of her pj's bagged at her ankles. "It's some kind of scam. You haven't sent this woman any money, have you?"

"My mother would never ask for money." Esther feared losing her nerve as she had every time before. If she didn't fess up now, the moment would be gone, like when the breeze blows away dried-up dandelion seeds—off they fly.

"I was ashamed to tell you. I meant to." She raised the envelope's flap, released the letter from its prison, and unfolded the stiff paper, bringing with it a trace scent of smoke from a wood fireplace and a memory of her mother's homemade biscuits.

Holly said, "I don't mean to be disrespectful, but I don't have time to play twenty questions." She dropped another square of Kleenex atop the spilled coffee and jolted to her feet.

"Yes, okay, but hold on." Esther studied her daughter's sleep-creased face, her mussed shoulder-length chestnut-brown hair, her hazel-brown eyes with flecks of amber that always made Esther think of the Pennsylvania sky at dusk—and Holly's father. How much should she tell her? The whole secret, like ripping off a bandage? Excruciating, but temporary pain.

"My mother—your Grandma Anna—says she desperately needs me." Esther felt a slam of guilt—more like a skewer straight into her chest. Her mother had probably needed her thousands of times, but

Esther had ignored her pleas. "Someone made an offer on the farm that my mamm can't afford to refuse. My brothers—I've got five of them, all younger than I am—are planning to move to Montana where farmland is more plentiful. But Mamm says she's sick and doesn't want to leave her home and neighbors."

Esther could see apprehension darkening Holly's face, arching an eyebrow and creasing her smooth forehead.

"Mom, you're talking gibberish. First a mother. Now five brothers? Are you sure you're not becoming—how shall I put it?—absentminded? Remember how you misplaced your keys last week?"

"Alzheimer's doesn't run in my family." Esther forced a chuckle, although she felt not a shred of happiness.

"You said you used drugs when you were a hippie in Haight-Ashbury."

Esther shook her head; her neck was stiff, her shoulders rigid. "I'm sorry I ever told you about my stupidity. I promise, by the time I was pregnant with you and then moved up here with Dori and Jim, I'd stopped using pot and alcohol altogether."

The corners of Holly's mouth angled down. "Wait a minute. You've never worn a wedding band. Were you and Dad even married?" Her voice flared out harshly, like when she was a rebellious teenager.

"Yes, in a chapel in San Francisco."

Holly slitted her eyes. "I've never seen pictures of the ceremony."

"That was our way. We didn't take photographs."

"Give me a break. Dori and Jim's house is full of family photos. And you have a snapshot of Dad upstairs on your bureau. But suddenly you have parents and a carload of brothers?"

"One parent. My father died a few months after I left home. But my mother is alive. When you were a wee baby, I considered bringing you home, back to the farm to be raised by her with my younger brothers." In the depths of postpartum depression and grief, Esther had planned to end her life, but she knew the Lord Almighty would never pardon her for abandoning Samuel's child.

Holly snapped her fingers. "You would have given me up, just like that?"

"No, no, I never would." Why had she mentioned her thoughts? Now she'd hurt Holly's feelings. "With Dori and Jim's help, I moved to Seattle and lived with them until you were born, and then several more years." Esther unbuttoned her cardigan to relieve the heat accumulating across her chest. She fanned her face with the envelope. "I thought when you were old enough to ask questions, it would be time to reveal the truth. But you never inquired about my past."

Pacing, Holly's hands moved to her hips. "Are you insinuating your secret life—if it exists—is my fault?"

"No, I'm to blame. For everything."

The timer binged. "I'll check the muffins." Holly cinched her bathrobe's belt and strode into the kitchen with her mug. Esther listened to the oven door open and close, and the muffin tin settling on the cooling rack.

Holly returned with a couple of paper towels and swabbed the remaining coffee off the floor.

"I should have told you years ago," Esther said, but Holly didn't answer. She tossed the soggy paper towels and Kleenex into a wastepaper basket and loped up the stairs.

Esther heard the shower running. She couldn't fault her daughter for being incensed. What young woman wouldn't be? Over the years, Dori had encouraged Esther to unveil the truth, but this was a mistake. She felt like unraveling her half-finished sweater and pulling the crinkled yarn out stitch by stitch in an attempt to untangle her past and start over.

One thing was for sure: She wouldn't admit her part in Samuel's death. Ever.

Esther pushed the back of her head against the velour-covered La-Z-Boy, closed her eyes, and summoned up Samuel's youthful face in vivid detail. On the day of his induction into the army, she'd run her fingers through his shaggy hair—the same color as Holly's—kissed his lips, and said good-bye to him for the last time. She'd never embraced another man since.

If she and Samuel had only returned home, as Esther's and Samuel's parents had demanded, Samuel would have been exempt from the draft. As a conscientious objector of the truest order, his nonviolent nature had been taught and nurtured since birth, imbedded in his DNA.

Her memories scrolling back to age fifteen, Esther recalled the resentment she'd harbored toward the non-Amish town kids. She'd rashly struck out when one of the boys knocked Samuel off his feet, his elbow gashed by the rubble at the side of the road. The boy knew Samuel wouldn't defend himself. At the sight of Samuel's blood, Esther's fist clobbered the kid's shoulder as if she'd been wrestling with her brothers all her life, though nothing could have been further from the truth. She'd also been instructed to turn the other cheek.

Hearing Holly's footsteps creaking overhead, Esther opened her eyes and scanned her mother's letter again. The last sentence reached out and seized her breath.

I'm begging you, come home.

Ten minutes later, Holly ambled down the stairs wearing a streamlined pantsuit and white blouse. She dug through her purse in what Esther figured was a ploy to get out the door without continuing their discussion.

"Please take a moment to read this." Esther rose to her feet and brandished the opened letter like a flag, but Holly made no move to take it.

She unscrewed a tube of lipstick and applied a mauve veneer across her full lips, then ran her tongue over her upper teeth. She finally gave the letter a cursory once-over. "No offense, Mom, but it looks like your handwriting, only a little neater. Are you sure you didn't write it?"

Esther inspected the note more closely. "I suppose our handwriting is similar. As a girl I wanted to be just like my mother. Until I turned fifteen. Then Mamm became a giant embarrassment."

Holly checked herself in the mirror and gave her hair a fluff, her soft curls framing her symmetrical face. "I guess we have that in common. When I was in high school, you drove me nuts." She grinned, the corners of her mouth perking up, but her eyes remained solemn, probing Esther's face, searching.

"I remember all too well," Esther said. So determined was Esther never to strike out like Dat had, she had repeatedly reigned in her anger and never even spanked Holly, no matter how ornery her daughter acted as a girl. "I was glad when we finally came to a truce," she said. Esther had dubbed Holly *Stormy*, but those tumultuous days passed when Holly graduated from college and then eventually moved back home. For the most part they got along splendidly. Until now.

"Please believe me." Esther stepped closer. "My mother—your Grandma Anna—sent this letter."

"I don't have the time or desire to read it." With a strident sweep of her hand, Holly zipped her purse shut and tucked it under her elbow, then grabbed hold of her briefcase. "Can you understand how shocked I am? It's like you want me to believe the earth is flat instead of round."

"Yes, of course. But—"

"Okay, Mom, for now I'll take you at your word. Your mother's alive and you want to visit her. By all means, do it. I've always thought it weird you never went back to Pennsylvania but figured you couldn't afford the trip."

"I can't go without you." Esther envisioned her childhood home, located in the outskirts of New Holland, north of Intercourse: the sprawling farmhouse, the barn, outbuildings, and two silos, the eighty acres of fields used for planting crops and grazing livestock. "For one thing, I've never ridden in a plane and I'm afraid of heights." She refolded the letter. "And who would run the shop?"

"I can't go with you, Mom. I need a new job. Just close the Amish Shoppe on the weekdays, and I'll open on Saturdays. Honestly, no one will care." Her brows pinched in the center, then lifted. "Or here's an idea. Aunt Dori can look after it. She's got plenty of extra time."

"But you must come with me to meet my mother and my brothers. And your father's parents. Maybe if they saw you, looking so much like their son—no, they'll never forgive me." Esther didn't blame Samuel's mother and father for holding her responsible for their son's demise. Over the years, Dori had tried to convince Esther not to feel guilty. Dori claimed the crazy era of flower power and war protests had lured Esther and Samuel away from the security of their Amish community; their rebellion was natural. But Esther couldn't accept that flimsy excuse. She felt like Lady Macbeth, blood staining her hands.

Samuel would have gladly remained in Lancaster County, gotten baptized into the Old Order Amish Church, then married Esther—the sooner the better. It was Esther who'd relished her newfound freedom during Rumspringa, the thrill of hitchhiking west to live in San Francisco. She'd adored the gaudy rainbow of her tie-dye skirts, crooning Bob Dylan songs on the street corners, begging for spare change. Once they'd landed jobs and earned enough money for their own place, she grew dependent on her electrical appliances: hair dryer, record player, and dishwasher—frivolities that meant nothing to her now.

"Why do you need Dad's parents' approval if they can't stand you?" Holly asked. "I don't blame you for feeling the same way about them." She checked her wristwatch and grimaced. "If your phantom mother has suddenly reappeared, email her and test the waters."

"She doesn't own a computer. No electricity. My family was—is—Amish. You know that."

"Then pick up the phone and call."

"No telephone in the house, or cell phones. But their Mennonite neighbors have one."

"What's a Mennonite? Never mind, I don't have time to find out now." She moved toward the back door. "Maybe you should invite Aunt Dori over when you make that call to Grandma's neighbor. Just in case she has bad news."

"Sure, I'll call Dori and ask her if she's free to look after the shop." But as far as contacting her mother and brothers, Esther didn't dare.

CHAPTER THREE

I'd felt dizzy ever since this morning, like a kid twirling round and around, staring at the sky, until she dropped onto the lawn. I yearned to talk to someone, but my closest girlfriend, Joanne, was on her honeymoon—a week in Hawaii, the lucky lady.

Now, after spending a day at work calling other brokerage firms hoping to find a new position, unable to piece together the remnants of my career, I was sitting in Starbucks in the University Village with Larry Haarberg.

Larry was a forty-year-old bachelor I'd known for several years from our church's singles' group. He was a handsome hunk, a banker, but had a dicey reputation as a ladies' man—love 'em and leave 'em—which was why I'd never accepted his invitations to go out on a real date. I figured he was much better friendship material. He'd called when he heard I'd soon be unemployed and wanted to get together to commiserate. I suggested we meet where chattering people and bright lights surrounded us.

The air vibrated with the aroma of steaming milk and roasted java beans. Instead of networking, I found I couldn't keep myself

from blabbing to him about Mom's preoccupation with Grandma
Anna, filling him in about the inexplicable letter from a woman I
thought long dead.

"If your grandmother wants you to visit, isn't that good news?"
Larry slid his hand across the table to take mine. His skin felt soft,
not a single rough spot—the hand of a man who'd never worked
with tools or dug in a garden. Which wasn't a crime, just not what
I had in mind for a mate. I'd always thought I'd marry someone
more hands-on, like my father or Dori's husband, Jim. Every man
I met carried some insurmountable flaw because he wasn't like my
father, whom Mom described as near perfect. But if Dad were such a
wonderful man, why did God steal him from us?

"Here's the catch," I said, feeling Larry's shoe nudge mine under
the table. I moved my foot away. "If Mom's being straight with me,
she's been putting on an elaborate charade my whole life, telling me
my grandmother was dead, while all the time she was alive. Wouldn't
that burn you up?"

"Yes, but I'd love to have Granny back. She died seven years
ago." He wasn't getting my point, but it was sweet he loved his grandmother so much.

I sipped my decaf latte. "I've never even seen a picture of mine."
Why no photographs? Mom had snapshots of me as a child that
Dori had taken but never owned a camera herself. "If I were my
grandmother, I would have hopped aboard a plane and come to visit
me years ago. Maybe she's mean and nasty. My mother said my dad's
family despises her for leaving home."

"That doesn't sound right. What's wrong with living in the good
old Northwest?" His expression turned sober and he leaned closer so

the couple next to us wouldn't hear. "Did your mother fall recently and hit her head? Could it be early-onset dementia?" He loosened his tie—he always wore one. "Any unusual trauma?"

"Not that I know of."

"Could she be running an infection? Have a fever?" He was bright, educated, and inquisitive. I should be crazy about him. But I wasn't.

"Mom hasn't had a sniffle in years. She's never acted odd before, just the opposite. With her, I always knew what to expect. Until this morning."

"Did you check the postmark on the envelope to verify it's the real McCoy?" he asked.

"No, I didn't think to."

"Some detective you'd make." His hand curved around my fingers. "A beautiful one," he added. Still, I didn't feel a zing of chemistry between us. "Where does your newly resurrected grandma live?" he asked.

"According to Mom, on the family farm in Lancaster County, Pennsylvania."

"Land of the Amish? I've always wanted to go there. Haven't you?"

"Not really." I took a sip, then licked the froth off my lips.

Since elementary school, I'd been embarrassed by my Amish background. In fourth grade, I'd unfolded one of Mom's quilts and spoke to the class about her upbringing on a farm where horses still plowed the fields. Bob Martin, the class bully, teased me relentlessly and got the other boys calling me plain as grain. Later, in my preteen imagination, I'd invented a colorful heritage for myself: half-French and half-Scottish. But Mom had forced me to study German in high

school and in college I took another two years. "Your father would
wish it," she'd said.

"I don't know much about them," I said. "My mother buys her
stock from Ohio and Indiana."

"I could try to help you find your grandmother's name in
Lancaster County," Larry said.

"I doubt she even exists." The word *scam* came to mind.

"I hope she does, for your sake. My granny made the best lemon
chiffon pie."

"Lucky you. Just thinking about pie makes me hungry. I was so
upset and distracted today, I skipped lunch."

"May I get you a scone or another latte?" he asked.

I admit I enjoyed Larry's attention. Maybe he was finally a blip
on my radar. I hadn't been out on a date for six months. A fellow at
work, Bart Neilson, had asked me out several times, but our boss
maintained strict rules about dating coworkers. "*Verboten*—forbidden," Mom would say. But Bart and I wouldn't be working together
much longer, and all of a sudden he didn't seem as attractive. Because
now he was available?

Okay, I had a problem with men. Five years earlier, after dating
several Peter Pans who'd avoided commitment, I'd gotten engaged
to a top-notch attorney. But our relationship imploded when I discovered he drank too much, and trolled bars and lounges searching
for—and finding—one-night stands. And he spent hours on the
Internet. Since then I'd been unable to warm up to any man, really,
although I wanted to.

"Tell you what," Larry said, "I'll come to your place and talk
to your mother. Sometimes an outsider can detect subtle problems.

At the bank, I've become an expert at reading body language and deciphering handwriting. I'll take a look at the letter and envelope. Does your mother have others?"

"I guess she's received many over the years, but I've never seen one come in the mail." I dreaded having to face her.

"Should I follow you home right now?" he asked, straightening his tie.

I was struck by his good manners and generosity. What was wrong with me? Didn't I want to get married, and soon? My bioclock was ticking toward its last tock.

"Not tonight. I wouldn't be good company." I poked my hands into my raincoat's sleeves. "But thanks for the kind offer. I'd better get home."

He walked me through the University Village's crowded parking lot to my twelve-year-old Subaru. Unlocking my car, I noticed a new door ding. I wished my car's minor injuries didn't matter to me, but they did. My life was spiraling out of control.

"Good night, beautiful one," Larry said and kissed me on the cheek. His hands glided around my back, and he pulled me into a hug and nuzzled my ear. "Let me take you out to dinner this weekend," he said. "Somewhere fancy, like Canlis. Okay?"

I'd always wanted to dine at the prestigious restaurant, but said, "I'll check my calendar." Which I knew was empty. Seriously, what was wrong with me? Larry could be my knight in shining armor. What did I really know about his bad-boy reputation? Maybe it was just rumors. His new Lexus, parked several stalls over, was polished and paid for. He was a vice president at a well-established, solvent bank.

"Let's talk in a couple days." I was glad the woman in the automobile next to mine was backing out so I could wriggle out of his embrace. "First and foremost I need to find a new job. I should stay home to work on my résumé to make me look more capable than I really am." For the last three years, I'd concentrated my efforts on learning the trade, dreaming of becoming a broker. Then the roller-coaster market had tossed me overboard. "Let me see, I have sales experience, if you count working twelve years in the Petite Department at Macy's."

"Why don't you let me help?" Larry said. "I'm great at writing résumés. I've read hundreds of them. After dinner this weekend, we could go to my place and put our heads together."

I opened my car door and got in. "I'm not sure how much work we'd get done." I'd be evading his amorous advances all evening.

Heading home, I dreaded the daunting conversation awaiting me over dinner with Mom. I drove in silence, my heart pounding against my ribs like a baby robin fleeing a crow.

CHAPTER FOUR

Esther praised God when Dori agreed to look after the Amish Shoppe while she and Holly traveled to Lancaster County.

Speaking to Dori on the phone, Esther pressed the receiver against her ear. "If Holly agrees to accompany me. She might refuse—a real possibility."

"Then we'll switch to plan B."

"You mean go by myself?" Distressing images assaulted Esther's mind. "I can't."

"Let's cross that road when we come to it," Dori said. "Say, do you mind if I hold my knitting class at the shop on Tuesday afternoon? Several of my gals have never been in your store. I think they'd love it." She spoke as if all were settled.

Esther tried to make her voice sound light-hearted while doubts plagued her. "Of course not. Make yourself at home. If you like, invite your book group Wednesday night too."

"Great, then Jim won't have to hide out in the basement all evening."

Esther heard the back door open and saw her daughter trudge into the kitchen. "I've got to run," she told Dori and hung up.

Esther had set the kitchen table with care, using cloth napkins and her best china, and had prepared one of Holly's favorites, beef and vegetable stew, hoping to put her daughter in a cheerful mood. But now she realized Holly might see her acts as manipulative. There was no way for Esther to win.

She watched Holly scuff the soles of her shoes on the floor mat. "How did your day go, sweetheart?" Esther said.

"The worst." Holly shrugged off her raincoat. "Tomorrow's my last day at work. To give my boss a break, I offered to quit. There was nothing left for me to do, anyway. Mel already reassigned my accounts. He was more than relieved—you could see it in his eyes. One less paycheck."

"I'm so sorry. I know how much your job means to you." Esther had never understood the appeal of the stock market, nothing a person could grasp hold of. Intangible numbers, charts, and speculations.

"Come have a seat," she said, pulling out Holly's chair. "Dinner will make you feel better. Your face looks drawn. Have you lost weight?"

"No. I weigh one hundred and twenty-five pounds, exactly what a five-foot-three woman should."

Why had she mentioned Holly's slim stature? Holly objected to remarks about her weight. She'd been a skinny adolescent, the last of her girlfriends to fill out, but as an adult she was near perfect in Esther's eyes. Most women would kill to have Holly's figure.

Esther brought the pot to the table while Holly hung her coat in the front hall.

Esther had fussed and worried all day. She'd channeled her excess energy into dusting the shop, rearranging displays, and washing the floors on her hands and knees. Still, she had no idea where to start a lifetime of explaining.

Minutes later, Holly sat at the table and scooted in her chair—partway.

Esther ladled stew onto her plate. "I've never mentioned this before, but when we were in our late teens, your father and I hitchhiked all the way to California."

Holly shook open her napkin. "You would have killed me if I pulled that stunt."

Had she already spouted too much? Esther prodded herself to continue. "I'm not saying it was a good idea." She served herself a small portion, more than she planned to consume. "In fact, it was the worst move of my life."

"That doesn't sound like you. When I was growing up, you were always uptight. A regular prude."

Esther knew Holly was hurting over the loss of her job. No matter, she refused to argue this evening. Turn the other cheek, she reminded herself. "As a teen, I was strong willed. Out of control, is more like it. But your father and I made it all the way to San Francisco, with the Lord's help."

Holly walked her chair in; the armrests bumped the table. "God's your answer to everything." Sarcasm hardened her voice.

"And for good reason. It wouldn't hurt you—" Esther sucked in her lips; now was not the time to lecture her daughter about her wavering faith. Holly attended church, but Esther hadn't seen her open a Bible other than in the sanctuary for years.

Her hands steepled under her chin, Esther bowed her head and prayed, "Thank you, Father, for our home and for this meal. Please help Holly find a new job." A multitude of requests inundated Esther's mind, but she calmed her thoughts and praised God. Then she begged him for forgiveness, even though her minister had assured her no sin was too great for God's pardon. Yet she felt compelled to confess her transgressions over and over again, a never-ending figure eight.

Holly also tipped her head forward, her longish bangs covering her eyes, but Esther wasn't sure she was praying, even when Holly muttered, "Amen."

Holly sliced into a square of meat. Her knife grated against the plate, the scraping sound heightening the tension. "I can't believe your parents let you hitchhike. Wasn't that dangerous even back then?"

"They had no idea until it was too late and we were long gone." The words were like puffs of steam from a kettle escaping into the atmosphere. "After four or five days, I finally wrote them a postcard from Arizona. Imagine, how selfish I was. I'd do anything to take my actions back." She pushed a morsel of diced carrot around her plate with her fork. "I didn't write my parents again for another two months, from San Francisco, and left no return address. My mother must have been frantic, worried sick."

"That's sad they passed away before you could apologize." Was Holly testing Esther's memory? Did she still not believe her grandmother was alive?

Esther felt like a barnacle clinging to a boulder at the bottom of Puget Sound. "I never spoke to my father again. He passed away soon after." She set her fork aside. "Once my Samuel got drafted into the army and I realized I was pregnant, I moved up here with Dori and Jim. My mother and I stayed in touch through letters. She implored me to return to the farm, but I was ashamed. I decided to wait until Samuel got discharged. But he never did."

Holly gave her a crooked smile—her father's mouth. "Instead of going home, you opened the Amish Shoppe in Seattle? Sounds rather dubious." Grasping her knife like a dagger, her words spewed out. "So why do you call yourself Pennsylvania Dutch to our customers?"

"Some Amish came from the Netherlands." Esther patted her mouth with her napkin and found her upper lip trembling. "The Dutch part is really *Deitsch,* meaning German. The Amish immigrated mostly from Germany, Switzerland, and what later became Alsace-Lorraine." This conversation was veering off track; Esther needed to adhere to pertinent facts. "In any case, I was raised Amish."

"So you say." Her words were spoken with distrust, as if sampling zesty East Indian food for the first time.

"It's true. Your father, too."

"Then why don't you ever talk about your childhood?"

"This shop and all that's in it, the buggy out front—I thought you understood."

Not true. Esther had intentionally kept her background vague, like on a foggy morning when she could barely see the buildings across wide Fifteenth Avenue Northwest.

CHAPTER FIVE

To find my mother had been fibbing to me all my life was like discovering Santa Claus and the Easter Bunny were dead. No, ten times worse: like Mom had revealed Jesus didn't really die for our sins. Maybe he didn't, if everything Mom had taught me was a lie.

I'd always struggled with the concept of a heavenly Father because I never had a dad. My main male figure growing up was Dori's husband, Jim—a nice enough fellow who generously lent Mom money as a down payment to buy her house and start her shop. But he wasn't my dad.

As for God, my prayers never got answered. For instance, what happened to my stellar career, and where were my husband and SUV teeming with children?

My appetite nonexistent, I forced myself to swallow a mouthful of stew.

Mom twisted in her chair, reached to the side table, and picked up a Keds shoebox held closed by a rubber band. Setting it between us, her face took on a rueful expression, like the day back in middle school when she'd told me my beloved terrier mix, Maxwell, had died and she was waiting until I got home to bury him.

She rolled off the rubber band, lifted the lid, and prodded the shoebox in my direction. Inside lay letters—dozens of them—in stamped envelopes like they'd arrived yesterday. But they emitted a musty smell and brought on a sneeze.

I dabbed my nose with my napkin, then flattened it across my lap. "Must we continue?" There was no law forcing me to peruse Mom's Pandora's box.

"Please, have a look." She seemed pathetic—how I must have appeared at work today.

At random, like an archaeologist—more like a snoop, one of those for-hire detectives tracking down wayward husbands—I removed one from the middle and took a moment to examine the postmark, thanks to Larry's tip. Two years old, mailed from New Holland, Pennsylvania, no return address on the upper left-hand corner. It was sent to Esther Fisher, in care of Dorothy Mowan— Dori. Odd. And frightening. Because how many other secrets was Mom keeping from me?

The hairs on my arms prickled. "A letter came from my grandmother two years ago and you didn't show it to me?" I was fuming, my heart hammering in my ears. I had every right to be angry.

I unfolded the paper and studied the fluid cursive script.

Dearest Esther, it started, giving me the confidence to continue. But just to make sure I wasn't stepping into some futuristic sci-fi movie, I scanned to the end to see it was signed: *Your loving Mamm*.

I inflated my lungs—guess I'd stopped breathing—and started again. Someone claiming to be Grandma Anna discussed aunts and uncles and cousins I'd never heard of, and Lancaster County trivia, like unseasonably cold weather. She mentioned their milk production—they had dairy cows?—and Cookie, an aging standardbred going lame, making me sad because I'd always loved horses, even though I'd never ridden one other than a docile pony at Woodland Park Zoo.

"I have cousins?"

"Yah. Many."

In the back of the envelope lay a folded newspaper article clipped from the *Lancaster New Era*, a publication I'd never heard of, mentioning the skyrocketing price of farmland, a problem with break-ins, and several paintball shootings aimed at buggies. Nothing I could relate to.

"People still drive horse and buggies, like the one on our front porch?" I asked, and Mom nodded.

"Please, read them all," she encouraged.

"Mom, you've hidden these from me for years. The letters can wait!" My fist pounded the table harder than I'd meant, rattling our water glasses. "Why didn't Grandma write directly to you here? None of this rings true. Like one leg of this chair is suddenly three inches shorter." I was tempted to unleash my frustrations and rip into my mother, who was obviously not the nicey-nicey woman she pretended to be. "Does Grandma Anna even know I exist? Or are you embarrassed of me?"

"No, darling, I'm proud. I've told her all about you. Maybe I exaggerated a little bit."

"Meaning you told her I'm happily married and have a dozen kids. Don't the Amish have large families? Seems I learned that fact somewhere."

"Most of them do." Mom grinned, like she used to when I was a little girl who'd just nabbed an extra snickerdoodle out of the jar and hidden it in my pocket. "I have five younger brothers, but we weren't considered a large family."

"Five brothers and this is the first I'm hearing of them?" Glaring at her, I tried to recall what little I knew about the Amish, other than what I'd learned scanning the brochures accompanying products we sold in the store. I'd seen a movie once, but was the Hollywood version remotely factual? I envisioned my teenage parents hitchhiking to San Francisco during the hippie era like a couple of vagabonds. "Did you and Dad get kicked out of the Amish community? Shunned—isn't that what they call it? Is that why you couldn't go back?"

"No, we left before getting baptized into the church. My mother would still like me to return and be baptized, even at this late date. My assurance to gain entrance into heaven. But I've learned, since I've lived here, we are saved through God's infinite mercy."

Her religious speeches annoyed me; I should be lecturing her on honesty. Not that I'd always been up-front with her.

I creased the letter and article and jammed them back into the envelope. "Why are you unloading this soap opera on me, right when I should be concentrating on finding a new job? You want me to have a nervous breakdown?"

Her knowing smile told me she didn't buy into my theatrics. Did she think I could handle anything? I wasn't putting on a dramatic performance. As a matter of fact, I was coming unglued. Unhinged.

"I'm sorry about your job," she said. "I realize how much it meant to you." At least she was listening. "But with you out of work, this makes the timing ideal. You and I will visit my mother and brothers. Together. I can't face them alone. Not after all this time."

"And you think I can?" Random thoughts flicked through my mind. I had to find a way to avoid being sucked into her scheme. "Under their microscope, I wouldn't know how to act or what to say."

"Just be yourself."

"I'm sure they won't like me."

"Of course they will."

I recalled the fifth commandment: Honor thy father and thy mother. I'd tried to show Mom respect while living under her roof, all the time wishing I could luxuriate in a studio apartment in the heart of bustling Ballard or near Dori and Jim on Phinney Ridge with a grand vista of the Olympic Mountains. But I could no longer afford Seattle's high rent; I was stuck sharing the second floor with my mother like a little kid.

Mom stood and cleared the plates. Neither of us had eaten much. "So, your last day of work is tomorrow?" She set them in the sink.

"Yes. I'll clear out my desk and leave the only job that ever meant anything to me."

She walked to my side and placed a hand on my shoulder, then sank back onto her chair. "I hope you know how badly I feel about your job. But, as I was saying, this makes the timing perfect. You'll come with me to the farm." Her eyes were wide and expectant, like I was the one who held the answer to her unsolved crossword puzzle clue. Newsflash: I didn't. I felt like I'd tumbled off a speedboat and was treading water, gulping for air. And sinking.

"When should we leave?" Mom said, apparently not noticing my distress.

"Are you sure this is what you want to do?"

"Yah, I must."

I eyed the shoebox. She'd always told me honesty was the best policy. Did I even know her? "Why so sudden?"

"It isn't sudden. I've been living with remorse for years."

Call me codependent, but I couldn't say no to her, seeing her look so despondent, her eyelids drooping.

My arms flopped to my sides. "Okay, I'll go with you," I said, then wished I could retract my words. "For a short visit only."

"Did I hear you right?"

"Yes, I might as well give in now. You're going to break me down eventually. You always do. And I can't imagine your traveling by yourself." How would she react when she arrived to find her former life had disappeared? I owed her support as she'd given me my whole life. She'd attempted to be two parents in one.

I set my napkin on the table. "Let me get online right now and see about buying a couple discounted plane tickets."

With Mom trailing me, I left the kitchen and moved to the computer behind the counter near the front door. I'd have to charge the tickets on my nearly maxed-out credit card. I knew Mom didn't have spare money, just enough to buy inventory and make her mortgage and utility payments.

"Must we ride on an airplane?" Mom glanced at the crack on the ceiling.

"Yes, I'm not traveling across country by bus or train." I signed on to cheaptickets.com. "Let's get this over with. Although I can think of a hundred places I'd rather travel, preferably with warm weather and salt water." I scanned the screen. "Here's a nonstop to Philadelphia. Is the day after tomorrow too early?"

She let out a gasp. "That soon?"

"I'm serious about finding a new job, even if it means working at Starbucks. When I do, I may not have time off for a year."

"All right, then, buy the tickets."

"You can set things up with Dori in less than twenty-four hours?"

"Yah, I spoke to her and she agreed."

"What if at the last minute she says no?"

"Then I'll lock the front door and put up a Closed sign until we get home."

I punched in my credit card number, then printed out our itinerary and receipt. "It's settled. Let's get this ordeal over with so I can start the rest of my life."

I plodded upstairs, removed my pinstripe pantsuit and blouse, and eased into sweatpants. I glanced down at my beloved pantsuit, deflated on my bed, and my heart sank. I was determined to wear my downtown outfit again in the near future at an interview—for what, I had no idea. Using a wooden hanger, I folded the slacks and hung up the jacket with care.

The next evening, after a supper of leftovers, I opened my bureau drawers to pull out a pair of jeans, corduroy pants, and navy slacks.

I dumped them, a blouse, a sweater, and several T-shirts atop the patchwork quilt Mom made for me as a girl. On a whim, I dropped a bathing suit on the bed. Not practical for mid-October, but for all I knew we'd end up staying at a motel with a heated pool. Then I stuffed four days' worth of clean underwear and socks into plastic ziplock bags. I hadn't mentioned to Mom we were only going for five days, including travel time. Which could be four days too long.

I heard Mom mounting the stairs. A minute later she poked her head in my room and frowned at my bathing suit. "You won't be needing that," she said.

"Then tell me, what shall I pack? Cowboy boots?" I released a weary sigh. Saying farewell to my coworkers and emptying my desk this afternoon had been an emotional roller-coaster ride. "I haven't taken a vacation for years. Shouldn't we be jetting off to somewhere sunny and lazy like the Baja or even San Diego?" I bet Larry Haarberg would whisk me to a posh resort. But I'd sworn not to go down that road again unless I was on my honeymoon.

Mom smiled at the word *vacation*. "This time of year, most of the crops have been harvested," she said. "But there's plenty of chores to be done."

"Like plowing fields and milking cows? We'll be working the whole time?"

"No, for the most part the men take care of that. As a girl I helped my mother clean house and preserve fruits and vegetables to get us through the winter. And I fed the chickens and gathered eggs." Her words brought a fresh gush of turbulence to my chest. The closest I'd ever been to barnyard animals was the Puyallup Fair and the petting farm at the zoo.

"I still don't have a clue what to bring," I said.

"Mostly casual clothes. No revealing necklines. And a modest bathrobe. Your Grandma Anna installed an indoor bathroom, but it's on the main floor."

I let out a gasp. "You grew up using an outhouse? Even in winter?" No wonder she and Dad wanted to escape to California.

"You get used to it."

"I never would. And the smell? Yikes."

"Your grandmother still doesn't have central heating or electricity. In her kitchen, she uses a gas stove and a gas-generated refrigerator, and kerosene lamps."

"No dishwasher or coffeemaker?" I said. "How can she stand it? What about Internet connection and recharging cell phones? I can't go anywhere without my phone and laptop."

"We'll find you an Internet café in New Holland."

"Won't you miss your favorite TV shows?"

"No, I mostly watch TV to fill the time."

"Yeah, right. I bet we'll both be bored stiff. At least you have your knitting."

"Yes. In fact, I'll knit on the plane to soothe my nerves."

"Good idea. I still have a hard time believing you've never ridden in a jet, or that you were raised in a community where people were proud to be called plain." I was transported back to fourth grade. "Plain doesn't sound like a complimentary remark. Who wants to be ordinary? I sure don't."

"The Amish live that way intentionally. Humbly, not trying to outdo their neighbors. It's a trade-off. What they lose—cars, electricity, and telephones in the home—they gain in quiet family time. Board games after dinner and volleyball on Sunday afternoon."

I wasn't buying her explanation. "Wait up, Mom, you love watching the Mariners on TV. Any time you want to play a board game, let me know. But I think you'd be bored." I quoted the word *board* with my fingers, but she didn't catch my pun. She rubbed her palms together like they were sticky.

"What makes you more nervous?" I asked. "Our sketchy family reunion or stepping onto an airplane?"

"I don't know." Her hair had straggled out of its bun and fallen to the middle of her back. She gathered it up, winding it around her fingers and pinning it into place.

I decided not to push her further; she had enough to fret about. I realized I needed to call Larry to tell him I'd be out of town. He'd probably find another dinner date. Our church singles' group was swarming with unmarried women, and he was considered a prime catch.

No time to worry about Larry now. I was about to take a trip and needed to find a way to entertain myself on the flight. I scooped up a novel I'd been meaning to read and hoped it had a happy ending. I was in no mood for mystery or suspense. I had enough uncertainty in my life.

Letting my thoughts leapfrog ahead, I imagined the awkward moment when I met Grandma Anna. Or went to the graveyard and saw her headstone. Gee, I hoped she was still living, but curbed my enthusiasm. Would a grandma never send a birthday card?

"When we get there, I'll rent a car and be the designated driver." I let resentment steer my tongue. "Were you always this helpless? I still wish you'd learn to drive."

Before age sixteen, I was at the mercy of my girlfriends' parents to ferry me to soccer practices. Unless someone gave me a ride, I rode the bus to school until I got my license. Then I insisted Mom buy a used car. It was a clunker, but had four wheels.

"Eventually I'll move out and how will you get your groceries home?" I said.

"Ach, 'tis too late."

"Meaning it's too late for me to get married and start a family?"

"Stop that. You're distorting my words."

I heard the front door swing open.

"Yoo-hoo," Dori called in her alto voice. "I brought the carry-on suitcase."

"I'll be right there," Mom said, and scowled at my bathing suit. I tossed it back into the bottom drawer with my other summer garments. I left my helter-skelter of clothes on the bed and meandered down the stairs to see Mom handing Dori a ring of keys and a two-page list of instructions.

"Don't worry about a thing," Dori told Mom, then noticed me. "Hi there, honey bunch. Isn't this exciting? I'm going to run the store in your mother's absence and you're going to meet your grandmother."

"It's exciting all right, but maybe we should let sleeping dogs lie." I wondered if Mom or I were more anxious and bet I was; the floorboards beneath me seemed to sway.

Dori's smile was broad and confident. "Now, now, it will be a marvelous adventure. A time of new beginnings." Her arms stretched out to hug Mom like they shared a common pact. Or a conspiracy.

My brain swarmed into a bee's nest of worry. I had no job and was flying across country to see relatives I didn't want to meet, not after all this time—if they existed. I thought about my father's parents, the Fishers. Did they know about me? Were they still living in the area? If so, would Mom and I be greeted with contempt? Mom and I were about to stir up a whirlwind of trouble. I felt like I was wandering out on thin ice, headed toward the center of Green Lake, which even on Seattle's coldest days rarely froze solid.

CHAPTER SIX

The next morning, Esther heard Dori rapping on the Amish Shoppe's front door to drive Holly and her to the airport. When Esther opened the door, Dori zeroed in on the suitcase she'd lent Esther and extended the collapsible handle.

As if reading her thoughts of doom, Dori said, "Your customers will understand you needed a vacation. Although I have the feeling your clients are the least of your worries."

"You're right." If the Amish Shoppe burned to the ground, it wouldn't cause Esther half the torment she was about to endure. She'd never been more terrified in her life. "I wonder, am I doing the right thing?" she said, an internal conflict waging. "Well, of course I am—what I've been telling myself for years. It's time to face the consequences of my actions. And my mother."

"I agree," Dori said. "Get those skeletons out of the closet."

"Holly's unusually quiet this morning," Esther whispered, watching her daughter lug her suitcase down the stairs.

"Hey, Mom, seeing you two together gave me a wonderful idea." Holly flashed them a smile. "Dori should go with you instead of me. I'll run the shop. After all, I am the woman who needs a job."

"Come on, gals," Dori said, corralling them into her VW parked at the curb. "You're acting like you're being shipped to the Middle East for combat duty."

"I think I'd rather be," Holly said. "Am I too old to enlist?"

As she drove them south to the airport, Dori kept the mood light by describing Jim's plans to remodel their living room. "While I'm working at the Amish Shoppe, he's going to build new bookshelves on either side of the fireplace." She parked at the passenger departure zone, and made sure Esther and Holly each had suitcase and purse, treating them as if they were children on their first day of kindergarten. And that's how Esther felt—immature and disoriented.

An hour later, Esther and Holly passed sock-footed through security at the airport. The guard investigated Esther's knitting needles and confiscated them.

"I told you to bring plastic needles," Holly said with a snap. "Never mind, we'll buy you new ones when we get there."

If we get there, Esther thought.

Finally seated on the aircraft, Esther tightened her seat belt. She grasped the armrests as the jet muscled through a mattress of clouds, reminding her of snow-covered Lancaster County in January. The entire flight she worried God would punish her by smashing them out of the sky before they reached Pennsylvania.

After a harrowing five-hour flight and a bumpy landing at the Philadelphia International Airport, Holly rented a small Nissan sedan with a GPS system. The tangerine sun had sunk behind a curtain of foreboding clouds an hour ago, while they'd still been in the air.

"I don't want you attempting to negotiate a road map and getting us lost," Holly told Esther as she agreed to pay extra for the navigational device. "Although I figure once we get to Lancaster County you'll transform into a homing pigeon and direct us straight to Grandma Anna's."

Esther stood in the darkened parking lot watching Holly juggle their bags into the trunk. Rubbing the back of her neck, Esther bet she'd aged ten years since this morning. She noticed her raincoat was fastened lopsided, the buttons in the wrong holes.

Holly rounded the car and plopped into the driver's seat, but Esther lingered, the chill evening air creeping up her sleeves, making her shiver. A sprinkling of rain misted down, then escalated into a full-blown torrent, reminding Esther of her youth—scampering barefoot out of the vegetable garden up the back steps.

"Come on, hurry up." Holly's voice sounded tetchy. "Is this typical Pennsylvania weather? It never rains this hard in Seattle."

Esther finally got in, clutching her purse.

"Sorry, Mom, you must be wiped out from your first ride on a jet."

Esther rebuttoned her coat. "Yah, confined to our seats most of the time."

"The choppy ride didn't rattle me as much as what lies ahead." Holly thrust the key in and turned on the engine.

"Me, too." Ever since she'd entered the plane, Esther surmised her life would never be the same, her thoughts harassing her like the first day of the flu.

Holly found the windshield wipers and the headlamps, and backed out of the stall. "What's Grandma's address?"

"She lives on Hollander Road, north of 340. But my mother doesn't know we're coming."

"Are you nuts?" Holly jammed on the brakes. "You plan to show up without warning her first? I refuse to pick my way across the state to what may be an empty house."

"She'll be home. It's after dark and my mother leads a simple life. There's no way she'd be out on a cold, wet evening. Let's go."

"But I'm exhausted and not in the mood for a scavenger hunt."

"Someone will be there. The kitchen door will be unlocked."

"No way." Holly's upper lip lifted into a snarl. "Are you sure—and we're talking positive—Grandma Anna still lives on the same farm where you grew up?"

"Yah, I'm sure."

Holly rifled through her purse and whipped out her cell phone. "We'll call her. Oh, that's right, you claim your mother doesn't have a telephone. Well, then, we'd better find a cheap motel for the night."

"I have an idea," Esther said, her lips going numb. "We could call my mother's Mennonite neighbor, Beth Fleming." She reached into her pocketbook and pulled out a scrap of paper. "Here's her phone number."

"I don't get why Mennonites use phones, but Amish don't."

"Old Order Amish will speak on them, but not keep them in the home. You'll see. They have phone shanties tucked away from the house for emergencies. But from what I hear, Beth's quite modern. Her house is fancy schmancy. A convection oven, plasma TV, and every kind of electronic gizmo. She often drives my mother and my brothers and their wives and kids into town in her minivan."

"Then why didn't you call Beth yesterday? Have you lost all common sense?"

"I should have, but we've never met. She moved here about the same time I left."

"She's all we have." Glancing in the rearview mirror, Holly maneuvered the car out of the stall. "Maybe she'll know a cheap bed-and-breakfast or a motel. I don't feel like sleeping in this cramped car. At least this Beth woman can confirm if Grandma is still alive—or not."

Esther recited the telephone number and Holly punched it into her phone. Esther's throat grew tight with anticipation and her forehead ached, like she'd swallowed ice cream too quickly.

"Good evening, I'm Holly Fisher, Esther Fisher's daughter, Anna Gingerich's granddaughter," Holly said when a woman answered.

Esther could hear the woman say, "What a lovely surprise. Did Esther give you my number?"

"Yes, in fact she's sitting right here next to me in a rental car at the Philly airport."

"Won't her mother be delighted to see you both!"

"I hope so." Holly's free hand gripped the steering wheel like a vise. "Um, does my grandmother still live in her house?"

"Yes. If I stand on my front porch, I can see it from here."

Holly's arm relaxed, bending at the elbow. "Then, Grandma Anna is alive?"

Beth let out a sputter of laughter, followed by a pause. "Yes, most certainly. What's this all about?"

"This is my first trip. I wanted to make sure."

"No matter. Isn't this exciting? An answer to Anna's prayers."

"We rented a car, but I think we'd better wait until tomorrow to pop in on my grandmother. It's been a hectic day."

"Then I insist you two stay with me," Beth said. "I have more than enough room. Just my husband and me in this big old house, and he's away on a business trip. Our three kids moved out years ago. I look forward to seeing Esther again."

Holly closed her phone, entered Beth's address into the GPS system, and headed to the checkout gate. She took a left onto the street, thanks to the GPS's directions. "Did I hear Beth right?" she asked Esther. "I thought you said you never met her."

"Well, I guess, maybe. A couple of times. But my mother acts like Beth's part of the Gingerich family."

"That's good, because we're spending the night at Beth's house."

Esther stared out the front window, like Holly was taking her to meet the principal to be suspended from school.

"Come on, Mom, we're here. It's what you wanted, isn't it?" She swerved onto a highway entrance. "What's wrong?"

Esther could tell Holly was furious she'd been forced to call Beth, a complete stranger, and beg for lodging. What would Beth think of Esther, the footloose daughter who'd danced off to become a hippie, and who never returned? Not even for her father's funeral. A woman who didn't know her own siblings; they were strangers to her. Esther dressed and spoke like an outsider now—an Englischer.

She dreaded the next day. The day of reckoning, she thought, not knowing what the phrase entailed. God's punishment on earth?

Holly aimed the car past hotels and factories, heading them west, traversing graceful hills. Esther felt a comforting warmth gathering in her chest, like recognizing an old friend, until she glanced over to see Holly's severe features, her mouth hard.

An hour later, after switching roads, they passed a golf course where a farm used to stand. In windy gusts, the rain slanted across a posh strip of car dealerships and a discount outlet Esther had never seen before.

The GPS's female voice instructed Holly to turn right, directing them northwest. The downpour increased, slapping down in sheets, puddling at the side of the road, beating upon harvested cornfields. Globules of water flung themselves at the windshield. Holly turned up the wiper blades; they flashed like daggers.

"I'll never complain about Seattle's weather again," she said. "This is awful."

"Can you see all right?" Esther asked, listening to raindrops clattering against the car's roof. "Are you sure we're going the right way?"

"Yes, according to this device. See? It's like a map."

In the blackened car, Esther examined the GPS's screen and saw undulating colored lines that must represent highways and names of towns she couldn't read without her glasses.

"Look!" Holly pointed out the windshield. "There's a horse and buggy on the road right along with the cars in this wretched weather."

"Be careful," Esther said, as if she had any right to tell Holly how to drive after spending a lifetime as a passenger. "My dat, your grandfather, died in a buggy accident. A truck hit him."

"How horrible."

"I'm sure it was. After all these years I can't bear to think of it." As a child, Esther had witnessed a buggy collision on the Ronks Road near Bird-in-Hand, the gruesome scene forever etched in her memory. The driver and his wife died. "If only there were a way to reinvent the past."

Holly let up on the gas pedal and reached over to briefly take Esther's hand. "You and I both lost our fathers too young. But at least you got to know yours as a child and had a chance to say good-bye to him at his funeral."

"Yes. I knew him as a girl. He was a strict but hardworking, diligent man." She couldn't bear to mention she didn't learn of Dat's death until weeks after his funeral, via Mamm's forwarded letter. Esther hadn't shown that pitiful tearstained note to Holly the other night.

Folding her hands in her lap, Esther's head fell back against the headrest. All is in your hands, God Almighty, she thought. She'd raised a child alone and owned a business. She was here to see her mother by choice. Why did she feel so helpless?

The traffic—cars, trucks, a tractor with rubber tires, RVs—grew less dense, and the rain lightened to a drizzle. Holly switched the wipers to the intermittent setting. She slowed the car to what Esther figured was the legal speed limit.

The deciduous trees—oaks, birch, maples, and elms—growing on either side of the road had discarded much of their foliage, allowing Esther to peer into the landscape to see a newly constructed Englisch housing development with streetlamps. Dozens of homes used electricity; incandescent lightbulbs brightened the porches and yards. A half a mile further, a recently built high school stood next to a sports stadium.

Approaching from the other direction, Esther spotted a pinto, much like the mare Samuel's family once owned, pulling an enclosed gray buggy driven by a man wearing a straw hat. The driver looked to be about Samuel's age when he and Esther skipped town.

She cracked the window and inhaled the aroma of damp pavement and soil. Her mind reeled with remorse and longing.

CHAPTER SEVEN

After the topsy-turvy day we'd experienced, I didn't know what to expect when we neared Beth Fleming's house. A ramshackle cabin with a beat-up truck and goats munching on weeds out front? No, that wouldn't be in keeping with what little I knew of Lancaster County traditions. Catalogues arriving at the Amish Shoppe illustrated expansive, well-maintained farms, like those we'd driven by. Impressive.

Mom had mentioned Beth was a Mennonite, a religious-type cousin of the Amish. Apparently, hundreds of years ago, while they were still in northern Europe, the Amish split from the Mennonites because they weren't strict enough—something to do with excommunication. Mom went on to say many Mennonites had adapted their lifestyles to the modern world and their traditional, conservative Christian beliefs were much as hers—and what she hoped were mine, most likely. But doubts about God's goodness and sovereignty still plagued me.

I felt apprehensive as I pulled into Beth's driveway and saw an early twentieth-century gray fieldstone home and a two-car garage, its doors shut. I parked next to a light-blue metallic Dodge Caravan. So far, so good.

"We're here, Mom," I said. "You nod off?"

She rubbed her eyes and looked around, yawning. "Yah, guess I did."

I opened my door. A black-and-white border collie, its tail flagging, bounded from around the side of the house and barked.

"Hello, there." I relaxed for the first time all day as I stroked its luxurious coat. "Mom, why didn't we ever get another dog?"

She climbed out and stretched her arms. "I offered several times, but you always declined."

I remembered my first and only dog. "Oh, yeah, never mind."

"You said you couldn't stand another loss, unless I'd guarantee the pup outlasted you. I bet no dog could take the place of Maxwell, anyway."

"You're probably right. And once I land another job, I won't have time to walk and care for one." I surveyed the sweeping lawn enclosed by a split-rail fence. "But if I lived out here, with a huge yard—"

The front door opened and a tallish woman about Mom's age strolled out wearing a midcalf-length skirt, a small-patterned flowered blouse, and a cardigan. Her blonde hair was parted on one side and held back with a clip. She descended from the porch. The dog romped over to her and pranced at her feet.

"Good evening, I'm Beth." She gave Mom a one-armed hug, and helped her haul her suitcase from the rental car's trunk. "I'm so glad to see you, Esther. After all this time. And you must be Holly. Your rooms are ready and waiting."

"Thanks for taking us in." I scanned a fenced-in vegetable garden—most already harvested—and a small barn out behind the garage. Turning back to Beth, my gaze settled on the rose bushes growing below the front porch; many had shed their petals, leaving tomato-colored rose hips.

"Beth, are you the gardener?" I hoped to get a conversation rolling on a topic all three of us might enjoy.

"I am, but my roses are past their prime in spite of our warm autumn. The nights grew chilly a couple weeks ago."

I expected Mom to comment about the weather or the flowers, but her lips were smooshed together, her gaze avoiding Beth.

"Don't feel shy." Beth spoke to Mom, who looked as bedraggled as I'd ever seen her. "Please, come inside."

Though tired to the bone, I held my ground. "First, can you show me where Grandma Anna's farm is from here?"

Beth pointed at a dimly lit home about a half mile away. "Down yonder." Her face broke in to a grin. "Want to go over there right now?"

Mom and I said, "No," in unison. I chuckled, not sure if my response was out of fatigue or trepidation.

But Beth's words gave me fortitude: If Grandma Anna actually existed, my father may have too. Mom might have told the truth. I'd lived with a deep-seated fear I'd been born out of wedlock, a love child sired by a druggie living in a San Francisco commune.

Growing up, even my best friend Joanne had no clue about my family's true origin. In middle school, I'd fabricated tales about my father, born in Normandy, bragging he was a racecar driver who died in a NASCAR pileup. That scenario got the boys' attention. I never revealed Dad probably hadn't learned to drive a car. Or maybe he had in the army—maybe he was forced to operate a tank or a jeep. How could I find out? Were any of his army buddies still alive? No way to locate them now.

Back in the 1970s, soldiers drafted into Vietnam were given bad media coverage. As far as I could tell, everyone denounced that war and its final outcome. We lost, deserting our allies. My dad died for nothing. Not until the Vietnam Memorial Wall was erected in Washington, DC, did the public begin to change its opinion.

Another thought unfolded its wings: Was Dad's name engraved on the monument's marble surface? I wondered if his parents knew. But I shouldn't let myself contemplate meeting them. According to Mom, they wanted nothing to do with her. In fact, Dad's parents could have died or moved away years ago.

One piece of the puzzle at a time, I told myself.

The dog flounced over to me and licked my fingertips. I scratched it under the chin. "You're a pretty one, aren't you?"

"Her name's Missy," Beth said. "She's expecting her first litter in a month."

"What fun." I noticed Missy's wide girth. I remembered the joy of carrying my eight-week-old Maxwell the first day we brought him home. "I bet they'll be darling." The only fragrance sweeter than a puppy was the back of a baby's neck.

"We can't wait," Beth said. "Here, Esther, let me help you with that." She insisted on lugging Mom's suitcase up the porch steps.

What was my mother's problem? She didn't smile or thank Beth.

I grabbed my carry-on and my suitcase, and followed them into the warmth of the house.

CHAPTER EIGHT

Esther felt like a zombie. Counting backward, she calculated it was four o'clock on the West Coast, but she was wide awake, no falling back to sleep now. In Beth's guestroom, once her daughter's bedroom, Esther had tossed most of the night, her legs tangling in the sheets.

Around midnight, she'd listened to the pattering rain on the rooftop and tried to subdue her racing thoughts, but images of her mother barring her from the farmhouse swirled around the room like a Frisbee ricocheting off the ceiling and walls. Every hour or so, Esther's bleary eyes checked the digital clock, then her thoughts spanned the country to the Amish Shoppe. Could Dori handle sales transactions? What if a customer came in with a return? Esther expected new merchandise, and it would need to be priced and displayed. Next month, November, introduced the Christmas shopping season, Esther's bread and butter.

She climbed off the bed, her feet sinking into the carpet, and dressed in her skirt and a clean blouse.

Taking hold of the banister as she descended the stairs, Esther asked herself if the Amish Shoppe had turned into the center of her universe. No, she loved Holly a zillion times more than any business.

In the living room, she glanced out the front window at fog rising off the lawn, lifting through giant maple trees, half their garnet- and sienna-colored leaves strewn at their roots.

She followed a man's voice into the kitchen and saw a tall and slender fair-haired man sitting at the dining room table chatting with Holly and Beth over coffee. Holly's voice sounded cheerful; Esther hoped her mood had improved.

Esther made sure her blouse was buttoned properly and tucked in. She'd arrived the image of a bag lady last night, in front of Beth of all people. Esther reminded herself she needed to improve her attitude. Had she adequately thanked God and her daughter for escorting her here safely? No. She hadn't even thanked Beth for her kindness. In Seattle, folks seemed friendly on the outside, but rarely invited strangers into their homes—certainly not to spend the night.

Not that she and Beth were really strangers.

Esther entered the dining room, with its oval table, sideboard, and glass-fronted cabinets chock-full of Depression glass and china. A cleanly shaved man in his midthirties stood and put out a hand to shake hers. His hair was styled short, and he wore a collared shirt and khaki slacks.

Driving last night, Esther had explained to Holly that Amishmen held their barn-door style trousers up by suspenders, and married Amishmen wore beards but shaved their upper lips.

"Good to meet you, Mrs. Fisher. I'm Beth's son. Please call me Zach." He gave Esther's hand a firm shake. "Sorry to dash off so quickly. I should be at the clinic." He nodded to his mother, who remained sitting, and gave her a wink.

"Thanks, honey," she said.

"Bye, Zach," Holly said—a casual farewell. "Nice to meet you."

"I hope we run into each other again." He gave Holly a lingering look, making Esther smile. Men coming into the Amish Shoppe often paused to admire Holly's appealing features—her eyes, trim silhouette, and wavy hair. But Holly didn't seem to take note of Zach's attention. Esther bet her daughter was jet-lagged and suffering from the same jitters she was. And Esther definitely didn't want her daughter falling for a man from around here and leaving Seattle to be with him. Especially Beth's son. A catastrophe. She hoped the young man Holly knew from church—was his name Larry?—would hold her fickle attention until she got home. But Esther hadn't noticed her daughter checking her cell phone for text messages.

When Zach was out the door, Holly told Esther, "He's a veterinary doctor. Isn't that cool?" So she had noticed him. Holly had always loved animals—from afar.

"Yes," Esther said. "Quite an accomplishment."

"We're very proud of him." Beth stood halfway to glance out the window to watch Zach roll his pickup out the drive with caution to avoid Missy, who trotted back to the house once Zach neared the road. "Being admitted to and making it through veterinary school was an enormous feat. Now, he has a thriving practice."

"He'd never want to leave that," Esther said, thinking aloud.

"I should hope not." Beth sat and straightened her blouse at the neck. "My two daughters live a ten-minute drive away, so I get plenty of time with my grandchildren. But my Zachary hasn't met the right woman yet, so it seems. He's thirty-seven and was engaged once—"

"Holly's age," Esther said, and received a scowl from her daughter.

"You two must be hungry," Beth said, abruptly. "They don't feed folks much on airplanes anymore. Ready for breakfast?"

"Thanks, but it feels too early," Holly said, and yawned. "I don't even want to contemplate what time it is in Seattle." She was clad in skinny jeans and a clingy turtleneck sweater. Esther imagined her daughter through her mother's eyes and decided Mamm would not approve. Should Esther suggest Holly change into a less revealing outfit? Maybe lend her a sweater a couple sizes larger? No, a negative comment might spin her daughter right back to the airport.

"We should get moving," Holly said. She raked a hand through her hair.

"What's your hurry?" Esther wanted to delay the inevitable. She peeked through the doorway into Beth's kitchen and saw modern amenities, including a Cuisinart food processor, a refrigerator with an icemaker, and a glass-top stove you'd never find in Mamm's kitchen. The cupboard doors were painted buttermilk yellow, and a pink and lime-green flowered apron hung from a hook by the wall phone.

"I haven't had coffee yet," Esther said. "It surely does smell good."

"I'll get some." Beth stepped into the kitchen and returned with a brushed aluminum coffee urn and an empty mug.

"I hear Grandma Anna's house doesn't have electricity," Holly said to Beth. "Would you mind if I left my laptop here to charge the battery? I forgot to plug it in last night."

"That would be fine, dear. An excuse to come back." Her hand reached across the table and patted Holly's. "You're welcome anytime."

"Thank you, Beth. You're the best. I don't know what we would have done without your hospitality last night."

"I enjoyed your company. When my husband Roger's out of town I get lonely."

"Do you think there's room for both of us at Grandma's?" Holly set her elbows on the table, cupping her chin like her neck wasn't strong enough to hold up her head—exactly how Esther felt.

"Anna's house is of good size. The far end, the *Daadi Haus*—where your grandparents once lived, Esther—is vacant. Anna sleeps on the second floor now, with the children. Your Uncle Isaac and his wife, Greta, use the *Kammer* on the first floor, the bedroom behind the parlor. Four of Esther's brothers own homes of their own, but the men are out of town looking to buy land in Montana."

"Are you sure?" Esther's back arched. "They're moving? Mamm never mentioned it in her letters. You must be mistaken."

Beth's shrugged. "I dropped them off at the railway station five days ago."

"Sounds like you know them well," Holly said.

"We've spent plenty of time together, that's for sure. When I was a young woman, Anna taught me how to garden, to can and preserve, and how to quilt, among one hundred other skills. In return, I helped look after the boys. When I got my driver's license, I became the family's chauffeur and go-for, the least I could do."

"Like a second daughter?" Holly said, making Esther gulp her coffee too quickly, then cough.

"I feel like one of the family," Beth said. "Soon after my parents moved here, when I was fourteen, my mother died, leaving my busy dad to raise me. Anna was a godsend."

Esther knew she had no right, but an ocean of jealousy roiled in her chest, churning like a river at the bottom of a waterfall. Of course her mother would adopt an orphaned girl after her own daughter had willfully deserted her. In her sorrow, Mamm would have been grateful for Beth and grown to love her as her own.

Esther's vision took in the room and she wondered if Mamm's hands had woven the runner on the sideboard. What was she doing here? Why had she agreed to come to Beth's, of all places?

Holly poured herself more coffee and added a slurp of milk. "Beth, is there anything we should know before going to my grandmother's?"

"Not that I can think of. The house should be relatively quiet. One of your uncles, Isaac, your mother's youngest brother, stayed behind. He and his wife and kids live there."

"If you think about it, they live together in a commune." Holly smirked and glanced at Esther. "Like you and Dad did."

Esther crossed her legs, smacking her knee on the table. "It's nothing like that, I assure you. Please excuse my daughter's sense of humor."

"You did live in a commune," Holly said. "It's not a secret, is it? I assume everyone who knows Grandma Anna has heard about your outlandish past."

"A little." Beth filled her coffee cup to the rim. "How about I scramble some eggs and make whole wheat toast. Sound okay?"

Esther unfolded her napkin. "Yah, *denki.*"

"Denki?" Holly said, and sniggered. "Where did that come from?"

"I meant, yes, thank you." Esther's first language, Pennsylvania Dutch—she'd tried to erase it from her mind, but still spoke phrases in her dreams—was creeping back. "Need any help, Beth?"

"No, thank you, sit and relax," she said, leaving her coffee on the table.

Hearing an engine gaining momentum on the road, Esther saw Zach's pickup motoring past. Ach, had he stopped at Mamm's to announce her and Holly's arrival? How had he described them? How did Mamm respond?

After she and Holly finished breakfast, Holly stood and headed for a shower. "I can't believe I ate so much." She patted her stomach.

"A couple extra pounds wouldn't hurt you one bit," Beth said.

"You think so?" Holly seemed pleased with Beth's assessment.

Since when did Holly take unsolicited advice from strangers? Esther didn't dare open her mouth on the subject. Instead, when Holly left the room she offered to help *redd* up Beth's kitchen— another expression from Esther's childhood.

"No need, you run along. Anna will be overjoyed. It's been a difficult year for her. Seeing you and Holly will cheer her day."

The morning was coursing along too quickly, as if Esther had run a marathon and needed to catch her breath. Her joints—especially her newly bruised knee—felt stiff. "I wish there were something we could do to help." And delay their departure. "Shall we remake the beds?"

"No, leave everything as is."

Because Mamm might change her mind and send them away once she saw Esther and Holly dressed Englisch? Esther wondered what she'd think when she learned their visit was temporary. As a girl, Esther's parents' bishop had instructed the congregation to forgive seventy times seven. But by now, Esther's mother might have run out of forgiveness.

A chill ran through her like an arctic blast; Esther wrapped her fingers around her coffee cup.

Fifteen minutes later, Holly descended the stairs from the second floor and wheeled her suitcase to the front door. "Mom, are you packed?"

"Not yet."

"Aren't you the woman who insisted I drop everything and fly all this way? Don't expect me to visit Grandma Anna without you."

"Yah, okay, I'm comin'." Esther climbed the stairs, each leg as heavy as if she were wearing waterlogged fishing waders. She folded her belongings into the suitcase and zipped it shut, catching the edge of her cotton nightgown.

Feeling light-headed, she perched on the bed and tried to picture her mother's countenance when she and Holly knocked on her door. Mamm and Dat had never been what Northwest folks classified as easygoing. "Go with the flow," Holly had remarked last week when Esther fussed about receiving an incorrect order from a furniture factory in Illinois, a magazine rack stained mahogany instead of oak.

Growing up, Esther's parents had insisted she and her brothers obey stringent rules because God expected humility and obedience. Had Esther fled to escape their iron hand? After all these years, she still wasn't clear, only that her life had felt like a prison. How could she explain her actions to her mamm when she didn't understand them herself?

In her mind's ear, Esther heard Bob Dylan's "Blowin' in the Wind," a tune she and Samuel performed on San Francisco street corners to earn change. At first, Samuel played his harmonica, the only musical instrument the bishop allowed back home. Samuel's tenor voice outshone Dylan's by far.

Esther dragged herself off the bed and carted her suitcase downstairs. Finally out in the nippy morning air and sitting in the passenger seat, she could scarcely inhale. Had she buttoned her blouse too tightly at the neck? She loosened it, but found no relief.

Holly coasted the car down Beth's lane and turned onto North Hollander Road, driving past harvested corn and a bountiful field of emerald-green alfalfa.

Moments later, Esther spotted the farmhouse. "There it is, on the right." Her voice sounded scritchy, like she was coming down with laryngitis.

The car felt oppressive, the heater cranked too high. The closer they neared her childhood home, the faster Esther's heart galloped, until it seemed to curl in on itself and lurch to her esophagus, cutting off her breath. She thought she might faint.

Holly craned her neck for a better view of the white austere clapboard home, standing in front of the gable-roofed cow barn, the larger main barn, the outbuildings, silos, and windmill. She pulled onto the graveled patch near the mailbox. Esther decided not to tell her most visitors used the back door exclusively. No use making Holly uncomfortable; she'd learn the routine quickly enough.

Esther scanned the hundred-year-old home where she'd literally been born and raised. The two-story structure looked the same. Green shades covered the windows of the smaller Daadi Haus off to the left, connected to the main house at a corner to provide light to all rooms. But she noticed subtle differences: a new white picket fence and a curved arch now graced the entrance leading to the front porch.

Esther lowered her window partway, allowing air to surround her, filling her nostrils with the heady aromas of sod and drying cornstalks. But she didn't open her door; her hands wouldn't move.

"Mother, what's wrong?" Holly bopped out, rounded the hood, and strode to Esther's door, just as Mamm bustled onto the porch, wearing a navy dress and black apron.

Esther hesitated, knowing she must appear to be one of those fancy folks Mamm used to complain about with distrust. And Holly? Would Mamm see her as an *alt maedel*—an unmarried spinster trapped into caring for her aging mother?

"*Willkumm!* It's *gut* to see you!" Mamm hastened down the steps. The strings of her prayer cap were tied under her double chin, a sign the old ways hadn't changed.

Esther tried to smile through the window, but her upper lip stuck to her teeth. Using all her concentration, she opened the car door, swiveled her knees, and stood, barely able to maintain her balance. Mamm swooped closer, her arms reaching to embrace Esther, who leaned back against the car and waited for a verbal assault, since she hadn't written or left a message on the phone shanty before arriving.

"I've been expectin' yous," Mamm said. She'd aged considerably and added inches to her middle. Esther could see her thinning hair, blanched the color of dust, through her heart-shaped prayer cap. Fine lines mapped her face and a veneer of tears moistened her once bottle-green eyes, now faded like driftwood.

Mamm patted her breast. "Zach drove over to tell me you were in town so I wouldn't faint when I saw ya."

Esther stared at her mother's animated face. Hadn't Esther intended to recite a significant phrase to reverse the decades? She finally mustered up, "I'm sorry to hear you've been ill," rather than hugging Mamm as she longed to do—or fall to her knees and beg for forgiveness. She didn't deserve her mother's love. "I regret it's taken so long," she said. A shallow remark, and not true. Half of her didn't want to be here, even now.

"This is gut," Mamm said. "A gift from God. Ain't so?"

Esther nodded. She wondered if God had orchestrated her homecoming or if Mamm was trying to make her feel guilty. She couldn't feel smaller than she did already, the size of a mouse. Would that she could scurry away.

"Truly, 'tis of God." Mamm grinned, showing crooked teeth, then turned her attention to Holly. What must Holly think of her grandmother's sing-songy accent? Her grandma must sound like a country bumpkin.

"I want to hear all about my precious *Grossdochder.*" Mamm's plump arms encircled Holly, who stood the same height, but half her girth. Esther was surprised Holly hugged her grandmother back. She hadn't received an authentic embrace from Holly for ages—just pecks on the cheek.

A gamut of emotions—feelings of isolation, nostalgia, shame—inundated Esther's mind, quickening her breath. She'd deprived Holly of her grandma, yet all these years she'd been certain she was making the right choice.

Mamm stepped back, her gaze glued to Holly. "Let's have a look at ya. You're a fine young woman, as pretty as any in the county."

Who looks like her father, Esther thought. The morning light sloping through the branches of the oak trees on the other side of the road highlighted Holly's hair, much the hue of the sorrel mare grazing amongst the neighbor's herd of Holsteins—Samuel's rusty-brown hair. He'd be older now too: Esther's age. Would a day ever pass by when she didn't long for him?

"I hope we're not intruding," Holly said.

"Nee!—no! Silly me," Mamm said, her hands steepled. "I should have invited you in immediately. *Kumm rei*—come in. Esther needs no invitation. This will always be her home. Her old room's *redd* up with two beds in it these days."

The three women climbed the porch stairs. Esther expected to hear the second step creak as she had as a child, but the boards must have been replaced and repainted. New planters housing pink chrysanthemums stood on either side of the front door.

They passed through the entryway, lined with bookshelves, the floor covered with threadbare throw rugs that must be fifty years old; Esther recognized several. Mamm had always been frugal, but maybe she was living in poverty, barely scraping by. To the left stood the closed door leading to the Daadi Haus; to the right lay the sitting room, illuminated by a gas lamp.

Esther's attention turned to Holly, who scanned the house's drab interior; she wondered what her daughter saw. The surroundings were the opposite of the Amish Shoppe, its every inch decorated and prettified, and the electric lighting intense.

"We apologize for not contacting you first," Holly said.

"No apology needed. I've waited so long." Mamm's voice quivered with excitement. She fixed her gaze on Esther, until Esther looked away. "What can I give yous ta eat?" Mamm asked. "*Kaffi* or hot chocolate? Whoopie pie? Essie, remember how much you loved my whoopie pie?"

"No one made it better." Esther inhaled the familiar aromas of warm chocolate, rising bread, and baking squash. "Maybe later, thank you, we just had breakfast."

Followed by Holly, she wandered through the sitting room into the kitchen—the hub of the house. The same long table, with six chairs and a bench crowded around it, dominated the room. She noticed a gas-run refrigerator and oven where the icebox and sturdy iron wood-burning range once resided.

"Where's Isaac?" Esther peered out the window above the sink and saw the chicken coop, mended in several places, and the barnyard she'd once crossed daily to collect eggs.

"He's looking after old Cookie." Mamm brought a stack of plates to the table. "It wonders me that mare has lasted this long."

"I want to see her," Holly said. "I've never been in a barn."

"Well, then, I'll ask Isaac to give you a tour after breakfast. He'll be in soon. He'll be pleased to see ya both." Mamm was speaking of Esther's youngest brother, only five years old when she'd left home. Esther had once helped prepare his meals, laundered his clothes, and baked him cookies. She'd left Isaac without a farewell hug and never written, not once. And she'd disgraced the family by not getting baptized into the Amish church. Why would he be glad to see her? If anything, he'd resent her return.

Mamm arranged the plates—nine of them. "Did Beth tell ya your other brothers have gone to inspect property in Montana? Clear across the country."

"Yes, she did." Hearing Beth's name, Esther's stomach knotted. She imagined Beth bringing her children and grandchildren here to help Mamm make pies and cookies. Having a grand old time in this very room.

Mamm turned to Holly. "Other Amish communities have moved to Montana, but I can think of half a dozen locations I'd prefer, if we must leave. Like New York State, Indiana, or Ohio. I'll miss this house."

"Then why leave?" Holly unzipped her jacket. "I don't understand."

"As the population grows, the county's shrinkin', meaning we're running short on land. One of your uncles, my oldest son, Adam, lives southwest of here in Gordonville. A development company made a substantial offer on his farm, and then recently a neighbor asked to buy our place, offering us enough money to purchase acreage ten times the size of ours, in Montana. Enough property for all my children and grandchildren."

The kitchen door leading to the utility room burst open and three kids bustled inside. The oldest couldn't have been more than four; the youngest was perhaps two years old. The barefoot girl wore the same clothes Esther had as a child, a below-the-knee apron over a dress. Straw hats covered the boys' heads and suspenders held up their trousers. They were giggling and jabbering in Deitsch. The scene was both comforting and off-putting, as if Esther's feet were sliding into her favorite bedroom slippers and finding a pebble at the bottom.

As if she were awakening from amnesia, childhood memories mushroomed, coming to life in 3-D. When Esther was young she assumed she'd remain in Lancaster County forever, but she'd suffocated under the weight of Mamm and Dat's expectations. Like a slingshot, she'd catapulted herself to the other side of the country and didn't belong here anymore.

CHAPTER NINE

"They don't speak English yet," Grandma Anna told me, describing the three preschool children trouping around me, chattering in Pennsylvania Dutch. "These are Isaac and Greta's *Kinner:* Joe, Luke, and Sarah." In their Amish outfits the two boys were hard to tell apart. No Mariner T-shirts or baseball caps here.

I caught snippets of what they said and was delighted they called me *Aendi* Holly.

Grandma Anna corrected them. "They think you're their aunt, but I told them you're my granddaughter. So you're their cousin."

"I probably look the age of their parents." I didn't care if they thought I was as ancient as Mount Rainier. The kids treated me like a celebrity. I wore jeans, blue flats, and a matching belt. And makeup—had I applied too much mascara this morning? I felt over my head and out of place, and also thrilled to be in the spotlight.

Grandma Anna removed the boys' straw hats and hung them on pegs at the back door. She turned to Mom, who stood watching us from afar. "This is Esther Fisher, *mei Dochder* from Seattle. Esther is Holly's *Mudder*."

The kids seemed to understand, because they smiled.

"Hello, children." Mom's eyes—I knew her every look—told me she was glad I was fitting in, but her shoulders and feet angled toward the front door like she couldn't wait to scram.

I had to ask myself again: Was Mom's memory failing? Unlikely. She ran the Amish Shoppe, rarely missing a beat when it came to checking in orders and recalling customers' names. What was her problem?

I heard footsteps on the staircase leading to the second floor. A moment later, a woman wearing an eggplant-colored dress and black apron entered the kitchen cradling a baby. Grandma Anna introduced us to Mom's sister-in-law—Uncle Isaac's wife—Greta, her prayer cap veiling sandy-brown hair, her strings hanging loosely.

"Good ta meetcha," Greta said. "This here's three-month-old Lydia." Greta stroked the baby's rosy cheek. "Our older two Kinner are in school. Have ya met my husband, Isaac?"

"Not yet." I figured Greta was my age. While admiring her baby girl, I noticed Greta's gaze analyzing me from head to foot. I reminded myself: My mother was the prodigal daughter, come back from sampling the wicked world and returning with nothing except me, a fancy Englischer, which is what Mom told me Grandma Anna labeled anyone who was non-Amish.

"My sisters-in-law went to town to do the shoppin' and will swing by in a couple hours," Greta said, rocking Lydia. "If they'd known you were comin' I'm sure they'd be here to greet ya."

Grandma chuckled. "Ach, even I didn't know they were comin'."

"I look forward to meeting them," I said. "How will I keep everybody in the family straight?"

"We share the same last name as your grandmother Gingerich, since the women married her sons," she said with a smile.

"You're right." I tried to memorize Greta's round face and her fair complexion, and repeated her name in my head, a trick I used with our customers.

"I hear you, your husband, and kids live here," I said.

"For now, anyways. Until we move west."

"Then there can't be room for Mom and me." I was thankful I'd left the suitcases in the car. But I wasn't sure what we'd do now.

"Sure there is." Grandma Anna laid her speckled hand on my forearm. Her nails were clipped short and her fingers beautifully gnarled. "There's plenty of space. You'll sleep upstairs."

"I couldn't take someone's bedroom," my mother said, finally sounding halfway like herself. But she was wringing her hands.

"Mom, I'd like to stay." I moved to her side and whispered, "We can't afford a motel room."

"You should have come last night." Grandma Anna opened a drawer and selected flatware. "Why did you go to Beth's?"

"Holly and I didn't want to wake you." Mom stared at the linoleum floor.

"That makes no speck of sense," Grandma said.

"Don't blame Mom," I said. "It was my idea not to show up on your doorstep without warning last night. I'll have to thank Zach for stopping over to announce our arrival this morning."

No, I wouldn't. Although he was good-looking and friendly, I thought he'd acted like a busybody—a mama's boy.

"Zachary Fleming's the best vet in the county," Greta said. "And his mother is like one of us."

I imagined those words piercing Mom's eardrums and my chest felt heavy, like when I had pneumonia as a kid. But my mother had brought this situation upon herself by rejecting her parents. I wasn't sure she deserved my pity.

"I'm glad you have neighbors to count on," I said. "Beth's extremely nice. She took us right in without question." I envisioned her transporting the Gingerich family in her minivan, saving them the trouble of hitching up horses, which is what my uncles' wives must have done today. After playing in the buggy at the Amish Shoppe as a child, I had a hankering to ride in one, to hear real horseshoes clopping.

The kitchen door rattled open and a man wearing an untrimmed beard—minus the moustache—a wide-brimmed straw hat, black suspenders over a blue shirt, and black trousers sauntered in, bringing with him a gust of glacial air.

"Holly, here's your Uncle Isaac," Grandma Anna said. "Did I tell ya he's a preacher?"

He didn't look like any minister I'd ever seen. "You must be proud of him."

Her features stiffened. Had I said the wrong thing?

Isaac cut me and Mom a cursory glance. The two little boys ran over to him and hugged his legs. He tousled the tops of their heads, then removed his hat, exposing flattened brown hair trimmed in a bowl-like fashion.

"Isaac," my grandmother said, "did ya see your sister's come home?"

He hung his hat on a peg, stepped out of his work boots and into slippers, then scrubbed his hands at the small sink by the back door. Drying them thoroughly, he spoke over his shoulder. "Hullo, Esther."

I sensed a mixed message; his voice was polite but aloof. Maybe he begrudged Mom's arrival. I might feel the same way. My mother had no doubt caused Grandma Anna years of anguish.

"Nice to see you, Isaac." Mom stared at his feet.

Seeming to ignore Mom—the boys were speaking Pennsylvania Dutch again—Isaac turned to me. "You must be Holly." His stern features—bushy brows over green eyes—softened somewhat. "I'm Esther's youngest *Bruder*."

He frowned as he scanned my straight-legged jeans and my sweater. Was he always grumpy? I told myself he'd been up milking cows since dawn and deserved respect.

He moved to the chair at the head of the table and stood with his hands on the seatback. "Ya comin' home to stay, Esther?"

Mom's face blanched as white as Grandma's prayer cap. "No, just a visit."

"And it's a gut thing she's here," Grandma said. "Ain't so?"

"If it makes ya happy, Mamm." His stare bore into Mom. "What took you so long, Esther?"

"Hush," Grandma Anna said to him. *"Sei net so rilpsich."*

"What did you say?" I asked her. "I can't understand."

"I told him not to be rude." Her mouth produced a thin-lipped smile. "This should be a time of celebration, not arguing."

Lydia started fussing. Greta laid the baby over her shoulder and patted her back.

"Please, have a seat," Mom told Greta. "Holly and I will help Mamm set the table. I like keeping my hands busy."

"*Ich bedank mich*—thank you." Greta settled onto the bench and Isaac seated himself at the head of the table. My cutie-pie cousin, Sarah, and her brothers, Joe and Luke, sat next to their mother.

I hoped for an opportunity to hold Lydia later. Growing up, I'd weeded and mowed neighbors' lawns to earn money, but never babysat. I was awkward around babies; Greta would have to show me what to do.

Mom and I helped Grandma Anna lay out a plentiful noon meal: meat pie, steamed vegetables, noodles, homemade bread, and jams and jellies much like the preserves we sold at the Amish Shoppe. Mom imported her stock from several states, but never from this area. Now I wondered why.

The kitchen door opened and another bearded man, taller than my uncle, stepped inside.

"This is our neighbor, Nathaniel King," Grandma said. "He lives next door, the opposite way from Beth. Esther might recognize him from when yous were kids."

Nathaniel removed his straw hat, revealing espresso-brown hair cut in the same bowl-over-the-head fashion as Isaac's. No wedding ring. But then Isaac didn't wear one either.

"After he milks his herd, he spends half days working here while my other sons are gone," Grandma Anna said. "We're most thankful."

I took in Nathaniel's face—tanned from fifty-some years working under the sun. Warmth filled my chest, flushing up my neck to my cheeks. Was I actually blushing upon meeting this bearded local yokel? Larry Haarberg would laugh his head off.

Nathaniel seated himself at Isaac's elbow, next to Grandma Anna.

"Will your wife be joining us?" I asked Nathaniel.

"He's a widower," Grandma Anna said. "With two grown daughters, both married."

"Two children, how wonderful," I said, and Nathaniel nodded. Another Oscar the Grouch! He seemed to be snubbing me, but glanced over to Mom with what appeared to be recognition.

"And you?" Isaac asked me. "A husband? Children?"

"No, never married, no kids. Perpetually single."

"Holly," my mother said. "We'll have plenty of time to talk this through in private. These men and children are hungry, and we need to pray first."

"He's the one who asked." I figured she was embarrassed about my marital status. So was I, but I'd taught myself to hide my discomfort behind an I-couldn't-care-less facade.

Isaac cleared his throat—a guttural sound—and all at the table bowed their heads for a minute, followed by "Amen" when he cleared his throat again—a silent grace. Mom apparently knew the routine but never prayed this way at home.

Grandma's face filled with elation as she passed me a serving spoon. "Eat yourself full," she told me. "You look on the thin side, Holly."

Ordinarily I balked when people implied I was skinny, because I'd been a scrawny kid. But not today. I had a real live grandma!

CHAPTER TEN

Sitting across from her mamm and Nathaniel, Esther felt pent up, a lamb being carted off to market.

Isaac dominated the table, sitting where their father used to eat. Her little brother was now a preacher, chosen by lot, ordained by God. In letters, Mamm hadn't mentioned his highly respected status, a full-time unpaid burden on top of working the farm. Esther wondered if Isaac relished the power and prestige accompanying the position. He certainly wouldn't approve of her choices and lifestyle.

Judging from his gruff tone and lack of eye contact—with her, anyway—he had taken on their father's disposition. She recalled Dat's flaring temper, how the family would cower when he fell into a foul mood. Esther's mamm never shielded her children from his ranting nor did she speak up in her own defense. Not that Mamm could, according to the Ordnung—the bishops', preachers', and deacons' interpretation of the Bible. A woman must submit to God, her husband, and her father.

Esther repositioned herself on the pad-covered wooden chair, but couldn't get comfortable. She was glad she'd dressed in her conservative calf-length skirt and hadn't chosen her blouse with the embroidered front, nor worn earrings or a wristwatch. She didn't want to look more fancy to her mother and brother than she already did. At least her hair was fastened into a bun, much like Greta's, but without a prayer cap.

The three kids gobbled their lunch, followed by fluffy molasses shoofly pie, then, after Isaac led another silent prayer, they congregated in the sitting room to play checkers before naptime. Their laughter reminded Esther of her childhood. At their age she had expected she'd help raise her brothers, do chores, tend the garden, get baptized, married, and raise a family, the more offspring the better.

She watched Mamm serve Holly another portion of shoofly pie and was surprised Holly didn't protest, "Hold on, that's way too much," but rather inhaled a mouthful and exclaimed, "This is the best pie I've ever eaten."

"Ich bedank mich." Mamm's eyes lit up with delight.

"Guess I'll need to take a walk later to burn off the extra calories." Holly savored another bite. "I usually go to the gym and jog on the treadmill four days a week."

"No need," Isaac said. "There's plenty of work to be done around here. Ain't that so, Esther?"

Esther bobbed her head, her words trapped in her mouth along with the pie she was having a tough time swallowing. If she'd only come back a decade ago, this meal wouldn't be so excruciating. But each year, she'd found an excuse. The Amish Shoppe couldn't operate without her; Holly was studying for her SATs, applying to colleges, and graduating from high school. Not enough money, no time, no backbone.

She checked the battery-run clock on the wall. The minutes seemed to tick at half speed. She remembered herself as a preteen; at the noon meal, time crawled while she longed to streak out the back door barefoot, run across the field, and wade in the creek. But no, she must wait for everyone to finish eating, put away leftovers, and clean the kitchen. After, weeding the garden awaited her.

Esther's hands scrunched her napkin, then she flattened it across her lap as best she could. Last week riding the Metro bus home from the Fiber Gallery, a yarn shop, hadn't she thought her days too stressful? At her annual physical, her general practitioner advised, "You should consider blood pressure medication, although I'm guessing anxiety is the culprit."

Esther pushed the rest of her pie around her plate with her fork as the others chatted about Nathaniel's organic farm. She recalled Nathaniel King from childhood. He was a couple years younger than she and Samuel, but they'd studied together in the same one-room schoolhouse. She'd thought he was all moony-eyed over her those many years ago, but he probably didn't remember her anymore. She shuddered to imagine his opinion of her now.

"When I do the grocery shopping, I buy only organic," Holly said. She seemed interested in Nathaniel's farming techniques, but Esther could tell by the way her daughter's gaze flitted about that she found Nathaniel boring. And the house? She bet Holly saw it as unappealing compared to Dori and Jim's home, their walls adorned with family photos and prints of the Pike Place Market.

Setting her fork on the edge of her plate, Esther remembered how pretty and spacious her parents' house had seemed when she was a child. Compared to her little home in Seattle it was huge, and for good reason. The front rooms' wall partitions could be removed to accommodate the whole district community, over two hundred on one preaching Sunday a year, rotating throughout the parish. As a young girl, she'd been thrilled when church members brought food dishes and thick-crusted pies to eat after church service.

Esther was an alien today. It occurred to her she should have brought her mother a gift—a hostess present, at the least. Self-centered Esther was still only thinking of herself.

"More pie, Isaac?" Mamm asked.

He belched and Holly turned to look at him. "Yah, please," he said.

Mamm smiled and sliced into it. "Anyone else?"

"Me, too," Nathaniel said, adding a belch.

Esther wished she'd warned Holly belching was considered good manners, a sign the person was enjoying his meal.

She wondered what had happened to Nathaniel's deceased wife. Giving him closer inspection, she saw slate-blue eyes the color of the yarn she'd recently chosen to knit Jim a sweater vest, framed by strong eyebrows and lashes any woman would covet. If only Holly could find a fine man like him; he'd be suitable husband material. No, Holly would never marry a bearded fellow wearing suspenders and baggy trousers, let alone become Amish.

"Do your children live nearby?" Esther asked Nathaniel.

"My Tina lives two miles east and has three children," he said, "and Hannah is down in Strasburg. No Kinner yet."

"You live by yourself?" Holly said, which seemed impolite to Esther.

"Yah, just me and my cows and chickens."

Holly tilted her head. "And horses?"

"A thoroughbred, four mules, and six Clydesdales. Not that I'm boasting, mind ya."

Esther wondered if he were courting anyone but knew better than to ask. Courting was kept strictly between the unmarried man and woman. Often family members and best friends were kept in the dark until an intention of marriage was announced at church a couple weeks before the marriage season commenced—next month in November and through December, on Tuesdays and Thursdays, now that she thought of it. As the notion rambled through her mind, Nathaniel glanced over at her and smiled, revealing laugh lines. She couldn't help but smile back. A butterfly fluttered in her chest. Was he flirting with her? No, not possible with her stunning daughter sitting close by.

She broke eye contact, took hold of her fork. "Mamm, your pies are as good as ever."

"Thank you."

"My mother bakes a mean pie, but she's never made this kind," Holly said. "Lunch was delicious, Grandma. Especially the biscuits. And the butter's creamier here."

The corners of Mamm's mouth curved up into a crescent moon. "I must admit, the butter's store-bought. But it's from a local dairy."

"Beth said she takes you shopping," Holly said, then sipped her water.

"Yah, she carries my groceries to her van and then into our house, and helps me put them away."

Esther gritted her teeth as she imagined Mamm and Beth chit-chatting on the way to the market. She wondered how much Beth already knew about her life, wondered if Mamm had brought Esther's letters along to read aloud.

CHAPTER ELEVEN

I felt I'd landed in a Northern Germanic country, transported hundreds of years back in time, immersed in rustic surroundings—although my grandma did have a refrigerator and stove, run by what I wasn't sure, since they didn't plug into the wall. My young cousins spoke only in Pennsylvania Dutch. I could catch bits of what they said.

After lunch, Greta addressed Mom. "I'll clear and wash the dishes if you'll look after our Lydia."

"Yes, please," Mom said. "I'd be delighted to hold her for as long as you need." Greta handed the baby to my mother's receptive arms and Mom began rocking Lydia and cooing.

If only I had my own child to include in this gathering. My mother had her daughter, me, to represent her branch of the family tree, but I was a desert. I might as well be barren; within years I would be.

Grandma placed a hand on Nathaniel's shoulder. "Would ya please take Holly for a buggy ride and show her the sights?" she said. "Looks like the sun's comin' out real nice."

"He's probably too busy." I didn't care for her suggestion. Was she setting me up for a date with an older man?

"I have much work ta do," Nathaniel said, hooking his thumbs in his suspenders, looking uneasy. "This late in the year, the sun sets early."

Isaac stood, then headed out the back door wearing his boots and hat, suggesting Nathaniel was right. Without modern equipment, Uncle Isaac must work twenty-four hours a day. And, frankly, who wanted to spend time with Nathaniel? Not I.

"The chores'll be waitin'," Grandma Anna said. She smiled at me, the way I'd always dreamed a granny would. "Maybe Holly can help out later."

"I know zilch about farming," I said, because I wanted to stay with her. Yet I needed a break from my mother. And I needed to move about after eating too much—I'd even polished off the morsels Mom said she didn't have room for. She'd hardly consumed her meal. I imagined Grandma Anna noticed but hadn't mentioned her skimpy appetite. So far, I couldn't find one detail not to like about my fabulous, picture-perfect grandmother. What had Mom been thinking all these years? Grandma Anna was the greatest.

"No hurry getting back, you two," were my grandmother's parting words to Nathaniel and me as I zipped on my jacket. "Have a *wunderbaar* time. Nathaniel, be sure to show Holly a covered bridge."

We left by the back door. Once outside, I felt the midday sun radiating warmth through a crepe paper–thin veneer of clouds. I inhaled the fresh farm air, laced with smoke from a distant fire. Nathaniel and I strolled down the road to his home, similar to Grandma's, about half a mile south. Behind it stood a freshly painted white barn, two silos, and a windmill.

I checked the far end of the house. "No Daadi Haus?" I said, pleased I remembered two words in Pennsylvania Dutch.

"Not yet. Neither my parents nor my former wife's parents dwelled with us."

I wondered why he'd never remarried and if he must wear a beard the rest of his life, even though he was single.

"I'm intrigued that you grow only organic crops," I said, not daring to bring up personal questions.

"Yah, organic only." He picked up his speed, his legs a foot longer than mine. Was he afraid a neighbor would see him with a stranger? Did he resent playing tour guide—my stealing him away from his duties? This was going to be a dreary afternoon as far as company went.

Tagging a few feet behind, I let my eyes embrace the serene landscape: pastureland, harvested fields, neighboring farms in the distance. I inhaled robust air unlike the city's smog and listened to trilling birdcalls I'd never heard before.

We rounded Nathaniel's house and I followed him into an area accommodating a barn he said was used for milking, a larger barn I guessed for storing hay and straw, small outbuildings, a chicken coop, and a gate leading to a lush pasture containing horses and two dozen black-and-white cows he said were Holsteins.

Behind them stretched another field of what looked to be drying cornstalks. Or was it wheat? I decided not to inquire and escape Nathaniel's one-word answers. Grandma Anna could fill me in later.

Nathaniel clicked his tongue.

A dappled-gray horse raised its majestic head, then bolted past the cows to receive a sugar cube from Nathaniel's hand. Nathaniel took hold of its halter and led the horse to a hitching post near an outbuilding lodging two buggies, one like ours at the Amish Shoppe and a smaller one without a roof.

"Which would you prefer?" Nathaniel asked.

I pointed to the open two-person buggy. "I'll get a better view." I wouldn't admit our brisk walk had warmed me.

The horse's tail flicked.

"Steady, boy, I'm movin' as fast as I can." Nathaniel harnessed the horse to the buggy.

"He's gorgeous." I admired the sculpted beauty, but was afraid he'd step on my foot or kick me. "Is he a stallion?"

"No, a gelding."

"What's his name?"

"Galahad. A retired racehorse I found at auction."

Nathaniel was not much of a conversationalist. At least I'd get a tour of the county and a retreat from my sulking mother.

"Sorry to put you to this trouble," I said.

Nathaniel extended his hand and helped me into the buggy. "'Tis no trouble." But his dour expression showed otherwise.

"I think Grandma Anna wanted me out of the house to give my mother and her a chance to speak in private. Finally. You know my mother's been gone."

"You both have."

"Our absence wasn't my fault. I honestly didn't know Grandma was alive."

He surveyed my face as if he didn't believe me. My, what beautiful blue eyes this man had. But not the greatest personality; no wonder he was still single.

He climbed into the buggy on the other side and took up the reins. The horses pulling buggies I'd seen so far appeared to trot demurely, but once Nathaniel spoke to Galahad and jiggled the reins, his feisty steed took off as if itching for an adventure. I felt every joggle and bump, then a joyous sensation as the horse cantered down the road.

My senses were heightened, colors magnified by the October sun sitting low in the sky, casting elongated shadows. Towering maple trees, their remaining leaves ranging from ginger to burgundy, blurred past. The wind swirled through my ears—invigorating. We overtook a gray covered buggy and an SUV full of tourists, I assumed, the way Nathaniel turned his face away when they took photos.

The farms and fields, pumpkin patches, meandering streams, and a stone mill I guessed was two hundred years old fascinated me. And Nathaniel? Yes, his steady grip on the reins piqued my attention. His knuckles were hefty and his nails in need of a manicure—a workingman's hands, seemingly able to tackle any job.

"You warm enough?" he said. "I've got a blanket." He stretched the woolen square across my lap.

"Thanks." Leaning back, I listened to the clip-clip-clopping and felt the soothing buggy swaying beneath me. Out of the corner of my eye, I gave Nathaniel a casual inspection. Except for his funky haircut and his scraggly beard—I'd never cared for facial hair, except a movie star's two-day-old stubble—he was ruggedly handsome. He possessed a manly quality, the opposite of Larry Haarberg back in Seattle.

With a spoken word and a subtle tug on the reins, Nathaniel steered the buggy off the main road onto a lane. We passed a herd of grazing sheep. I envisioned newly born lambs frolicking on the pasture next spring. Why did my mother leave this extraordinary place? Oh, yeah. No cars, electricity, or telephones. But still, why not visit her mother and brothers? Not to mention her outlandish lying to me.

Through a grove of partially bare elms, their limbs reaching to the sky like ballet dancers' arms, I spotted farmhouses much like Grandma's, also with green shades. And no electric wires running from telephone poles.

"I'm finally getting the hang of it," I said. "No electric wires means Amish live there."

"That's right."

"How can you stand living without electricity?" I thought of our TV—the five o'clock news and *Masterpiece Mystery*.

"Electricity brings in the outside world and separates our community." His voice turned forceful, emerging from his abdomen. "It separates us from God."

"Are kids required to join the church at a certain age?" I thought of my rebellious parents.

"They're given a choice," he said. "At age sixteen, they enter a running around period, what we call Rumspringa. By age twenty-one, around ninety percent of young adults raised Old Order Amish get baptized and commit themselves to God and the church." The man who hardly finished a sentence seemed primed to give me a lecture. But I wanted to learn about their ways, my parents' history.

"And once they get baptized?" I said.

"They're committed to remain Amish for life."

"I guess my parents didn't want to be baptized for some reason." I hoped Nathaniel would fill me in, but he clammed up, his focus directed on a bearded man in a field steering a team of mules.

Feeling cozy, I unzipped my jacket. As I watched a rabbit scamper across the road, my thoughts skittered back to Mom. I was thrilled my grandma was alive, but Mom's past behavior baffled me more than ever.

Dori had mentioned meeting my mother in San Francisco when Mom was first pregnant, but Dori hadn't divulged further details, only that my mother traveled to Seattle, where she gave birth to me. She'd lived with Dori and Jim for several years, until moving to her own home, later transformed into the Amish Shoppe with Jim's assistance.

Fifteen minutes later, Nathaniel slowed the horse and circled back toward his house. We hadn't crossed a covered bridge, but I could see one tomorrow. Now might be my last chance to grill him for information about Dad.

"Did you know my father, Samuel Fisher?"

He loosened up on the reins and Galahad slowed his pace. "I was a couple years younger, but we all went to a one-room schoolhouse together."

"Just checking. My dad really existed?"

"Yah. For sure."

"Mom has only one black-and-white photo, taken when Dad was eighteen."

His eyebrows lowered, and a look of disapproval morphed his face—why, I couldn't fathom. "She owns a photograph of him?" he said.

"Yes, on her bureau." Inquiries about Dad, everything from his personality quirks to his hobbies, crisscrossed my mind. Did Amishmen have time for hobbies? Mom had mentioned volleyball games on weekend afternoons. "What was he like?" I asked.

"It's been many a year." Nathaniel repositioned his hat. "I haven't seen Samuel since I was thirteen. As I recall, he was outgoing and energetic. You should ask Esther."

"I have, but she sidesteps the subject." I turned to face him; his hair and beard seemed more pleasing. "I wonder what his ambitions were. To be like his father? Mom said his dad was a farmer."

"He still is. Ready to retire. Samuel's parents live not far away. Maybe you and your mother will visit them while you're here."

Would Grandma Anna orchestrate that gathering, or did the Fishers hate Grandma, too?

"They may not know about me. They might think my father died childless." Nothing new, but voicing the facts made my throat constrict like I'd swallowed a tablespoon of salt.

"Of course they know about you. Anna would have told them years ago."

"But they've never reached out to me." Because of Mom.

Having no relatives in Seattle was an advantage, I'd always told myself. But I knew deep in my core it wasn't true. Thanksgiving and Christmas were humdrum without a houseful of family. Thank the Lord for Dori and Jim. But they had their own children, as well as siblings and cousins they often visited in Portland, Oregon.

"Out of curiosity, where do my dad's parents live?"

"Not far away." Nathaniel massaged the reins. "I could drive ya by their farm right now if ya like."

"No, we'd better not." I avoided conflict. Hated it, really. "Mom said they never wanted to speak to her again."

"I'm sure Samuel's parents have forgiven her. Holdin' a grudge goes against the teachings of the Good Book. Luke 6:37. 'Judge not, and ye shall not be judged: condemn not, and ye shall not be con-demned: forgive, and ye shall be forgiven.'"

"Mom's recited that Bible verse enough times, but why should I forgive mean-spirited bullies who teased me as a girl and never apologized?" Even if they'd forgotten all about me.

I supposed I hadn't forgiven my dad for dying, either. Which I knew was ridiculous. But still, it seemed like he'd deserted Mom and me.

"The Lord admonishes us to forgive." Nathaniel's home was still a good trek away, but he pulled up on the reins and Galahad halted at the side of the road. Maybe he was going to make me hike back.

When the reins went slack, the horse lowered his neck to munch grass and dandelions.

"Thank you, I've enjoyed our ride tremendously," I said. "This is a beautiful area. So peaceful, I forgot to check my cell phone for messages all day." Why was I babbling? Because I didn't want our outing to end.

Yet I couldn't help pondering my life in Seattle. I'd turned my cell phone to silent. I slipped my phone out of my pocket and saw four missed voice mails. Three from Larry, and one from my newlywed girlfriend, Joanne. Before leaving the city, I'd left her a message, nothing specific, only wishing her well and saying I'd be out of town.

So my old boss Mel hadn't called. I didn't expect him to, I told myself, but couldn't shake the melancholy sludge engulfing me. I made the decision not to dwell on finding new work again for twenty-four hours. Who needed a dynamic career, anyway?

I slipped my phone back in my pocket. "Our trip here was worth it if nothing more than this ride," I said. "Thank you for taking the time, even if my Grandma Anna forced you."

Now what would we two polar opposites talk about? I considered describing the Amish Shoppe and my mother's buggy, but Nathaniel would find it ludicrous. Then I wondered why I should care what he thought; I'd never see him again after this trip.

His fingers tightened around the reins and he gave me a challenging look. "You sure you don't want to mosey over to Samuel's parents' right now?"

"Why would you care?" I returned his gaze with defiance, a tug-of-war waging in my mind. "Although I admit I am curious to get a look at them, to see if my father favored either parent. This might be my only chance. No, I'd better not. I need to check with Mom first. She'd have a conniption. And my dad's parents might give me the cold shoulder." Too disappointing.

"Perhaps another time, when your mother's with us." He slapped the reins and Galahad headed home. Nathaniel directed him around the side of his house to the barnyard.

I hopped out—a long way for a shorty like me. Gathering my courage, I stroked the horse's rump, then moved to his neck to feel his smooth, moist hair, the warmth traveling up my arm.

CHAPTER TWELVE

Storing leftovers in the refrigerator, Esther listened to Greta coax her children up the stairs for naptime. Oh, how Esther adored the sound of their youthful voices. If only Holly got married and made her a grandmother. Grandchildren would finally bring Esther fulfillment, she was sure of it.

She removed unused flatware and cups from the table. She hoped to keep her hands and mind occupied while Holly dallied with Nathaniel. What was taking them so long? She shouldn't be aggravated, Esther told herself. But she was.

She noticed Mamm open the refrigerator door and rearrange the leftovers Esther had just put away. Apparently Esther still couldn't do anything right. Up to Mamm's high standards, that is. Although Esther saw no logic in Mamm's method of storing the vegetables next to the cottage cheese, nowhere close to the sour cream and yogurt. And her mother put cubes of butter in three locations.

"I'll scrape and wash the dishes," Esther said. She flushed hot water into the sink, followed by a squirt of liquid soap.

"Nee, I always do the dishes," Mamm said.

If she could see Esther's kitchen, its sink piled with soaking plates, she'd be shocked. Not to mention the empty soup and tuna cans. But no problem; Mamm would never visit Seattle.

"You didn't eat much," Mamm said. She closed the refrigerator door, then slipped the dishes into the sink. "Don't ya like my cookin' anymore?"

"Yes, as I mentioned before, it's as tasty as ever." Esther swiped the vinyl-covered table with a sponge. In truth, she felt like her taste buds had gone dormant. "Beth fed us breakfast this morning. And I've gained some unwelcome weight recently." She attempted to lighten the mood by adding, "Either that or my skirt's waistband is shrinking." Who needed a diet? With her jangled nerves, if she ate every meal in this kitchen, Esther would be down to a size eight lickety-split.

"Don't go blaming your measly appetite on Beth."

Esther wished she hadn't brought up Beth's name and vowed not to repeat it. If all went well, their paths wouldn't cross again. Ever.

"Now, what was I doin'?" Leaving the dishes in the sink, Mamm set about transforming the kitchen back to its tidy self. Decades had evaporated, but her insistence on tidiness and order persevered. Esther wondered if her mother wanted a woman-to-woman talk now that they were alone. Did she expect Esther to do the listening, as if she were still an obedient child? For better or worse, Esther was a completely changed person and used to speaking her mind.

Over the years, Esther's letters had stated emphatically she had no intention of returning here. "If you want to see us, hop on the train to Seattle," Esther had written, knowing the trip would never happen. Esther recalled she'd sent Mamm Holly's graduation picture and several others. Had Mamm tossed them in the fireplace? Well, Esther knew she'd plunked Mamm in the impossible position of disobeying the Ordnung, the rules passed down from generation to generation, by which Old Order Amish must live, especially with Isaac being a preacher.

And now here Esther was, in spite of all her refusals to return—because Mamm had tricked her, feigning to be on her deathbed.

Mamm minced around the room swabbing counters. She bent down to pick up an errant crumb, then straightened, her hand on the small of her back as if feeling a zap of discomfort. Was she putting on a show for Esther? Yes, Esther had been duped into coming to rescue her vigorously healthy mother.

"I'm glad to see you're doing so well," Esther said.

"Today's a *wunderbaar* day—ain't?"

Anna Gingerich could be a Hollywood actress, Esther thought, watching Mamm rinse the sponge and set it at right angles to the drying board. Still no dishwasher, but even if the bishop allowed it, she doubted Mamm would accept one. Her mother had always taken pleasure in washing the glasses and dishes, then polishing them spotless. As a girl, Esther hated housework; she would have preferred to be in the barn helping the men. She'd felt excluded and uninformed when Dat, her brothers, and the hired men gathered for conferences.

Right now, she knew she should be asking about Mamm's life after Dat died, how she'd managed raising five sons without a husband or another woman in the house to help rear the boys. At age sixteen, Esther had refused to care for her brothers anymore, slaving all day and picking up after them. But now, Esther should demonstrate compassion. After all, she'd felt empathy for Holly and Dori many times, as she had for complete strangers on the street.

Please, Lord, forgive me and fill me with tenderness toward my mother, she prayed, but she felt disconnected from God. Instead of compassion, resentment coiled through her mind, spurring her tongue into action.

"Tell me about your health, Mamm." Esther knew she was goading her mother, but felt she deserved straight answers.

"The excitement and joy of seeing you and Holly lifted my symptoms today. What a gut job you've done raising her." Mamm's gaze probed Esther's eyes. "But you deprived her of her Amish heritage. Her People. If only you'd come home we could have helped ya." Her lower lip tightened. "Or was there a man?"

"Are you asking if I remarried or found a boyfriend?" Esther retucked her blouse and smoothed her skirt. Glancing out the window above the sink she saw Isaac shouldering open a gate, then steering four draft horses into a field to bale hay. She bet her youngest brother wished Esther would vamoose. Since he had an insubordinate sister, she was surprised he was ever nominated to become a minister.

"There's never been another man." Esther said. "Only Samuel."

Mamm lined up the chairs, evening the spaces between them. "I see Samuel's parents every once in a while. Shall I invite them over for dinner?"

"No! They made it clear they despised me."

"People change." Mamm removed her spectacles and polished them with her apron. "I agree, his father was too hard on Samuel, but old Jeremiah has mellowed."

"And his mother? She only saw me as a distraction to Samuel's dawn-to-dusk chores." She couldn't help smiling when she recalled the Sunday evening Singings and later riding in Samuel's courting buggy, entwined in each other's arms.

Mamm set her glasses back on the bridge of her nose. "His mother's still standoffish, I s'pose ya might call her."

"Both Samuel's parents were too strict." No use bringing up that Esther's own dat was easily provoked over minor misdemeanors like not stacking the wood neatly. Esther had avoided Dat's switch or belt by blending into the woodwork or hiding behind Mamm's skirt.

"People change." Mamm clustered the sugar bowl with the salt and pepper shakers on the table. "Fortunately, neither you nor Samuel were yet baptized."

"His parents shunned me in their own way. Please don't force Holly and me into an awkward situation. They wouldn't like being reminded of their son's death, nor seeing us."

"Not meet their granddaughter? They'd be delighted."

"No, they'd say something cruel, I know it." Esther wouldn't allow Samuel's parents anywhere near Holly.

Mamm finally tackled the dishes and handed Esther a dish towel. "Would ya mind?"

"The water must be lukewarm by now," Esther said.

Mamm added more hot water. "*Simbel mir*—silly me—I get distracted."

Esther got to work drying the plates, stacking them in the cupboard in the same configuration as when she was a girl. She was relieved to have her hands active again.

"Now that I think of it," Mamm said, "comin' up is a nonpreaching Sunday, an afternoon to visit our neighbors. Maybe head over to Samuel's parents'."

"Absolutely not, I refuse. I'd rather hide in my room all day." She remembered the Fishers' words of chastisement, calling her demonic when she and Samuel announced they were taking a road trip, hitch-hiking across the country to San Francisco. "We want to see the Pacific Ocean," she'd told them, the words of a song popular at the time playing in her ears, encouraging her to wear flowers in her hair.

Samuel had never seen her long hair, always hidden under her prayer cap, until they left Lancaster. Esther had adored the idea of weaving daisies into her wavy tresses, a provocative frivolity forbidden by the Ordnung. Mamm nurtured colorful flowers in the yard, but not for picking. Wearing flowers was like wearing jewelry. *Verboten.*

Flower power! Esther had repeated in her mind.

"No wonder the Fishers detested me for luring their only child away," Esther said. "Their only child, dead. Any parent would be devastated."

Mamm drained the sink. "When Samuel passed away, what would you have done in their place? Eventually, you'd forgive, ain't so?"

"No. I'd hate me." Esther polished a coffee cup so hard she worried about cracking off the handle. She stowed it in the cabinet and returned to the drying rack. "In fact, I still do, for luring him away. The journey was my idea, not his."

"You didn't force him to go with you. He had a mind of his own."

"I used every persuasion." More than she'd admit.

"No use frettin' about the past. 'Tis *unsinnich*—senseless. If you see them, be polite and assume they'll return the courtesy."

Esther envisioned Samuel's parents' outraged scowls of disdain. Her thoughts spinning like a windmill, her hands went limp. Mamm's favorite oval serving bowl slipped from her fingers and crashed to the floor, smashing into shards.

Esther's jaw dropped open. "*Dabbish* fingers—I've never been so clumsy. I'll find a replacement. There's an online company that specializes in missing china."

"Never mind, 'tis only a bowl," Mamm said, a broom and dustpan soon in hand. "Lately I've been droppin' things too."

As Mamm swept, using quick motions, Esther imagined coming face-to-face with Samuel's parents—a fiasco. "We may not even be here," Esther said, feeling a wave of relief. "I'll check with Holly to see when we return. I didn't think to ask about our tickets."

"This is your home. Don't ya go away so soon." Her mother bent to use the dustpan. "Stay awhile."

Esther felt her invisible horns locking with Mamm's, like when she was a teen. "Have you heard nothing of what I've told you? I have a business to run."

"What sort? I still don't know what you do. Only that your friend is helpin'. Is this the same woman who carried you off to Seattle?"

"Dori didn't carry me anywhere. She's my best friend. When Samuel was drafted, she and her husband kindly took me in. I had no one else."

"Are ya *ab im Kopp?*—off in your head? You could have come home any time."

"To live under your domineering thumbs?" Esther spurted out.

Mamm dumped the broken bowl in the trash can. "Let's not quarrel. Tell me about your business."

Esther didn't dare admit she was making a living off the people she'd discarded. She couldn't bear an onslaught of her mother's criticism.

"It's a small retail store in my house. Holly and I live on the second floor. I order merchandise, price and display it, and help

customers—it's what puts food in our mouths and pays the mortgage, especially now that Holly's lost her job." Esther bit her lower
lip. "I shouldn't have mentioned that. She'd have a fit if she knew I
told you she'd been laid off."

"I don't understand. What kind of job did she lose? Why should
anything about the two of you be kept hush-hush?"

Esther reminded herself she was the woman bearing secrets.
Or did Mamm also keep one tucked in her apron pocket? Staring
into her mother's eyes, she felt like she was being sucked into
a vacuum, transported to childhood, a little girl looking up at
her parent who made all the decisions. Esther felt her strength
weaken. She couldn't face seeing the rest of the community, especially Samuel's parents. She wouldn't! She'd rather face Napoleon's
army.

"I should let Holly explain her career," Esther said. "I don't
really understand it myself. But I know she wants to go home and
start job hunting right away."

"Surely you'll stick around longer, won't ya?"

"No, I can't possibly stay when Holly leaves."

"Since she's without a job, both of you should remain until we
move to Montana, ain't so?"

"I'm too tired to debate the subject." Esther faked a yawn. "I
think jet lag's catching up with me."

"Go, put your feet up. I might take a nap myself."

Esther had never known her mother to snooze in the afternoon
when there were chores to be done, but she reminded herself of
Mamm's age. Esther followed her out of the kitchen to the bottom
of the staircase.

Mamm rested her hand on the banister. "I put you and Holly in your old room. Did I tell ya there are two beds in there now? I'll be up in a minute."

"Yes, okay." Her mother was repeating herself, but Esther sometimes did the same thing.

She climbed the staircase she'd skipped up and down thousands of times in her youth. Why had Mamm added another bed to her room? Perhaps hoping for more children? No, not possible after Dat died. Maybe Greta and Isaac's children had been sleeping in it, making Esther wonder why Mamm hadn't moved into the Daadi Haus years ago.

Greta or Mamm had made up the twin beds, each covered with one of Mamm's colorful quilts—Esther recognized her mother's precise craftsmanship. She breathed in the aroma of the cedar floors and stepped across rugs she recalled from her childhood. The same pull-shades hung in the windows.

Figuring her mother was close behind, Esther ignored the clean, pressed prayer cap on her bureau next to her old hairbrush and comb. The night she'd run away, she'd thrown her *Kapp* out the window in a show of defiance.

The trunk Dat had made for her sat at the foot of her old bed; she recognized the headboard. Was the chest still packed with gifts for her future marriage?

Esther opened the trunk, its lid heavy in her hands, and recognized pillowcases, tablecloths, and a baby quilt, making her feel like a *Laus*—a louse. Was her diary buried at the bottom? The night she and Samuel ran away, she'd thought she'd sequestered the journal. But the first night on the road, after digging through her backpack, she couldn't find it. Her mother had probably discovered and read the diary, meaning Mamm knew she had worked part-time at the restaurant where tourists stared at her and that she'd pocketed her tips instead of giving the money to Dat. She'd even driven a car on a bet. Not to mention the many times she and Samuel sneaked off on Saturday nights, or stayed up until dawn after Sunday Singings. Esther could have listened to Samuel's pure tenor voice for hours and relaxed in his arms forever.

Noticing movement out of the corner of her eye, Esther realized her mother had followed her upstairs and stood watching her.

"You should use this chest and linens," Esther said.

Mamm leaned one shoulder and her head against the doorframe. "It's been waitin' for ya. I knew you'd come home eventually."

"Mamm, I'm too old for a hope chest."

"Nee. You're young compared to me, and still beautiful. Why did you never remarry?"

"I could ask you the same question."

"I had a few men come round, but none could take the place of your father. Anyway, I had five sons to run the farm." She sighed, her chest sinking and her volume decreasing. "Without you here, I was too busy for courtin'." Hands on the doorframe, she turned and tottered toward her bedroom at the end of the hall.

Glad for a break, Esther closed the trunk and tiptoed downstairs. She padded outside onto the front porch and noticed a mare pulling a buggy, making her once again ponder Holly and Nathaniel's whereabouts.

CHAPTER THIRTEEN

"Thank you, you've been most kind," I said from my side of the buggy.

Was I flirting with Nathaniel? At home, I never gushed or inflated my praise. Just the opposite. What would friends think if they heard me carrying on?

"Before today, the closest I've come to a horse was riding a pony at the Woodland Park Zoo when I was seven or eight." I glanced down at my hands, folded in my lap—also not like the usual me—holding my cell phone.

My vision caught sight of a goat pen. "I wish I knew more about livestock."

"You can easily learn by doin'." Was he referring to me—as in him and me—here on this farm? Fat chance. If only Nathaniel could see me dressed for work, speeding my car down the freeway, radio cranked up.

"I won't be here long," I said. "We need to get back home. My mother owns a retail store and I've got to find a new job."

"Plenty of jobs here."

Brokerage houses? I thought, but didn't wish to hurt his feelings. Besides, he was growing better-looking by the moment, now that I could see past his beard and archaic hairdo. And he didn't seem like the kind of man who'd run out on a woman. He'd remained a widower for fifteen years after his spouse's death—a tad strange when he could have had a wife spreading a feast out on the table. And keeping him warm at night.

"I hear you've been a bachelor a long time," I said. Mom would cringe. Since I'd been a kid, she'd advised me to count to ten before speaking, but I rarely did.

"You certainly ask a lot of questions." He unhitched the horse from the buggy. "Say, you could help me out since you're here. How about brushing Galahad?"

"Me? Groom a horse? I guess, if you showed me how. He doesn't bite or kick does he?"

He guffawed. "Nah, he's a pussy cat. Most of the time." He led the horse into a stall in the larger barn—the other stalls were empty. He replenished Galahad's water and poured a scoopful of oats into his trough.

I scanned the barn's spacious, tidy interior, and inhaled the dusty aroma of hay. Not bad. In fact, I wouldn't mind hanging out here.

"I should let you get back to work," I said. "I've taken you away from Uncle Isaac. He's probably miffed. Don't want him sending Mom and me packing."

"'Tis too late now. I have my own chores. But, as I said, you could brush Galahad. He needs it, for sure."

"Okay, if you'll give me a lesson."

Nathaniel fetched a currycomb and demonstrated how to brush the horse. Then he handed it to me and I lazily stroked Galahad's neck and shoulders—Nathaniel called them *withers*. I enjoyed every moment.

"That's good. No need to be *naerfish*—nervous." Nathaniel said.

Dad's image came to mind—a fuzzy picture at age eighteen. If he'd stayed here, he would have embraced this life and I might have siblings galore. I'd be the oldest, like Mom was. Would I have left home? I didn't think so, not with my father loving and encouraging me.

I felt my blood pressure and my shoulder muscles relax for the twenty-five minutes I brushed Galahad's silky coat. Lavishing the horse with attention, I removed bits of dirt, loose hair, and debris. I had no idea so much effort went into grooming, but I luxuriated in the job. Maybe when I got home I'd work in a stable instead of a brokerage.

I stayed my hand for a moment. What was I thinking? I needed to climb back on the stock market saddle and resurrect my career.

Nathaniel returned carrying a pitchfork and leaned it against the wall. He looked the horse over. "*Des gut.*" He pointed out a side door to a gate across the paddock. "Time to put him out and get you back to your family."

I was proud of my grooming accomplishment, but Nathaniel didn't remark on my fine job. Or thank me. I guessed brushing horses was an everyday occurrence around here. Nothing out of the ordinary. Like me. Ho-hum.

My toes felt damp. I looked down at my mud-covered shoes. "What a doofus. Why did I wear these?"

"I keep extra work boots in the backroom, belongin' to my daughters," Nathaniel said. "Sorry, I should have offered them earlier."

"Not your fault." I was curious to hear about his daughters. Were they my age?

While we were in the barn, the sky had brightened to a cobalt blue. With me on the other side of the horse, Nathaniel led Galahad out of the barn to the pasture and opened the gate. A young goat captured my attention with a high-pitched "Ma-a-a-a."

Nathaniel unbridled Galahad and the horse's head jerked. He arched his forceful neck, his luxurious mane flashing, startling me. Back-stepping, one of my heels sank into a patch of mud. I slid a few inches. My arms swung out to counter-balance my weight, but to no avail. My second foot flew out like a toboggan on an icy slope.

I hovered midair for an instant before my rump landed with a splat onto spongy slush. My palms sank in up to my wrists.

"Oh, no!" Mud covered my rear and hands. A swearword I hadn't uttered since high school almost escaped from my mouth, but fortunately I contained my temper. Nathaniel would not appreciate foul language. And his approval mattered to me, I realized.

"What a klutz." I chuckled, but wanted to cry.

He secured the gate, then turned to me. "A little dirt never hurt anyone."

"Easy for you to say." I felt moisture seeping through my jeans. "I can't go back like this."

Springing to my feet too quickly, I slipped again, this time floundering forward onto my knees. "Now look at me!" I'd never been such a mess.

He let out a belly laugh. "Maybe I can help. My daughters left extra clothes upstairs in their old rooms. They won't mind if you borrow them."

"Sure, why not?" When in Rome.

He walked me to the porch and into a utility room. "I'll be right back," he said, and loped through the kitchen. He returned minutes later with a towel, a long sapphire-blue dress, and a black apron, and set them on the kitchen table. By this time I was shivering.

He fetched a shopping bag for my mucky garments. "'Ta give ya privacy I'll be in the barn," he said, handing it to me.

Ditching my drenched shoes and socks, I wiped my feet on the mat and entered the kitchen barefoot, feeling the cool linoleum floor.

During our buggy ride, I'd noticed a woman walking barefoot and had contemplated giving up shoes for the rest of our visit. I'd toss my orthotics away.

Looking around the kitchen, I saw a rectangle table with six chairs and a kerosene lamp in the center. No decorative touches—only an outdated stove, a refrigerator, and built-in cabinets. The kitchen didn't smell enticing like Grandma Anna's. What did single Amishmen feed themselves? I was tempted to peek in his refrigerator, but needed to clean up first.

I wriggled my legs out of my jeans; they felt like a second skin. I hoped Grandma Anna could clean the mud out with her decades-old washing machine I'd noticed in her utility room. Then, would my clothes hang on the line on the front porch for all the world to see?

I changed into the dress and smock, not sure how to fasten the waist. I called out the back door and asked Nathaniel for instructions.

"My daughters use straight pins," he said from afar. "I left them on the counter."

Was he pulling my leg? Careful as I was, I jabbed myself several times inserting them. Why not a zipper, buttons, or Velcro?

Finally clad much like Greta and my grandma, I savored the aged fabric; it felt like velvet cascading against my legs. I liked my new—make that old—attire, even if it didn't flatter my figure. I thought of the Amish Shoppe and wondered why Mom never hung a dress in the store for customers to view.

I looked around for a mirror, but couldn't find one. I reminded myself no one cared about my appearance. Certainly not Galahad. Hey, I'd overcome a fear and groomed a horse.

I heard knuckles rapping on the back door.

"Nate?" a woman said, and I opened it.

A perplexed-looking Amish woman in her early twenties carrying a wicker basket full of baked goods—oatmeal cookies, cornbread, apple strudel—peered over my shoulder. "Is Nathaniel in?"

"He's outside, maybe in the barn."

"Who are you?" Her stare traced my loose, mussed hair. Apparently one woman in the county cared what I looked like. And she was not amused.

"May I invite you in?" My mouth watered for a cookie or a bite of apple strudel.

"Nee, denki." She twirled around and stomped down the steps. Over her shoulder she said, "Tell him Lizzie will come back later."

CHAPTER FOURTEEN

Esther sat on a wicker chair on the front porch where she hoped Mamm wouldn't find her. Her mother's questions had pounded down upon Esther's head like pellets of hail. She was thankful she'd avoided the most daunting: Why did you leave us and never return?

Esther wouldn't admit she didn't understand her actions herself, only that her survival seemed to depend on living as far away from her parents as possible. And when Mamm had asked about Esther's business, she couldn't bring herself to confess she owned a shop specializing in Amish goods imported from states other than Pennsylvania—a fact Mamm might take as a slap in the face.

Gazing down the road, she spotted a bearded man carrying a grocery bag walking with a barefoot younger woman. Was he escorting his daughter, as her Dat had insisted? Once Esther had reached puberty, Dat rarely let her out of his sight unless she was helping Mamm. He didn't trust her, and he turned out to be correct.

Rebel without a cause, Esther thought, recalling an old James Dean film about a defiant teenager. On a daredevil, reckless game of chicken, a young man tragically died.

She moved to the edge of the porch to get a better look. The couple was striding in her direction at a breezy clip. The woman wore a traditional midlength Amish dress and apron, no doubt a pattern passed on from generation to generation. Esther was surprised to see the young woman's cinnamon-brown hair was *schtruwwlich*— disheveled—not tucked into a traditional white cap.

The woman waved, wriggling her fingers, then giggled. No one but Holly laughed in that graceful free-and-easy way when she was happy, a mood Esther seldom enjoyed.

Esther stood, slack-jawed, as the two approached. She was flummoxed—unsure what to do.

"Holly, is that you?" Yes, she clearly recognized Holly with Nathaniel, but neither looked her way or answered.

She considered trotting down the stairs and sprinting over to them, but restrained herself. Holly wouldn't appreciate the intrusion. Why was her daughter in an Amish dress and apron?

Waiting, Esther wondered why no one had thought to include her on the buggy ride. Nah, she was thinking like a nitwit. A handsome man like Nathaniel—his posture confident, his shoulders broad—wouldn't wish to spend time with a woman in her late fifties, not when lovely Holly was available.

Esther's spine stiffened as she realized she was musing about Nathaniel's rugged good looks, the first man she'd considered attractive since she'd lost Samuel. Over the years, men had asked Esther out to lunch, dinner, or a movie, but she'd usually begged out. Today, she just might accept an invitation from Nathaniel. No, no, he'd never enter a movie theater. But he might dine in a restaurant.

What was happening? Had her mind gone haywire?

The front door swished open, and Esther turned to see Mamm bustle outside and descend the steps as Nathaniel and Holly came to a halt a few feet from her.

"Why, Holly, don't you look beautiful," Mamm said.

Holly curtsied. "I had a slight accident." She grinned at Nathaniel, who smiled back, like they shared an inside joke.

"On the way over, I made up several colorful scenarios," Holly said. "But the truth is, I fell in the mud. I warned everyone I was a city gal."

"And Nathaniel loaned you clean clothes?" Esther was not sure what riled her the most. "How very kind of him." She forced a stingy smile, like she bestowed upon difficult customers who insisted on entering the shop after closing time.

Esther wondered if Nathaniel had set his eyes on Holly as a future bride. A widower would need a wife in this community. Someone to take care of him.

Nathaniel set down a brown sack. "Holly may keep my daughters' clothing."

"At least through tomorrow," Holly said. "Okay?"

"Yah." He tipped his hat. "As long as ya like."

"They suit her, ain't so?" Mamm said.

Esther felt ready to explode. "What on earth are you up to, Holly?" Esther's words grated through clenched teeth. "Pretending to be half-Englisch and half-Amish?"

"She looks *lieblich*—lovely." Mamm lightly clapped her hands. "Now, we must find her a Kapp."

Esther wouldn't mention the prayer cap sitting on her old dresser. Would Mamm entice Holly into trying it on? The first moment she had a chance Esther would hide it, that's what she'd do.

"Did you two enjoy your ride?" Mamm asked.

"Yes," said Holly. "Absolutely."

"And the covered bridge? Did ya like it?"

Nathaniel kicked a pebble with the toe of his boot. "We didn't make it that far."

"I hear tell there are twenty-eight covered bridges in the county." Mamm waggled her finger at Nathaniel, but her face displayed pleasure. "You can see one next time."

"What took you so long, then?" Esther clamped her arms across her chest.

"Never you mind," Mamm said. "Nathaniel, next time you owe Holly a ride to a bridge. I bet you don't find covered bridges in Seattle."

"Or air that smells so sweet," Holly said.

Mamm turned to Esther. "Have I told ya? My four other daughters-in-law are stoppin' by. It must be God's will, because I invited them before I even knew you and Holly would be here."

Esther felt a crescendo of anxiety as she envisioned her brothers' wives scrutinizing her. Lancaster news spread like swarming bees. Mamm had probably gotten Greta to use the phone shanty to call everyone they knew. Esther could imagine the chatter flapping amongst the community. "She's like a fancy ghost back from the dead," she could predict neighbors and relatives saying. "Samuel Fisher's parents will be mortified."

Please, dearest God, not Samuel's parents, Esther prayed silently.

She found herself staring into Nathaniel's eyes. Their vision locked for a beat too long. Was he hoping to get acquainted with Esther so he could court Holly? No, an upright man like Nathaniel wouldn't marry an unbaptized non-Amish woman. But with Mamm's support he might attempt to convert Holly.

Esther looked away, forcing herself to admire the multistoried purple martin birdhouse in the yard, standing tall like an apartment building. Esther had always loved watching birds and listening to their trills and chirps, but at this moment they held no interest. All she cared about was going home—wherever that was.

"Grandma Anna?" Holly said.

"Please, call me Mommy Anna," Mamm said.

"Okay. Mommy Anna."

"That's better. Now, to complete your outfit, let's find you a prayer cap. I'd offer you Esther's, but she may still want it." She turned to face Esther. "I notice you've kept your hair long."

"Out of convenience." Her hands reached back to make sure her hair hadn't loosened from its bun. No, it was secured in place.

CHAPTER FIFTEEN

Apparently my mother thought I looked goofy in my borrowed Amish attire. But I was grateful for the dry, comfy clothes, and that Nathaniel hadn't doubled over with amusement when he first saw me in them. If anything, he looked pleased.

Gathering my muddy belongings together in his kitchen earlier, I'd asked if he owned a washing machine.

"I do, but I don't use it. A neighbor helps me out."

A neighbor or a single beauty looking for a husband? I'd wondered and said, "I think I met her. Lizzie? She was carrying a basket filled with baked goodies, but when she saw me she skedaddled and said she'd stop by later. I hope I didn't scare her away."

Not true. I wanted her long gone, replaced by a homely married woman my mother's age.

"I don't remember being so happy." Mommy Anna said, bringing me to the present. She smiled at me, her face radiating love, but I noticed tension at the corners of her eyes. She looked tired.

"What can I fix yous to eat?" she said. "*Kumm,* everyone." In slow motion, she turned to climb the porch steps.

I followed her. Peace and tranquility surrounded me. I thought about Nathaniel's daughters—Hannah and Tina—both wearing and then outgrowing this dress and apron. Again, I wondered about his former wife. How did she die? I was nosy enough to ask him, or maybe not. Mommy Anna would be a better source of information. Or Beth. I needed to zip over to her house for my laptop and to recharge my cell phone. I'd immediately liked her last night because she knew and loved Mommy Anna, and had taken my mom and me in, a couple of waifs without a hotel reservation.

My dear Mommy Anna trod up the staircase. *Labor* was a better word to describe the effort each step seemed to require. She paused halfway and grasped the railing.

Her knees buckled. She toppled backward.

I darted forward, knowing I was powerless to do more than cushion her fall. I felt Nathaniel's arms scooping us up like we were a couple of baby chicks. Once I stood on the porch, he glided past me and slid an arm around Mommy Anna's stout waist.

My mother dashed up the steps and stabilized Mommy Anna's other elbow. She and Nathaniel ushered her to the nearest chair, where she came down hard. Her hand moved to her forehead.

"I get dizzy sometimes," she muttered. I could tell she was using all her energy to keep from slumping over.

"You call that dizzy?" My mother's forceful voice cut through the air. "*Was fehlt dir denn?* You wrote saying you're sick but you've been a bundle of activity ever since we arrived, so I assumed you were fine."

Mommy Anna untied the strings of her prayer cap; they fell limply like scraps of mom's yarn. "Yah, well, I'm light-headed every now and then. And my bones in my arms and legs ache."

"Why hide it?" Mom's hand steadied my grandma's shoulder.

"I wrote ya, didn't I? My sons and their wives know, but they don't understand. They're busy workin', all their energy focused on moving."

"We could take you to a doctor right now," I said. "I have a rental car. I bet Nathaniel would help us."

"No, he's got his chores and milking ta do. And Holly, dear, I've already seen several medical doctors. They say my problem's old age."

"You're not that old," Mom said. "Two of the women in my friend Dori's knitting group are in their late eighties. One is ninety-four."

"Like I told you before, you should try my naturopath or a chiropractor," Nathaniel said, scratching his chin. "They always help me out gut." So he knew Mommy Anna was sick, too, but hadn't mentioned her condition.

"I'm fine now." Mommy Anna drew in a chest-full of air, then let it out like a collapsed balloon. "I got overly excited seeing Holly dressed so *wunderbaar*. Like I dreamed she'd look."

I figured she was putting us off, trying to spare us worry the way my mother did when she was in a bind. "What exactly is wrong with you?" I asked her.

Mommy Anna shook her head. "No one but the good Lord knows."

"Was this a trick to lure me home?" my mother asked, with what sounded like scorn. I felt like raising my skirt's hem and kicking her in the shins.

"'Tis true, Esther. More than anything, I wanted to see you before we moved and you came home and found someone else livin' here. You'd never find me."

"But you have my address and our telephone number, if you'd ever use a phone," Mom said. "You could have let me know where you were. None of this rings true."

"I regret nothin'. I have you and my Holly here, at last." Mommy Anna took my hand. Her fingertips were icy cold.

"'Tis a blessing I got to meet Holly." She held my hand tighter. "Even if I don't have much time left on earth."

I got a panicky feeling in the back of my throat. She was going to die? But I'd only just met her!

CHAPTER SIXTEEN

Thirty minutes later, Esther heard a motor vehicle stop in back of the house. From the kitchen window, she saw four Amish women and a gaggle of preschoolers file out of a twelve-passenger van.

Three of the women looked to be in their early or midforties and one was nearing fifty. They each carried either a toddler, a grocery bag, or both. They were conversing in Deitsch, sounding jovial and carefree. Everything Esther wasn't. She wanted to dodge out the front door, but there was no way she could pretend she didn't see them.

With Mamm resting in bed upstairs—Nathaniel had literally carried her—Esther had agreed to help entertain her brothers' wives during their visit. The Amish enjoyed gathering to chitchat. She bet over the years she'd been the topic of many a storytelling during work frolics.

Earlier, Mamm said, "Offer them cookies and lemonade," as Nathaniel lowered her to her bed. Was she truly ill? Mamm seemed to have Nathaniel hoodwinked. But then maybe he knew more than he was letting on.

Esther had been impressed by his gentle strength and show of respect for Mamm. Every so often, his gaze landed on Esther's face to take in her features. Unless she was mistaken, he seemed somewhat in awe of her. More likely, he was astounded how much she'd aged since their childhood days.

While peering in a mirror earlier, Esther had reminded herself of Beth's shriveled rosebush. Beth still appeared vibrant and in the prime of life, even though she was just a few years younger. Should Esther start wearing makeup and get a chic new haircut to accentuate her high cheekbones as Holly had urged? "Life is not over in your fifties, Mom," she'd said.

How would Holly know?

In Seattle, Esther had convinced herself she enjoyed living unnoticed by the opposite sex. Holly was irascible some days, but Esther was content sharing the house with another woman: no pressure to keep up her appearance. She didn't need or want men ogling her. But here, her world felt like a pineapple upside-down cake, flipped over before thoroughly baked.

Esther heard Greta and her children upstairs, and Holly running water in the bathroom.

She watched the women and children head for the back stoop, led by a tall, angular brunette. They were chattering in Deitsch. She hoped they'd switch to English for Holly's sake. For her own, as well. Esther didn't want to back-slip into her childhood dialect. Esther and Holly were not Amish, in spite of Holly's ridiculous endeavors at looking like one. Why hadn't she changed into her other pants and a sweater? The moment Holly opened her mouth the women would know she wasn't from these parts. Did people in Seattle speak with an accent? Esther wondered, then tossed the random thought aside. Her mind was twirling with inconsistencies and questions.

Hearing footsteps enter the utility room, Esther squared her shoulders. If she could deal with customers at the Amish Shoppe, she could converse with her brothers' wives, whom she'd probably never see again after today.

She placed her sweaty palm on the doorknob. Forcing a show of bravado, she swung open the door. "Hello, everyone. I'm Esther Fisher, Anna's daughter."

The laughter fell silent. Apparently no one had warned them of Esther's arrival. A strawberry-blond toddler carried by a woman with the same color hair stared at Esther; the little boy's face puckered like he might burst into tears.

Did Esther appear frightening? To him, she might.

"Please come in," Esther said. "Looks like you've been busy."

The oldest and tallest of the women, a brunette hauling a shopping bag, stared down her beakish nose. "We were buyin' fabric and stockin' up on groceries."

Esther wondered which brother she'd married; probably lanky Marvin, two years older than Isaac. Yet in this family, Isaac was the preacher. The youngest son held seniority and made the final decisions.

"Here's my daughter, Holly," Esther said when Holly entered the kitchen barefoot, wearing the dress and apron.

"Hey, you guys cruised up in a van." She sidled next to Esther. "I thought Mommy Anna's friends were horse and buggy only."

"We may hire cars when needed, but not own or drive them," the woman carrying the toddler said. Her reddish-blonde hair peeked out from beneath her Kapp, and Esther guessed it curled like her son's.

"Yah," said a blonde woman wearing a plum-colored dress and black apron who shared Holly's petite stature. "We brought food for Anna, too."

"Thank you," Esther said. "I'm sure Mamm appreciates your kindness."

"The driver will be back for us in an hour, then we'll pick up our school-age children," the last woman announced. Her brown hair above a high forehead was parted down the middle with precision, making Esther recall the hours she'd spent brushing and parting her own hair as a girl.

"And grandchildren," the tall brunette cut in. "I have nine children and seven grandchildren. The older boys are either in school or helping their fathers on the farm this very minute."

"You sure have a big family." Holly raked a hand through her hair; a speck of dirt the size of a pea fell to the floor.

"Holly!" Esther scooped up the dried mud and hid it in her closed fist. "Show your aunts respect."

"Sorry, I didn't mean to be rude. I've always wanted aunts—the more the merrier."

The women went quiet again. They stared at Holly's wavy loose hair, then at Esther.

"I'm Mary Ann," the tall brunette said, her voice stern. "This here's Francine, Martha, and Julie." Each woman donned a meager smile, their lips compressed. Esther couldn't tell if they were shy or in shock.

"Happy to meet you." Esther found her legs quaking. Knowing her palms were moist from nervous perspiration, she didn't offer to shake hands. And she needed to throw the wad of dirt away.

"Nice ta meetcha," the women said in unison, reminding Esther of her childhood. As a girl, she'd been taught not to draw attention to herself.

"Let's go into the front room," Esther said. "Greta left us a plate of cookies and lemonade. Mamm's upstairs."

Mary Ann set down the grocery bag and followed her. "So, you're Esther," she said. "Where've you been hidin' yourself? Indiana? Ohio?"

Esther figured Mamm had informed Mary Ann where she lived, but her sister-in-law was going to rub it in.

"Seattle," Holly said. "In the Pacific Northwest."

"Ach, so far away." Mary Ann screwed up her mouth like she was gnawing on a lemon wedge.

"Are there any of our People livin' there?" Sandy-haired Francine settled her wiggly child on a rag rug.

"No Amish settlements in the state of Washington that I know of," Esther said. The toddler crawled over to unlace her Naturalizer shoes.

"There can't be many Amish in Montana, either," Holly said, cocking her head.

"Yah, a few," Francine said. "We're hopin', anyways."

Esther wondered if these women wanted to leave Lancaster County any more than her mamm did, but wouldn't ask. She didn't wish to put them in the spotlight of disagreeing with their husbands. Or Isaac.

Holly poured lemonade into glasses. "In the city of Seattle, the only thing Amish is Mom's retail store, the Amish Shoppe." Esther squinted her eyes, trying to send her daughter a keep-quiet message, but Holly didn't seem to notice. She said, "We even have a gray buggy sitting on the front porch—like the ones around here."

Francine covered her mouth and giggled. "Yous own a store named the Amish Shoppe? And a buggy?"

Martha also set her toddler on the floor; golden-blonde strands escaped from her prayer cap as she leaned forward. "What kind of horse do ya keep?" She broke a cookie in half and gave it to her little boy.

"Horses aren't allowed in the city, except those owned by the police department," Holly said, and handed a cookie to Francine's child.

"Are ya joking' with us?" Mary Ann's glower spread crevices across her face. "I bet you're pullin' our legs."

"No." Holly held the cookie platter out to Mary Ann. "I mean, yes," she said quickly. "Mom does own the Amish Shoppe and sells Amish products, but we don't have a horse."

Paying no heed to the cookies, Mary Ann narrowed her eyes like she didn't believe a word Holly said. She bulleted her words at Esther. "After all this time, what brought ya home? Other than seeing your poor Mudder, what ya should a done decades ago."

She's bent on embarrassing me, Esther thought, her cheeks radiating with heat; they must be cranberry red. Should she mention her mother's illness? Did her sisters-in-law know Mamm lived in pain and was faint headed? It was her mother's responsibility to inform her family, if she really were ill. Esther still wasn't convinced. One minute she was bursting with vigor, the next collapsing; maybe Mamm was faking for Esther's benefit.

As Esther sipped lemonade, she reminded herself she'd seen Mamm crumple down the stairs an hour ago. If Nathaniel hadn't come to the rescue, both her mother and Holly would have fallen like Mamm's oval serving bowl. Feeling a sliver of shame impale her, Esther was struck by the fact that Mary Ann was perfectly right. If Esther had returned earlier, she could have taken Mamm to specialists.

"I hear both of you are single," Mary Ann said, then finally selected a gingersnap cookie and chomped into it.

"Here to find a husband?" Julie asked, with a wry smile. She was either rotund or carrying child. Her loose clothing made it difficult to tell, not such a bad style in Esther's opinion.

Holly shook her head. "Heavens, no."

"This is the best place on earth to find a beau," Greta said, descending the stairs carrying baby Lydia, two of her youngsters at her heels.

Martha swallowed a mouthful of lemonade. "Have you met Nathaniel next door? He'd make a fine-gut husband for either of you."

If Esther wasn't mistaken, Holly looked uncomfortable, the way she shifted her weight back and forth. Or was her borrowed Amish clothing pricking her at the waist? Had something happened between her and Nathaniel? It shouldn't bother Esther, but the thought of them together made her bristly inside. Pangs of jealousy? she had to ask herself.

Esther noticed movement in her peripheral vision and saw her mother descending the staircase one step at a time, her hand on the banister.

"Talking about husbands?" she said. Reaching the first floor, Mamm lowered herself onto the couch next to Greta and her baby.

"First a woman must be baptized. No Amishman will marry a woman outside the church."

"A man can't switch churches?" Holly asked, making Esther wish she'd educated her better about the Amish ways. She'd been a miserable mother to her daughter.

"Nee," Martha said, with a look of dismay. "A man and woman must be equally yoked and marry within the Amish church."

Francine said, "Now, if a girl were Englisch, Beth's son Zachary would be fair game. There isn't a more eligible Englisch bachelor in the county. His veterinary medicine is a blessing to every animal owner. He even donates his services to the poor."

"Yah, yah, he's very kind and committed," Mamm said. "But not Amish, Holly, so keep your distance." She lifted Lydia from Greta's arms and reswaddled the baby. Cuddling Lydia, Mamm directed her words to Holly. "A young Amish woman once tried to convince Zachary to convert, without success. 'Tis almost impossible to become Amish in midlife. Very few do. He was fond of that girl but wouldn't give up his modern technology. Plus, he isn't fluent in German, and that's necessary for reading the Bible and understanding sermons."

"His mother, Beth, sure is nice," Holly said, making Esther wince. It seemed Beth could do no wrong. "But I notice she doesn't dress or live like you."

"The Flemings are devout Christians, I can attest to that," Greta said. "But their Mennonite church is worldly as far as dress and lifestyle go."

"They have telephones and electricity right in the house," Julie said.

"And drive cars and tractors in the fields," Martha said. "Against the Ordnung, for sure."

"Don't you go chasing after Zachary, Holly," Mary Ann said, her hands planted on her ample hips.

"I bet a lot of women do," Holly said. "Having Beth for a mother-in-law wouldn't be so bad. But I have no intention of chasing after her son."

"Gut," Greta said. "You should marry Amish."

"Yah, our blood flows through your veins," Mamm said.

Esther wanted to stop the women from pestering Holly, but held her tongue.

"Holly, both your parents were Amish," Greta said. "My Isaac says he wants you to move in with us. I could use your help raising Lydia. You want to hold her?"

"Okay. Sure." Holly inched over to Mamm and lifted the baby, supporting her tiny head. "Am I doing this right?"

"Yah, perfect," Greta said. "She likes bein' walked and rocked. Yes, just like that."

Esther was blanketed with sadness; she could deceive herself no longer. Holly ached for a child of her own. Of course she would. Esther should have encouraged her daughter to find a husband in Seattle.

Mamm's face beamed. "You're part of our family, Holly."

"That dress was made for you." Julie nodded. "It couldn't suit you more."

"Can ya speak and read German?" Mary Ann demanded.

"I studied it in high school and college. But it's been a while."

"I bet you'll pick it right up again in no time," Greta said, clapping her hands.

"Anna can teach ya Deitsch," Francine said.

"Sure, a few new words a day," Julie said.

"*Mei Kinner*—my children—can help," Greta said.

Much to Esther's consternation, each woman in the room gave Holly her unasked-for biased opinion.

"Hold your horses, everyone," Esther said, her voice sounding frayed. "Holly has a marvelous life in Seattle." An exaggeration, since Holly seemed to be blossoming here before her eyes.

But if Holly stayed in Lancaster County, how would Esther survive?

CHAPTER SEVENTEEN

A motor vehicle stopped out back of the house and honked. Mary Ann gobbled another gingersnap. "Julie, Martha, Francine. Time ta go."

After one last cuddle, I laid Lydia on Mommy Anna's lap, then Greta and I helped my other aunts gather their children, then stream through the kitchen toward the back door.

The driver, a middle-age fellow, wearing modern clothing and sideburns, leaned out his window. "Everyone ready? I'm running late."

"We're comin'," Francine said, carrying her toddler. She paused to kiss my cheek. "So gut to meet ya, Holly. I hope this ain't good-bye forever."

"Me too. I wish you could have stayed longer."

"Move with us to Montana," Julie said. "We could see each other every day."

The women hastened down the steps and into the van. They spoke to their children in Pennsylvania Dutch; I picked up bits and pieces. Could I learn the language? Yes, given enough time.

The last to leave, Mary Ann gave me a sparse kiss that hovered several inches from my cheek. She clasped my upper arm and said, "Don't ya let Esther go runnin' off again and break Anna's heart."

When I thought about it, I supposed I did have influence. Why had I arranged our trip with such a short turnaround time? Oh, yeah, I didn't want to come to begin with. But now that I was here, I felt a kinship to my newfound relatives and this beautiful history-filled county where my father was born and raised. If we stayed another week I might learn more about him.

My aunts' driver revved the engine. I waved good-bye, but as he sped away I doubted the women could see me, packed in as they were with sacks of groceries and wriggling preschoolers. And laughter. I compared their get-togethers to my life in Seattle. I had one best girlfriend, but when she got home from her honeymoon, she and her husband would be eager to spend every moment together. Who could blame them? Sure, I knew Larry and people at church and through the Amish Shoppe, but our relationships were superficial—my fault, no doubt.

I stepped inside, made my way to the sitting room, and saw my mother gathering the drinking glasses, one at a time, like she was sapped of strength.

"I'm headed to Beth's house," I said. "I left my laptop at her place to recharge the battery."

Her face bunched in on itself like a prune. "Dressed like that?"

"Sure, why not?"

"I agree," said Mommy Anna from the couch. She handed baby Lydia to Greta, then pushed herself up to a standing position. "Why would Beth mind Holly lookin' like one of us?"

"I haven't seen you on your cell phone," Mom said, standing between Mommy Anna and me like a brick wall. "Does it need charging too?"

"Thanks for reminding me."

"Have you spoken to your young man from church group?" Mom asked, and Mommy Anna craned her neck to get a look at me.

"He left a couple messages." Phooey, why had I admitted there was a man? Mom could always extract information from me. She was sneaky that way. "If you're talking about Larry, I consider him a friend," I said. "We've never gone out on a real date." Although I did accept his paying for lattes. If I were honest with myself, I was leading him on.

"He may have written you an email," my mother added, as if trying to drive home a point for Mommy Anna's sake. Were they both vying to marry me off?

I reminded myself: I should be on the prowl for a spouse. And kids. At least one, before my menopausal timer binged. But not here in Lancaster County; that would be like searching for a rooster in the middle of Lake Washington.

Steering my rental to Beth's house, I felt drained of energy. I'd appreciated my aunts' attention, but wasn't used to a barrage of advice. Would these dear women drive me nuts if we got together on a regular basis, or would I merge into their conversations, finding their words a sign they cared about my future?

My thoughts turned to Dori, whom I'd always considered an aunt. But she wasn't, really. With three hours' time difference, she'd be working in the Amish Shoppe right now. Saint Dori, I might dub her for managing the store in Mom's absence. Odd, Mom hadn't asked to use my cell phone to call her. My mother's thoughts usually encompassed her business; she verged on being a control freak when it came to the Amish Shoppe. And her knitting. She hadn't begged me to purchase her new needles nor had she borrowed a pair from Mommy Anna or Greta—not that I'd seen either woman knitting.

Pulling to the side of the road, I punched in the store's telephone number. It rang four times, then Dori answered with a breathy, "The Amish Shoppe. This is Dori speaking." She told me she was having a blast, but was too busy to chat. "I'm in the middle of ringing up a sales transaction. I sold a bench—the one by the fireplace—and two pillows. Got to run."

Minutes later, I parked in Beth's driveway. Again, I admired the look of her home's stone facade, extensive lawn, and garden. I spotted Beth raking maple leaves onto a plastic tarp. She waved, then gathered the tarp's corners and tossed the leaves into a compost bin at the side of her garage.

Her dog, Missy, trotted toward me with wagging tail. Beth set the rake aside, propping it against the garage. "What a lovely surprise." Her gaze canvassed my dress and apron. "Don't you look—different."

I stroked Missy between the ears and she leaned against my leg. "It's a loaner from Nathaniel, left over from his daughters. And a straight pin is sticking into my waist at this very moment." I reached behind my apron, extracted the pin, and slid it in the apron's pocket. "My mother was horrified when she saw me dressed like this."

"Understandable, after all this time. I imagine she has many memories. I'm glad she has you to keep her company."

"Oh, we've had plenty of that. Four aunts stopped by, all wanting my mother and me to get baptized Amish and move to Montana with them."

Beth chuckled. "There's no shortage of advice around here."

Missy nuzzled her nose against my hand, begging for attention, which I gladly bestowed upon her.

"May I speak to you in confidence?" I asked Beth. I'd decided I could trust her.

"Yes," she said. "What you tell me stays here."

"I don't believe Mommy Anna wants to move." I ran my fingers across Missy's satiny ear. "I can't help wondering if my aunts do, either. Don't they have a say in their future?"

"Yes. But ultimately, the bishop, preachers, deacons, husbands, and men in general hold higher positions on the hierarchy."

"Couldn't Mommy Anna stay, somehow?" I assumed Beth knew of Mommy Anna's health problems. Or did she? Since Beth wasn't Amish, she might not be privy to family issues.

Beth lifted her chin to survey the two-story garage, its taupe exterior turning apricot from the setting sun. "I suppose Roger and I could rent her the bedroom and bathroom over the garage. The upstairs would only require cleaning and a coat of paint, and new space heaters. It even has a phone, which Anna could use since this would be a rental. We could charge her a nominal amount. In fact, she could pay us back by baking bread, on days she feels up to it. She'd be more than welcome to use my kitchen."

"That sounds perfect."

"She was a lifesaver when I was at my lowest. I'd do anything for her. But honestly, I think Anna would miss her children and grandchildren too much. And I'm not sure she's strong enough to live by herself."

"Yet she's too frail to travel across the country," I said.

"I have no say there. If I had my way, I'd drive her to Philadelphia to a physician who specializes in fibromyalgia. Not that we don't have fine doctors in the area and a top-notch hospital. One reason my father moved here when I was a teen."

"Which brings me to another question, if I'm not being too nosy. I did the math in my head. I figure you and my mother lived next door to each other for at least a year."

Beth took the rake, turned it upside-down, and picked dried leaves from its tines. "Yes. At that time, my mother had lung cancer, which ultimately took her life." She leaned the rake against the garage, but it tipped over, landing on her foot. I retrieved it and propped up the handle.

"Your mother was stepping into Rumspringa, joining what's called a gang," she said. "In all fairness, I was younger. I don't think Esther noticed me. If I'd been Amish, maybe our paths would have crossed more."

"And you would have been friends?"

Her face drained of color. "I don't know if I'd go that far."

"How could she not notice you, her next-door neighbor?" I asked.

"The truth? Esther never seemed to like me." Her words took me by surprise.

"After my mother died, while Dad was working—he had to support us—I was on my own after school," she said. "Soon after Esther left, I ventured down to Anna's and she took me in. She had a heart for the sad and lonely, maybe because she was so despondent herself, what with missing Esther and losing her husband." Beth glanced down the road toward Mommy Anna's farm. "Anna hired me after school and on the weekends to help look after her sons and clean house. She paid me back with eggs and milk, and sewing and cooking lessons. And hugs." Beth wrapped her hands around her forearms. "I needed those the most."

"And your father?"

"He lives in a Mennonite retirement center not far away. He gave Roger and me this house as our wedding present."

"He sounds great."

"He is. I hit the jackpot in the father department."

Unlike me, I thought, then reminded myself Beth had lost her mother at an early age.

With Missy at her side, Beth moved toward the kitchen door. The dog bolted ahead, letting out a yip.

"She wants her dinner," Beth said. We followed Missy on the stone path.

"I wonder how many pups she'll have," I said. "I bet they'll be adorable.

"Zachary thinks six. He's usually right about everything when it comes to animals."

"No wonder she's hungry. I wish I could be here when they're born."

"According to Zach, she's got another month to go. Can you wait?"

"I'm guessing a border collie wouldn't make a good stay-in-the-backyard-all-day dog while I'm at work."

"You're right. She demands constant activity or she'll entertain herself. Like chasing the chickens or herding the neighbor's sheep."

"My mother's in the shop during the day—"

"Then a fluffy, cuddly lap dog might be best for her," Beth cut in. "If Esther even likes dogs." For the first time, her voice took on a raspy tinge of sarcasm. She paused, as if deep in thought, then moved to the kitchen door around the side of the house. "Have you come to use your computer?"

"Yes, if it's no trouble." I'd temporarily forgotten about my laptop. I preferred conversing with a woman who might answer my many questions.

First on the list: Why had neither my mother nor Beth mentioned they'd lived almost next door to each other? Another thought: Had Beth known my father? She must have noticed him passing by her house before he took off. Not to mention my queries about Nathaniel and his deceased wife. Had Beth known her? How did the woman die? Had Nathaniel remained single by choice? Was he infatuated with Lizzie?

Missy circled back and wove between Beth and me as we proceeded to the kitchen.

"Is your husband home?" I asked.

"No, not yet. Three more days in LA at a conference. Roger's in construction equipment, the regional manager. He's always traveled, so I'm used to it. Which doesn't mean I don't miss him."

"I imagine you would." I tried sounding sympathetic, when in fact the only man I had to miss was my dad.

"Absence makes the heart grow fonder." She gave me a sly wink. "But I have our three children and two grandchildren. How about you?"

"I'm still single." I slouched my shoulders like I felt sorry for myself. I suppose I did.

"Waiting for a knight in shining armor to come riding up on a white steed?" she said.

"No, I'm more realistic than that. But it does seem a component is missing from every man I meet." At least Nathaniel owned a horse, I reminded myself.

"I know an eligible young man," she said. "My Zachary's coming for dinner tonight. Would you care to join us? Ham, string beans from the garden, and scalloped potatoes."

"Sounds delicious. I'm tempted." I glanced down at my Amish apron and dress, and pictured myself through Zach's scrutinizing eyes. "My aunts certainly think highly of your son." I imagined he was used to having women fawn over him. He probably considered himself superior; that's how he came off this morning. A Mr. Know-It-All. No, I was being overly critical.

"I'd better get back to my grandma's for supper," I said. "She's taking a nap right now."

"I can't blame her for wanting every moment with you, but I doubt she's awake yet."

"You know more about my grandmother's habits than Mom and I do." I felt like a book missing its cover and half its chapters.

She pulled open the kitchen door as Missy zeroed in on her empty food bowl.

I inhaled the bouquet of baking ham, cloves, and brown sugar. "Smells delish. After my huge lunch, how can I contemplate eating again?"

"That was hours ago. And it sounds like you've had a busy day." She poured kibble into Missy's dish and the dog dove in.

"Did I tell you about my buggy ride with Nathaniel King?" I said.

"Nathaniel took the afternoon off? That doesn't sound like him. Although it's not every day Anna's granddaughter comes to town."

"My grandma practically forced him, but I think both Nathaniel and I had fun. And I got to borrow this outfit." Never mind that I'd scudded across the mud like a walrus to earn it.

She tilted her head. "Which buggy did you use?"

"A small, open one."

Her eyes widened. "Sometimes called a courting buggy."

"Courting, as in next step wedding bells?"

"Yes, but Amish people of all ages use them, not just young couples looking to get married."

"I hope he didn't get the wrong impression." But I had been profuse when thanking him, and I'd accepted his daughter's clothes.

CHAPTER EIGHTEEN

Esther entered the kitchen and found Greta at the sink rinsing carrots. "Is Mamm still napping?" Esther asked.

Using her fingers as a strainer, Greta drained the water. "I haven't heard a peep from her."

"Should I go check to make sure she hasn't gotten up and fallen? But I wouldn't want to wake her."

"Just between you and me, Anna often snoozes before dinner." Greta set to work scrubbing a carrot. "She's had an exciting day."

"Yes, we all have." Staying with Mamm was *ferhoodling* Esther's brain, not to mention coping with her sisters-in-law, particularly Mary Ann.

Listening to Greta open a drawer to extract a knife, Esther's thoughts scuttled like a squirrel up a hickory tree. "I need to ask Holly the date of our return tickets," she said. "I've grown compliant, allowing her to make our travel decisions. Has she come home yet?"

"No, I think she's still at Beth's house." Greta sliced the carrots on a wooden board.

"I'm not about to go running over to Beth's," Esther said, hearing her volume intensify.

Greta glanced up, her face registering concern. "Maybe Isaac could run ya over there in the buggy if it's too far to walk."

"No, thank you. I'd rather wait."

Greta arranged the carrot sticks on a ceramic platter Esther remembered from childhood. She imagined Beth in this room comforting Mamm and in subtle ways turning her against Esther. Had Beth assisted Mamm when writing letters to Esther? Had Beth bought the stamps and stationery?

She knew she should be grateful to Beth. But she wasn't. She recalled Beth's crush on Samuel when they were teens. He hadn't minded her flirtatious attentions one bit. Even though too young to court, Beth had been twice as pretty as Esther, and still was, with her fair complexion and hair the color of spun gold. When she waltzed into a room, all marveled at her radiance. Esther figured Beth had hoped Samuel would tire of Esther and return from San Francisco to court her once Beth turned sixteen. She probably held Esther responsible for Samuel's death too.

What was the use of rehashing the past? Esther asked herself, when she had plenty to worry about. Like where Holly was. Surely she didn't have that much to talk about with Beth. Maybe she'd decided to drive around or take the clothes back to Nathaniel. Esther didn't want her daughter to be late for supper.

"Anything I can do to help?" she asked Greta. She remembered her family ate a hearty breakfast and noon meal, then a light supper in the evening. "Early to bed, early to rise," she could recall Dat saying.

Greta dried her hands on her apron. "A casserole's already in the oven and I made a fruit Jell-O salad. 'Tis in the refrigerator."

"Sorry, I should have thought to ask earlier." Esther looked around the room for a chore to keep her busy.

"*Es macht nix aus*—it doesn't matter," Greta said. "But ya look *sclimm*—sad in your face. Worried about your mamm?"

Esther pressed the heel of her hand against her forehead and massaged it. "Yes. And I'm used to being busy. 'Idle hands are the devil's workshop,' Mamm told me many a time."

"I'm sure my Isaac can find a job for ya, if you're serious."

Work alongside her brother? Esther had purposely avoided the barnyard so he wouldn't make her muck out the pigpen.

"No, thanks." Now what? Esther was too fidgety to knit and realized she hadn't replaced her confiscated needles. It wasn't like her not to knit every day. She should have asked Holly to drive her to New Holland or Intercourse.

Esther wandered around the kitchen. Her life felt like a row of dominos about to topple down upon each other. How many careless decisions could she make? She never should have brought Holly here. She could have taken the bus or train by herself. She would have relaxed and knitted the whole trip. A sweater would be finished by now, a present for Greta. The garment would be too small for Mamm, who might find fault with Esther's stitches, as she had when Esther was young. Mamm was always on her case, as Holly would say.

"Unless you need me, I'm going for a walk before Mamm wakes up," she told Greta.

"It's turning chilly. You're welcome to borrow my jacket and scarf, hangin' at the back door."

"Denki. I need to use the phone shanty." Esther glanced out the window and saw the magnificent salmon-orange sun poised to set. She needed to stretch her legs and to inhale fresh air. She would snuggle into Greta's jacket and stroll by Nathaniel's house. She hoped to speak to him about her mother's health, if the subject arose. And she was curious about his and Holly's buggy ride, and her daughter's impulsive interest in dressing Amish. Esther admitted to herself she wanted to see him, plain and simple. Maybe he'd be standing right out front, making the encounter seem spontaneous and casual. Then Esther would call Dori.

Surprisingly, the Amish Shoppe hadn't niggled Esther's mind as she'd thought it would. In Seattle, she was used to her comfortable schedule, consumed with stocking and arranging merchandise. But she'd hardly thought of the shop all day.

Nearing Nathaniel's on foot, she admired his house, barn, and outbuildings, and his stately windmill, its blades catching the copper-colored glint from the setting sun.

She climbed the steps and rapped on his front door. Hearing footsteps inside, she felt her heart beating faster.

Nathaniel opened the door wearing work clothes and slippers. His eyes brightened when he saw her. "Hullo, Esther. What a fine-gut surprise. *Wei gets?*"

"Sorry if I'm interrupting."

"Nee. Truth be known, I was thinking 'bout ya. *Kumm rei.*"

Esther couldn't fathom why he'd be thinking about her, of all people. Her throat tightened and her mind went blank, but she managed to say, "I was on my way to use the phone and thought I might find Holly returning your daughter's clothing. But her car isn't here." She couldn't see past him, only that his front sitting room was scarcely decorated, except shelves laden with library books and a calendar with a river scene across the bottom. At one time, his wife and his two daughters lived here, but Esther saw no feminine touches. Maybe his housekeeper had put their belongings away because she hoped to be the next Mrs. King.

"I haven't laid eyes on Holly for hours," he said. "Not since I helped Anna into bed. Would ya like to come in for coffee or hot apple cider?"

She rubbed her fingers together, then blew into her hands; they were icy. "Sounds good, but I best be on my way before it gets too dark." She smoothed Greta's scarf over her hair and refastened the knot. "We don't want folks getting the wrong idea." Not that Holly hadn't been here earlier changing her clothes. Imagine that! Holly had yet to describe how her muddy calamity occurred. Why had her hair looked *schtruwwlich?*

"A young lady comes most every day to clean and straighten and prepare my meals," Nathaniel said. "*Breddicher* Isaac says it's fine. She can use the income and I surely do need the help." More proof Esther's brother Isaac, a preacher, one notch below the bishop, held the final word. "I'm a widower, you probably know."

"I'm sorry for your loss." If anyone could relate, Esther could.

"Ich bedank mich. It's been near fifteen years, but I still miss *mei Fraa* on nights like this. Now that my girls are married and livin' on their own, the house gets lonely." He looked right into Esther's face, as if expecting her to say something, but Esther felt tongue-tied. She could understand how Holly might get swept away by everything about him. Thank goodness she wasn't here.

He stroked his beard. "Forgive me if I'm being too forward, but I hear ya lost your spouse too."

"Yes, I did." The words half choked her, even after all this time. Because she never wore a wedding band, few people in Seattle knew she'd been married.

"I've been a widow longer than you." Esther knew the circumstances were different; he hadn't indirectly caused his wife's death. Not even Dori understood Esther's role in Samuel's demise. Dori and Jim considered themselves conscientious objectors because they'd opposed the Vietnam War, but they hadn't been taught since childhood never to retaliate. Esther wanted to weep when she envisioned her Samuel being forced into a military uniform. Had he refused to touch an M16, or had he caved in under pressure? Had he closed his eyes and prayed for forgiveness when he shot the enemy?

Still, she was curious about Nathaniel. He and his wife had only two children and no doubt had wanted more—several sons to help work his farm. Why hadn't he remarried?

She smelled warm berries and buttery crust. "Am I keeping you from your meal?" she said, hesitating to move inside, but wanting to continue their conversation.

"Lizzie put chicken in the oven an hour ago. I'd be happy to share it with ya." He back-stepped into the house. "And blackberry pie."

"You make it hard to resist, but I need to stop at the phone shanty and place a call to a friend who's tending my store."

"Another time, then," he said.

"All right, thank you." Was he hoping she'd bring Holly back with her?

"I'm going to hold ya to it." He glanced outside into the darkening sky. "You wanna borrow a flashlight?"

The sun had dropped behind the distant hills, leaving the world a crisscross of shadowy pockets. "What was I thinking?" she said. "Is it too late to find the phone shanty tonight?"

"Not if I walk you there. 'Twill take but a few minutes. Give me time to stoke the fire." He came back wearing boots, a black wool jacket, a black felt hat, and carrying two flashlights. He handed her one. "Take it home with ya. I'll fetch it in the mornin'."

"I've lost track of these parts," she said. "We didn't have a phone shanty when I left, and many of the trees have doubled in size."

"Like I said, 'tis no trouble walking you there."

As they strolled side by side, Nathaniel said, "I was wondering. Forgive me if I'm prying. Are you planning to join the Amish church?"

She swung around to see if he was serious. "Get baptized at my age?"

"Yah. 'Tis never too late." His elbow brushed against hers.

"But I live in Seattle. And I attend a church that encourages Bible studies and memorizing scripture. As a girl, the bishop frowned upon such practices."

"Never mind about that." He slowed his pace. "You could come home, Esther."

Trying to read his expression, she stopped to face him and felt the ground shifting. "Right when my brothers are moving?"

"You could stay right here, with me."

"So you could marry Holly?" The first thought to crowd into her mind flew out her mouth.

He chuckled. "Nee! It's not Holly I have my sights set on. 'Tis you I wish to court."

CHAPTER NINETEEN

"I'll be right back," I told Beth, as I strode up the stairs to fetch my laptop.

I carried my Mac to the kitchen table. "Do you mind if I check my mail here? I don't think my grandma would appreciate the computer in her house because it feeds off electricity. Plus, no Internet connection."

"Go right ahead. We're wireless anywhere in the house."

I sat at the table as Beth filled the kettle with water and set it on a burner. "What kind of tea do you like?" How did she know I was thirsty?

"Something herbal that won't keep me up tonight. It's been a long day. Fun, but exhausting." Like a twisting river: sudden bends, rapids, and undercurrents.

Beth opened a box of tea bags. "Here's one called Sleepy Time."

"Sounds perfect."

A knock-knock on the kitchen door lured Missy away from her food dish. Her mouth half-full of kibble, she guzzled it down, then bolted toward the opening door to welcome Zach.

"Hello." Zach's voice sounded upbeat and amiable. "I saw Holly's rental in the driveway." When his gaze landed on my attire, he did a double take.

I was struck by his good looks. This morning, through my bleary eyes, I hadn't noticed his strong rectangular jawline, his erect posture. But I didn't care for his gaping at me right now.

"Come on in," Beth said, and gave him a quick hug. "Dinner's still an hour away."

"I finished up patients early."

"That doesn't happen very often. You're usually thirty minutes late."

"Meaning, I'll probably get a midnight call from the Schrocks. One of their mules may have sprained a pastern this afternoon, but they didn't want me to come examine it yet. They're icing the area to see if the swelling goes down." He sniffed the air. "Smells as good as Dienner's Country Restaurant."

"Thanks, honey."

He shrugged off his jacket, exposing a fit physique, then moved closer to me. "Good evening, miss. Are you the same Holly Fisher I met this morning?"

"Yes, the one and only." I felt squirmy under his scrutiny— he seemed to be looking down his nose at me. Zach the quack, I thought, and grinned to myself. But why be mean spirited? He was a skilled and respected veterinarian. And I was acting nitpicky for no good reason.

I was curious about the mule and about Zach's job. If the animal's owner were Amish, how would he contact Zach? Wake neighbors to use their telephone?

I imagined Zach answering his cell phone by his bed tonight—sleeping alone?—leaping to his feet, throwing on clothes, and dashing for his pickup, medical bag in hand. He struck me as somewhat arrogant, but I had to admire his dedication. And I admit, I was envious of his secure career. He owned a thriving business, was well respected, and didn't pay heed to the whims of Wall Street. He had it made.

"What happened here?" he said, sending me an ambiguous smile. "A transformed woman?"

"Are you mocking my Amish clothing? If you only knew what I went through to borrow them." I was grateful Zach hadn't seen me at my worst.

He chuckled. "I'd love to hear the story."

"Let's just say, I collided with a squishy patch of mud. If my dress and apron offend you, I can leave." In jest, I pushed my chair out a few inches.

"Please don't go. You'd look charming no matter what you wore." He sat across from me, his elbows on the table. "But you caught me off guard."

Beth removed the boiling kettle from the stove top, deposited a tea bag in a small pot, and poured steaming water over it. "Holly stopped by to check her email. Zach, don't you dare give her a bad time and scare her away."

"Since when is complimenting a woman on her dress tantamount to teasing?" he said.

"That was a compliment?" Beth raised an eyebrow in his direction as she set a tray housing a flowered china cup and saucer and the teapot on the table next to my Mac.

"Thank you, Beth." Thinking my time here might be short I opened my laptop and angled the screen so Zach couldn't read it.

I scanned my email and noticed Larry had written. Subject: Missing you. He suggested he fly to Philadelphia to visit an uncle, borrow a car, and make a day trip to see me. Larry Haarberg here? No offense, but we'd never actually dated or shared a goodnight kiss.

I pressed Reply and wrote: "Good news: My grandmother is alive, but not doing well. At times, she's alert and agile, but then she practically fainted—an invitation for a broken hip. I met my exuberant aunts, who decided I should move to Montana with them. Don't think Mom appreciated their meddling. Will fill you in when I get home. Larry, as far as your coming here, please don't take this wrong, but I'd rather you didn't. Life is already too complicated. See you next week."

I didn't mention I'd barely scanned his texts and hadn't listened to his phone message when I saw his number on my caller ID earlier today.

I poured tea into my cup and took a sip. While I was online, I could change our departure date—with or without Mom's approval. I hoped she wouldn't be livid but decided a few days wouldn't make much difference. She seemed distracted and might not even notice. And Dori had told us to take our time. "Don't rush back home on my account" were her parting words when I'd called her earlier.

"Can we tempt you to stay for dinner?" Zach asked me, returning my attention to the kitchen.

"Thanks, but I should get back to see how my mother and grandmother are doing."

My fingers tapping the keyboard, I changed our airline tickets, canceling our departure and making it open-ended. I gasped as I accepted the penalty charge.

"Holly, anything I can do to help?" Beth took hold of the teapot's handle and topped off my cup. "You look disappointed. Bad news?"

"My poor credit card—" I logged out. "I was laid off a few days ago and was hoping to hear from my old boss. He hinted he'd rehire me if the economy made a miraculous comeback."

"It gave you time to visit us," she said.

"Hey, I have a brilliant idea," Zach said. "I need someone in my office. My receptionist is so pregnant she can barely fit in her chair. She's quitting next week and I haven't even started looking for her replacement. How about it, Holly?"

"You want to hire me?" I didn't believe him. "Would that include making you coffee?"

"I'd have to taste your brew before I commit. I'm particular. I like it dark and strong."

"Zach," Beth said, "if you want to make her stick around, I can think of kinder ways of showing it. Where are your manners?"

I closed my laptop. "Thanks for the job offer, if you're serious—which I doubt. But I can't accept. I made our tickets open-ended, but eventually Mom and I need to get back to Seattle."

"Sure we can't change your mind about staying for dinner?" Zach said.

"Positive." I took a final sip of tea and walked my chair away from the table.

"In the meantime, you're welcome to leave your laptop here," Beth said.

"That would be fantastic. Or I could take it to a library or coffee shop with Internet access so I won't be a bother."

"I wouldn't hear of it." She gave my hand a soft squeeze. "I enjoy our visits."

"Okay, I'll come back tomorrow." When Zach wasn't here. "Earlier in the day," I added, then wondered why I wished to avoid him. Was the problem his or mine?

CHAPTER TWENTY

Nathaniel's courting proposal was as unexpected as a UFO sighting.

"Did Mamm set you up to this?" Esther said, her hand moving to the base of her throat. Courting was like getting engaged—next step: marriage.

"No. At my age, I didn't think to ask her permission. But I could go do it right now if you like. And speak to Bishop Troyer."

"Hold on. You and I hardly know each other, except when we were kids."

"I remember you with fondness, though you only cared for Samuel." He removed his hat. "I admired you from afar since first we met."

"But I'm not Amish."

"Like I was askin', are ya willing to join the church?"

"Then move here? Be your wife?" She felt dizzy headed, like Mamm swooning down the porch stairs.

"I know I'm comin' on fast." He set his hat back on his head. "But I feared you'd leave town before I made my intentions known."

"I don't know what to say." Until a week ago, her life seemed relatively content, even if nearing its end, a snowball rolling down a slope, melting as it made its final journey to the bottom of the hill.

"Will ya at least give my proposal some thought?" He took her hand, his twice the size of hers, but gentle.

"Yes—I suppose." How could she not?

His voice's steady cadence manifested honesty. Unless she'd misunderstood him. No, Nathaniel had offered to court and marry her. He wanted Esther to join the Amish church, to be followed by a wedding. As a favor to Mamm?

"I can't give you an answer tonight." She reminded herself of the hasty mistakes she'd made as a young woman, the travesties they'd caused. Esther dare not commit another. *Es Sclimmscht vun Narre*— the worst of fools—Mamm and Dat had no doubt called her. Court Nathaniel, and in doing so, possibly compete with Esther's own daughter? Holly had a crush on him, Esther was pretty sure of it— even if her daughter's whims were temporary. If Esther showed an inkling of interest in him, Holly would never speak to her again.

She tried to envision Holly's living here, riding a buggy into town, dressed Plain every day. But she couldn't picture it; Holly was a modern woman in every sense. Yet her daughter might be so discouraged after losing her job she'd wish to stay longer.

An owl hooted, and Esther's mind explored another avenue. What about herself? Only a couple days ago, she'd been positive she'd never consider moving back to Lancaster County. But the beauty of the area wowed her, its pristine farms, the men working the fields with draft horses and mules, gathering corn and hay for the upcoming winter. She'd convinced herself she hadn't missed Pennsylvania's frigid weather in January and February or the sweltering summer days. Seattle's temperatures remained mild. The seasons melded into one another.

Last December Holly had complained she wanted a dusting of snow on Christmas but didn't get her wish. On Christmas Eve Esther had caught herself reminiscing about snowflakes feathering to the ground and her riding in the family's sleigh, then ice-skating on a frozen pond. And in July and August she'd occasionally longed for kick-off-your-shoes blistering hot summer days.

Esther was avoiding a monumental issue: joining the Amish church, the last notion she'd have considered an hour ago. If she became a member, she'd have to submit to the bishop's and her preacher brother Isaac's decisions. Unless Isaac moved to Montana, and she and Nathaniel remained here. Would Samuel's parents block her membership? Would the bishop know of her devious past? Certainly she would have to publically repent in front of the whole community. On her knees.

She and Nathaniel stood, their eyes locked, until she looked away. She flicked on her flashlight, then turned it off again, wanting to hide in the darkness. She got an idiotic impulse to hug him, if for nothing more than to show gratitude for his compliment that he found her a marital prospect. For the first time in what seemed forever, she longed to be held in a man's arms. Not just any man's. Nathaniel's. Was it possible for the seed of love to sprout so quickly?

"There's a lot you don't know about me," she said.

"That goes for me, too. Thank the Lord, he forgives us our transgressions."

She bet Nathaniel held himself to a higher standard than her own. What could he possibly have to regret? Perhaps a harsh word to his daughters.

Esther and Nathaniel reached the phone shanty, a one-windowed, weather-beaten shack set well apart from the farmhouses, inconspicuously tucked amid bushes and shielded by a tree.

"Nathaniel—what you're asking—are you serious?" She bet many a single woman had her eyes set on him.

"Esther, I'm serious as can be. It's past time I remarry."

"This is so sudden." Her thoughts whirled like a windmill on a blustery day, spinning too quickly for her sight to pin down one blade.

She felt like turning on her heels and running away. "I'll be fine. You can go," she said.

"Are ya sure? I don't like leavin' ya alone."

"I can find my way home. *Gut Nacht.*"—Good night.

"Gut Nacht," he said.

In the phone shanty, Esther picked up the receiver, placed the call, then heard Dori's cheerful voice. "Good afternoon, the Amish Shoppe."

Nathaniel receded into the woods toward his house. He dimmed his flashlight, but she heard his footsteps, twigs cracking under his boots.

Had a hummingbird invaded her heart? She missed him, already. "Ich bedank mich," she called after him.

"Is that you, Esther?" Dori asked. "How's it going?"

"Fine—as well as can be expected." Esther was dying to tell Dori what had transpired between her and Nathaniel. A sounding board is what she needed, but she dare not mention it. By now he might already have qualms about his spontaneous suggestion and be wondering what ever got into him.

It occurred to her Nathaniel could have been drinking. No, he wasn't *gsoffe*—drunk. She hadn't smelled liquor on his breath and doubted he drank alcohol.

"How are you getting on?" Esther said. "Any problems?"

"Didn't Holly relay my message? She called a couple hours ago. I'm having the time of my life. I told Jim I wish he'd built this store for me instead of you. Not that I had your vision or ability, or knew one thing about the Amish. But now that our kids are gone and my days are free, I love working again. And Jim's planning to retire at the end of the year."

"You've been great, Dori. I can't thank you enough. But Christmas is around the bend. I need more merchandise in place by Thanksgiving."

"Don't you dare hurry home on my account, girlfriend. I've never had so much fun. Why not buy merchandise there and have it shipped home? I mean, you are in the heart of Lancaster County."

"How do you know so much about it?"

"Reading the brochures. And I got online and checked out a couple books from the library on the Amish. Couldn't you go to market or vendors, select merchandise, and send it here? You'd be the middleman and save on commission."

Esther had to tell her friend the truth. She hushed her voice to just above a whisper. "I'm short on funds. I hope to take out a loan when we get home."

"That's where my plan steps into action. How would you like a business partner? You and I get along so well, and you'd still call the shots. We could make it a fifty-one, forty-nine percent partnership, if you like."

"What if it doesn't pan out? What if working together ruins our friendship?" But on the other hand, a partnership would open a world of possibilities. "Where would Holly and I live?"

"Exactly where you do now, for as long as you like. But face it, that beautiful daughter of yours is going to fall in love and get married one of these days."

"Maybe sooner than later."

"What was that?" Dori's alto voice rose in pitch. "Holly's found herself a sweetie in one day?"

"Possibly."

"I don't believe it. The Holly I know doesn't dive into relationships."

"You're right, she's overly cautious or she'd be married by now." Esther pressed the phone to her ear. "But you'd barely recognize her if you saw her today."

"She's dyed her hair black and gone Gothic?"

"No. I'll explain when we get home."

"Holly told me she's changing the airline tickets to open-ended," Dori said. "Meaning you don't need to rush back."

"Without consulting me first? She's gone too far." Treating Esther as though she were a child.

CHAPTER TWENTY-ONE

I returned my laptop to Beth's guestroom. Back in the kitchen, I said good-bye to Zach, who got to his feet. Did he think I looked bizarre in my Amish attire? I didn't know what to make of him and figured my appraisal went both ways. We couldn't be more different, except we both liked Beth. I had to admit I was envious of their compatible relationship—the flipside of Mom's and mine since she'd shown me the shoebox of Mommy Anna's letters.

At the door, Beth kissed my cheek. "Don't make yourself a stranger," she said. "Hope to see you soon."

"Thanks, I look forward to it."

"Let me walk you to your car," Zach said, helping me with my jacket.

"No, thank you, I'm fine." Stepping outside, the chill evening breeze traveled up my legs and goose bumps erupted on my calves. The sky was as black as soot. The air hung heavy with silence. With only a quarter moon, the stars twinkled vibrantly, not like in the city, where streetlamps and porch lights competed for my eyes' attention. I stood for a moment as my pupils dilated, open-ing themselves to embrace the heavens, the opposite of my hazy thoughts.

Like the old two-pan balance scale we kept in the shop window for display, my mind weighed Beth and my mother's relationship. Had Mom truly forgotten Beth? Back in Seattle I'd wondered if Mom suffered from memory problems. Maybe I'd been right. How did Beth's telephone number get in Mom's purse? Grandma Anna must have sent it to her.

Zach stepped outside with me. "My mother would never forgive me for sending you off into the night by yourself."

Aha, his gentlemanly manners were Beth's idea.

"I was serious about that job offer," he said. "I could run you by my office right now. It's not far away."

"I have no experience with animals or any idea how long I'll be here."

He reached over and touched my arm. "Hey, did you and I get off on the wrong foot?"

"Not at all." I ducked into the rental. "Thanks for the job offer." Which I figured was Beth's idea too.

Driving to the farmhouse, I recognized Mom striding on the dirt path at the side of the road hustling in my direction. She wore a jacket and scarf I'd seen on Greta and was carrying a flashlight.

I stopped at the front of the house and got out. When she noticed me, her hand jerked and she dropped the flashlight. "*Dabbish* fin-gers," she said—I guessed calling herself all thumbs. I'd noticed, bit by bit, she was using the language of her youth.

"Where have you been?" I asked.

"Using the phone shanty." She scooped up the light and aimed it at my face. "Why did you call Dori?" Her words came out an accusing blast.

"Hey, stop that." Squinting, I blocked the blinding flashlight beam with my hand until she switched it off. "I called Dori because I'm the one with the cell phone, which you could have used if you'd asked. You're the only person I know, in Seattle, anyway, who refuses to own one."

A dim gas lamp from the house illuminated her face. She hurled me a fierce look. "What right did you have to contact her?"

"I can't call my own home?"

"But you didn't tell me." Mom's cheeks appeared splotched; her breath was staggered. I wondered if she had been running away from something or had heard a spooky noise in the woods. I didn't appreciate her tone of voice.

"I'm a grown woman who lives above the Amish Shoppe too," I said. "One of my friends could have stopped by." Unlikely. "Or my old boss could have called." Even more unlikely. "Why are you so edgy?"

Two cars and then a covered buggy passed by. Ooh, I loved that clip-clop-clip-clop sound.

My mother craned her neck to search into the buggy as if expecting to recognize the driver, then turned back to me. "I was dumbfounded when Dori announced she wants to be my business partner. Did she tell you that?"

"No, but I think it's a terrific idea. Wouldn't having a partner like Dori, your best friend, be fun for you? Not to mention the financial benefits—let's face it, we're low on cash."

With her free hand, she readjusted the scarf to cover her ears. "I don't know anything, anymore."

"That sounds ominous. I've never seen you so jumpy. Did Dori mention I changed our airline tickets?"

"What right do you have to make these decisions without consulting me first?" She flicked the light back on and shined it into the trees, casting ghoulish shadows.

"I didn't think you'd mind," I said. "You can't desert your mother twice, can you?" I considered telling Mom about Beth's garage apartment and her offer to rent it. No, Beth was right: My grandmother wouldn't stay behind when her sons and daughter left.

"From what I've seen, Mommy Anna's too weak to travel," I said. I wondered how the family would manage the journey without U-Haul trucks. Would they hire professional movers? "She can barely get around. The first few months they'll be too busy to look after her properly."

"My brothers may purchase a large spread with houses and barns in good shape." She glanced down the road in the direction of Nathaniel's farm.

"Even so, I bet the men will be erecting fences, repairing roofs, and buying livestock, frantic before the first snowstorm, if it hasn't hit already. I've heard Montana winters can be brutal."

"It gets cold around here, too." She shivered for effect. "The womenfolk will look after your grandmother."

"Womenfolk? I've never heard you use that term in my life," I said. "My aunts will be chasing after their younger children and busy enrolling the older ones in school."

"Unless they can find a vacant school for sale or settle near another Amish district, they'll build their own. Remember, Amish only go through the eighth grade." Her whole demeanor—her shoulders, neck, and arms—drooped like a rag doll. "I begged my parents to let me go to high school."

"They wouldn't let you? I assumed you'd dropped out."

She shook her head, her chin lowered. Another covered buggy rolled by. Again, Mom searched it with what looked like anticipation—or dread.

"Growing up, I read aloud to my brothers," she said. "And any other book I could lay my hands on."

"Like someone's diary?" I wondered if it belonged to Mommy Anna. "I saw you looking through one earlier. Up in your old bedroom."

"Ach. In my haste I went off and left mine. What a *Dummkopf*. My mamm must have been furious, because surely she showed it to Dat, who would have punished me."

She moved toward the front porch and sat on the second step, her elbows on her knees. "*Simbel mir*. I'd detailed my dreams of going to college and studying everything from economics to music."

"You would have been punished for dreaming big?"

"Yah, I'd wanted to learn to play the harp and had written in my diary about asking Samuel to build me one."

"Your parents would have prevented him?"

"For sure. Except for harmonicas, musical instruments weren't allowed."

Wondering if she was being straight with me, my mind sifted through a hodgepodge of emotions, including sympathy and compassion. I wanted to believe her.

"Mamm would never stand up to my dat," she said.

In a flash, my sympathy for her dissolved. Her complaining about my deceased grandfather—Mommy Anna's husband, Levi—spiked into my ribs like a rusty nail. "How can you speak badly about your father?" I said. "Maybe he wasn't perfect, but at least you had one, more than I can say for myself."

"Daughter, I'd give up anything to change the past." She stood and reached her arms out to hug me. "You're right, I shouldn't speak ill of the dead, especially my own dat." She let out a throaty sob. "My brain's all addled."

She held me tighter, making me feel trapped in a straitjacket. Several inches taller than I was, Mom could almost rest her chin on my forehead.

"Ouch, you're pricking me." I wriggled out of her grasp. "I'll ask Greta how to put the pins in properly because, who knows, I might wear this dress again sometime."

Mom grimaced, but I ignored her sour expression.

"I'm going inside," I said, moving past her. "I'm hungry."

"Dinner should be ready by now. Isaac's probably still outside, not that he'd help with cooking preparations."

"What is it with you?" I spun around. "You've got a complaint about everyone in your family."

"Well, now, men don't help in the kitchen. Housework is for women. That's a fact. And in Isaac's defense, he's a preacher. Besides milking the cows twice a day and his many farm duties, people flock to him seeking advice."

"He does seem awfully serious." Disgruntled was more like it, but I wouldn't fan the flames of my mother's negative attitudes. I'd always wished for siblings. She had five and didn't even appreciate them.

"I'm thinkin' our being here doesn't help my brother's mood." She gave my apron a tug. "I've got to tell you, seeing you dressed that way might upset him. Please change back into your city clothes."

"No, Mommy Anna likes the dress." With Mom on my case, I didn't feel like being civil. "I might even part my hair down the middle and wear a prayer cap. Did I tell you, I've thought of growing my hair out? It would save a bundle at the hairdresser."

"Holly, please don't antagonize Isaac or give my mamm false hope. Or get duped into a lifestyle you know nothing about."

"How dare you, after conning me into your make-believe world? Since we're staying longer, I'll have time to meet my other grandparents. The ones you claim disowned you. Did you lie about them, too?

"No, I forbid you to see them."

"Don't tell me what to do." My hands balled into fists. "Now that I've met my aunts and their kids and my sweet grandmother, I want to meet Dad's parents."

I recalled Nathaniel and the buggy ride, traveling past immaculate farms and inhaling the aroma of harvested corn. "I wished I'd let Nathaniel take me to the Fishers' this afternoon," I said.

Her twisted expression told me she was appalled. Or was she afraid?

CHAPTER TWENTY-TWO

"My Nathaniel offered to drive you to Samuel's parents' farm?" Esther said, hoping she'd misheard Holly.

"Your Nathaniel?" Holly yanked her hair into a ponytail, her bangs flopping forward. "You're laying claim on him? He's not yours, Mother. But if you want to tag along with us, I suppose you may."

"No." Esther's throat squeezed her windpipe like wet leather left out in the scorching sun. The last time she'd gone to the Fishers' farm, Samuel's parents had barred her way, admonishing her never to return. A lifetime ago, but she couldn't face them again—as if sticking her head into a combine.

"Then never mind, I rescind my invitation." Holly's fingers combed her hair back into place. "If Nathaniel's too busy, I'll drive there myself." She let out a huff, but didn't march into the house as Esther expected.

Her daughter hadn't shown such hostility since high school when Esther'd caught her with cigarettes in her pocket and grounded her for a month. She was a wild one in her teens, much as Esther had been.

Esther gripped the flashlight. "I think I'll stay outside a few minutes." She considered rushing over to Nathaniel's house to put an end to her daughter's scheme to visit the Fishers. But not after he'd made his intentions of courting her known. He might already be suffering from remorse. Surely a younger woman like his housekeeper, Lizzie, would make a better wife.

Moving back to Lancaster County—with or without her mother and brothers living here—was ludicrous. An even more preposterous idea was that her heart longed for Nathaniel—like a teenage crush. He'd professed he'd admired her from afar; she took that to mean he would have courted her if she hadn't been head over heels in love with Samuel. She envisioned a weighty novel opening to a new chapter in her life, then two giant hands slamming the book closed again.

Esther shined her light on the mailbox. "Your grandma usually fetches the mail," she told Holly.

"No way she could get it today," Holly said stiffly.

For old times' sake, as she'd loved to do as a girl, Esther ambled out to the metal breadbox-shaped container and pulled its door open, its hinges squeaking.

Inside lay a legal-size envelope addressed to Isaac.

"*Guck emol dat!* I mean, look at that." What was wrong with her? It seemed she had no control over what came out her mouth. The longer she remained here the more she felt the lure of this secluded world she'd once avoided. She felt like the biblical brothers Jacob and Esau, sparring within their mother's womb.

Esther reached in and extracted the letter. She thought she recognized her brother Peter's handwriting, but after all these years was unsure.

"Who's it for?" Holly asked, drawing near.

Esther shined the flashlight on the postmark and said, "It's addressed to Isaac. From Rexford, Montana." She was tempted to open it on the spot. "I think it's from Peter."

"One of your brothers?" Holly said.

"Yes, one-and-a-half years younger than Adam. Such a good boy he was."

"Speaking of brothers, aren't you going to give the letter to Uncle Isaac?" Holly's tone sounded demanding, oozing with accusation.

"I will. For sure, I will."

"I don't trust you." Holly plucked the envelope out of Esther's hand like a bullfrog catching a fly. "I'll do it."

"Nee!" Esther snatched the letter back and hid it behind her waist. "Enough of your bad manners, young lady." She ascended the porch stairs, wrestled with the knob, and forced the door open. She saw Isaac on the easy chair in the sitting room reading *Family Life,* a monthly magazine.

"Have you been upstairs to see Mamm?" Esther asked him. He nodded, but kept reading. "A letter came for ya," she said, stepping to his side.

Without glancing up, his hand released *Family Life* and took the envelope from her. He slid it among the pages of the magazine, obviously not wishing to share its contents with Esther.

She knew her four other brothers wouldn't make a move without first consulting Isaac. In part, they couldn't. Not only was he a preacher, but as the youngest brother, this house and land would be passed on to him.

Esther doubted he'd give Mamm enough money to stay in this area. No, he'd insist on keeping the family together.

CHAPTER TWENTY-THREE

Maintaining my distance by a few yards, I followed Mom into the house. She crossed the front hallway to the sitting room and stood by Isaac—the first time I'd seen him actually off his feet and relaxing. My mother appeared timid, her eyes lowered, as she handed him the letter. She paused, then turned and trod up the stairs.

Shutting the front door, I inhaled the fragrant aroma of cooking apples wafting from the kitchen. I should help Greta with dinner preparations, meaning I must walk past Isaac, who sat opening the letter. Why was I reticent? Even though he'd been aloof, Isaac had treated me with respect. He seemed to be a good husband and dad. He might have a beef with my mother, but not with me.

Much as I loved Dori and Jim, calling them Auntie and Uncle, I'd always wished for genuine blood relatives. Like a banner waving out my window, my mantra growing up could have been: I want a humongous extended family!

In the past I'd kicked around the idea I might have distant cousins, but Mom had acted as if her entire family left Pennsylvania when her parents died. Address unknown. But really, I scolded myself, by using the Internet or hiring a detective, I could have pursued my relatives; their tracks would have trundled straight to this farmhouse. I'd been gullible, believing my mother's smoke-and-mirrors deception, and wasn't any closer to understanding her motivation. Unless she was a sociopathic liar or her drug use in San Francisco had erased her memory. Then Dori had convinced Mom Haight-Ashbury was no place for a pregnant woman. According to Mom, she'd moved with Jim and Dori to the Northwest and never looked back.

Once a runaway, always a runaway, I thought, hearing Mom's voice upstairs speaking to Mommy Anna. Did she even love my grandma?

I meandered across the entry's rag rugs.

Uncle Isaac stroked his beard with one hand as he perused the letter. He must know I was watching him. As far as I could tell he was ignoring me. Maybe Mom was right about my wearing the borrowed dress and apron; it was a mistake. I'd disregarded her opinion because I'd been infuriated when she bad-mouthed her father, my Daadi Levi, whom I'd never meet. All my life I'd imagined my grandfather a mixture of Santa Claus and John Wayne, but now I wondered if Isaac was a younger version of his father, authoritarian and domineering.

Not the shy type, I goaded myself to stroll into the sitting room, coming to a halt near him. "Hi, Uncle Isaac. How's it going?"

He folded the letter, slipped it into the envelope, and placed it on the side table.

"Care to share your plans?" I said. "If you wouldn't mind."

He tugged his earlobe. "What exactly are ya askin'?"

"For starters, why are you moving?"

"We need more land. We're stymied—nowhere to expand. This county is clogged with traffic jams, making it dangerous for horse and buggies."

"I haven't seen many cars."

"If you went through Bird-in-Hand or Intercourse, you'd see outsiders swarmin' like locusts." His eyes honed in on me like a hawk catching a glimpse of a rabbit. "We need to get away from picture-taking tourists. Gawkers, like you."

I maintained a poker face. "I'm not a gawker and I didn't bring a camera." I wouldn't mention my cell phone took pictures. Maybe he already knew. Although I'd kept my phone out of sight in the house.

He targeted me with his index finger. "You're mockin' us by dressing Plain."

I could hear Greta in the kitchen setting the table. I wished she'd call us for supper. "I didn't mean to insult anyone," I said. "Mommy Anna doesn't mind my dress."

"She's so glad to set eyes on ya, she wouldn't care what you wore." He sat back in his chair and leveled his gaze at me. "Is this your first step toward joining the Amish church and stayin' with us for good? There ain't many Englischers I'd extend that invitation to, but seein' as you're Esther's daughter and we need someone to help look after Mamm—"

"You'd want me to live with you as your mother's caretaker?"

"Unless Esther will. She owes it to Mamm, for sure." He ran a hand through his hair, flattened on top. "Ya can't imagine the sorrow she's caused our Mudder."

"Yes, I can." The conversation was galloping into dangerous territory. "I'd rather my mother speak for herself." I sat on a chair facing him. "Please forgive me for being nosy, but is that letter from one of your brothers?"

"Yah. But 'tis none of your business."

"But I care about my grandmother's future. She isn't well."

"Ya think I can't see that for myself?"

"Sorry, I didn't mean to insinuate anything." The last thing I wanted was an argument. I heard a jet's engine rumble in the distance, then recede.

"Sounds like a storm's rolling in," Uncle Isaac said. "Thank the good Lord, we got most of the corn in the crib today."

"What did the weatherman predict?"

He shrugged. "No idea."

"Can't you listen to battery-run radios?"

"Yah, but I choose not to. A bunch of *unsinnich* jabber. Senseless."

As the wind picked up, branches scratched the side of the house like untrimmed fingernails. The gusts multiplied, thrashing through the trees. I heard a cracking sound, like a limb breaking off. Rain pattered on the front porch, then gathered momentum—a river of water against the windows. The droplets crystallized into pellets, sounding like pebbles. I glanced outside and saw layers of hail hammering the lawn.

A beautiful sight until a blinding flash whitened the world like a strobe light. An ear-piercing crash louder than a shotgun's blast sent me bolting to my feet. Isaac remained in his easy chair as another lightning strike blasted down the road in Nathaniel's direction. I guessed the deafening sound was a tree splintering.

My ears rang. "We don't have many electrical storms in the Northwest." I crept to the window and saw Beth's lights in the distance flicker, then go out. A shroud enclosed her and another neighbor's house, but our kerosene and gas lamps burned steadily.

"Guess you never lose your power," I said, trying to sound fearless, when in fact I was trembling. "What about your cows?"

"They're safe, under shelter, and the horses are in their stalls. 'Tis unlikely the barn will be hit. The Almighty protects us."

"But the rain falls upon the just and the unjust."

"Ya know the Bible?"

"A little," I said. "Less than I should."

"Are you willing to submit to God's will?"

Good question. I was stubborn and always had been. According to Mom, even as a one-year-old I'd refused her help when learning to walk.

Where was God right now? I wondered. In the volleying thunder and lightning? Speaking to me through Isaac?

My uncle shifted his weight forward, his face nearing mine. "I believe the Almighty wants you ta be one of us. Your wearing the dress and apron tells me you're returnin' to your heritage."

"Give up my car keys and cell phone?" I recalled sitting in Starbucks sipping mocha lattes and my life in Seattle, an area I couldn't get enough of. But at a distance I saw my favorite city bulging with houses, condominiums, office buildings, and the air smoggy with exhaust fumes when the Metro bus chugged past the shop.

Isaac's hands gripped his suspenders. "Holly, you should consider moving with us to Montana."

"Exactly where are you planning to go?" I was stalling until Greta fetched us for supper. I had no intention of relocating with him anywhere.

"Near the Canadian border, close by other Amish districts."

"I went to Montana once. It was beautiful and untamed. But your mother's sick. You've got to find out what's wrong with her before you take her into the wilderness."

"She's old. Ain't much we can do about that."

I didn't buy his glib reply. "I want to take her to a doctor," I said, hearing the trees outside swishing like hula dancers. "Does she have health insurance?"

He shook his head. "None of us do. We pay out of pocket or the community will help us if we run dry of money."

The sky lit up, followed by a roaring sound like colossal waves on the Oregon Coast. I hoped the worst part of the storm had passed, but on the other side of the house, forked lightning pierced the ground and thunder rattled the windowpanes.

I wrapped my arms around myself. "Not even fire insurance on your home?"

"If God allows the house to burn, we'll build another."

"I guess you don't need car insurance," I said, attempting levity. But the corners of his mouth veered down.

"But your mother," I said. Now might be my only time alone with Uncle Isaac. I had to convince him. "I want to find her a specialist."

"The only way I'd let you take her to a doctor is if you were one of us," he said. "I mean truly one of us."

No way would I let him run my life. Yet he called all the shots in this household.

CHAPTER TWENTY-FOUR

Esther was *naerfich*—so nervous she wanted to bury her head under the goose-down pillow. With no central heating, the room felt tomblike, a good excuse to remain in bed. But she was determined to creep out of the house prior to sunup before anyone noticed her.

Though Esther's feelings were initially hurt last night, she was glad Holly had switched to Mamm's bedroom. Why had Mamm continued sleeping in the main house instead of moving into the Daadi Haus? Had she moved when Isaac married Greta, but returned to the main house because she was afraid to live alone, or did Isaac think she'd become disoriented or fall?

Right now, Holly was no doubt bathed in slumber, purring when she exhaled. Oblivious, while Esther tossed fitfully, worrying all night.

Holly had barely spoken to Esther over supper, but rather chatted with Isaac about the turbulent weather—by then, the storm had volleyed to the east—and asked Greta about their children, who would never display insolent behavior. They were submissive and obedient, as Esther was in her childhood

After the family had finished eating last night, Isaac, Greta, Holly, and Esther transferred Mamm's clothes and few belongings to the first floor of the Daadi Haus, attached to the main house, where Esther's maternal grandparents once resided, so Mamm wouldn't have to navigate the stairs to the second floor. "We should have done this years ago," Isaac had said, placing the water pitcher on the bureau, both family heirlooms for two centuries.

"Anna, we'll be close by should ya need us," Greta told her. "Leave the door open." She set a bell on the nightstand. "Ring this and I'll be right over."

Esther felt the burden of guilt weighing upon her shoulders for not predicting Mamm's needs, but her sister-in-law Greta knew Mamm better than Esther did.

"Since Mommy Anna's room is vacant, may I sleep in it?" Holly had asked, and Isaac nodded. Holly had sought his approval, apparently seeing him as alpha male, head of the household. Esther didn't trust him to make Holly's needs his priority. Who knew how he might influence her?

She tugged the bedcovers up around her throat. Her goal since Holly's birth was to protect her, to spare her pain, but the plan had gone awry. She'd been wrong; she saw that now.

Holly's remark about visiting Samuel's parents festered in Esther's mind. Holly and Nathaniel had evidently discussed the Fishers, yet he hadn't brought up their names to Esther.

Juicy news flocked across Lancaster County like starlings; Samuel's parents might know Esther was here. If Holly were determined to approach them, Esther must speak to them first, to dip her toes into the frigid waters.

She heard footsteps on the first floor, then moments later the back door opened and closed. Isaac, she thought, slogging out to milk the cows. Greta was in the kitchen preparing breakfast.

Esther rolled on her side and stretched her legs. She knew the route to the Fisher's farm, not far away, south and west, five minutes in a buggy, but fifteen on foot. When she was young, anyway.

Samuel had been the Fishers' only child, the previous three miscarried or stillborn. Esther felt a visceral round of pity for Samuel's mother, who was devoted to him but had mentioned to Esther she'd selected his future wife, the daughter of a close friend. If Samuel had lived, the Fishers might have grandchildren. A house thriving with activity.

Esther felt compelled to ask God's forgiveness again for stealing away their only child. She'd been *grossfiehlich*—bigheaded—when she'd left home. She knew she should accept the Lord's mercy. To refuse his forgiveness was ungrateful. A sin, Isaac's bishop might label it.

She wondered if Samuel's father, Jeremiah now an old man, still got up at dawn to milk their herd of black-and-white Holsteins. Unlikely, without neighbors helping him or hired hands. Esther doubted Samuel's narrow-minded father would employ Englischers to work for him.

She pushed the covers back and swung her legs over the side of the bed. Her bare feet hit the icy wooden floor. She hurried to the closet and chose a cream-colored blouse in need of ironing. Leaving her nightgown draped across the end of the bed, she shoved her hands into the blouse's arms then tugged a V-neck sweater over her head. She stepped into slacks—too cold for a skirt this morning. She didn't care what she looked like, but out of habit secured her waist-length brown hair into a bun.

She opened the window shade halfway. In the darkness, she could see that Beth and their Englisch neighbors across the field were still without power. Esther felt satisfaction for not depending on electricity and wondered if Beth had kept her fireplace burning all night for heat. But then Esther admonished herself for finding pleasure that Beth's electric coffeemaker was at this moment useless. Yes, Esther still held a grudge she should have released decades ago.

She noticed Isaac's lamp burning in the barn and a shimmering of frost on the ground, illuminated by the lights from the kitchen. Autumn was plunging into winter early this year.

Esther knew Isaac wouldn't eat breakfast until he'd finished milking. Were his older children and Nathaniel helping him? No, Nathaniel would attend to his own herd first. She must slink past his home to reach Samuel's parents' farm, if they still lived there. What age would they be? A few years her mother's senior? Childless.

She worked her feet into woolen socks and fished her fleece vest and her walking shoes out of her suitcase, then padded down the staircase. An enticing bouquet of coffee, rising bread dough, and baking biscuits floated from the kitchen, but she would wait to sample Greta's cuisine until after her excursion.

Crouching on the bottom step, Esther tied her shoes. She spotted Nathaniel's flashlight and opted to bring it along, planning to leave it on his back stoop on the way home.

After buttoning her coat, she stepped into the predawn gloom. No one would see her, Esther assured herself as she proceeded down the steps. She must hurry by Nathaniel's house—she hoped unobserved. To play it safe, she crossed to the far side of the two-lane road.

Skulking past Nathaniel's farm, their conversation dominated her thoughts, edging out fears of speaking to Samuel's parents. This morning, Nathaniel's marriage proposal seemed like a figment of her imagination. Not that she didn't find him good-looking and masculine. She did. And his eyes—

For a scant second, she imagined waking up and warming her legs against his. But always Samuel's youthful face, still age nineteen, smoldered in the back of her mind, a sign she wasn't ready to move on. Nathaniel had suggested she join the church and marry him, but she wasn't about to make either commitment. Later, Esther would march over to his house and put a stop to his silliness before he mentioned his intentions to Isaac or Mamm.

She couldn't imagine Nathaniel's reasoning, unless Mamm had coerced him into an arranged union of convenience. Esther's joining the Amish church would be Mamm's ultimate desire, and Nathaniel would gain a free housekeeper all in one. He couldn't love her or even be attracted.

Although she remembered his gazing across the kitchen table at lunch. Had she felt a tingle of electricity pass between them? Maybe Nathaniel was losing both his eyesight and perspective, not so hard to do around here, living apart from the contemporary world.

A sedan motored toward her, its headlamps on bright. Probably a factory worker on his way to a job, she thought, but she turned away and kept her head down to hide her face as it sped by. Other than the one automobile, the road stretched quietly, broken only by the sound of a sheep bleating and mourning doves cooing in a stand of maples.

With no streetlamps, she passed several Amish farms, their lights glowing, and an Englisch house cloaked in darkness. She took a left and continued alongside a plowed field. She recalled the storm last night, as erratic as her inner thoughts.

Her foot hit a dip in the road. She tripped forward, but righted herself before her knees smacked the asphalt. Her memories floundered back in time to her days living in San Francisco with Samuel. When they'd first arrived, they lived with other homeless youths in a commune. She'd been a babe in the woods, wandering from her parents' fold to a society that encouraged radical thinking. "Don't trust anyone over thirty," they'd warned her. One of those young men died of an overdose and two sisters disappeared, simply not returning. Esther wanted to believe they went home, wherever that was. Daisy and Violet never mentioned where they were from or if they'd assumed new names. Back then, it was practically impossible to track someone down without going to the police, whom the sisters called pigs. Police intervention was not considered an option.

On the San Francisco streets, Esther let her hair cascade across her shoulders in public for all to see. But when Samuel was drafted, Esther lost all desire to expose her hair and serenade on corners for change. Needing money, she landed a job in a restaurant that fed her lunch on her break. Esther found the drudgery of kitchen chores her mother had forced upon her came in handy; she could accomplish any task the restaurant manager asked, and do it well. The Purple Café was where she met Dori, a member of the Jesus Movement. Esther had mentioned to Dori how exhausted and nauseous she felt, attributing her fatigue to worrying about Samuel. "Could you be pregnant?" Dori had asked. "You'd better come live with me and my husband." They had an extra bedroom in their apartment and insisted she move in. That evening, Esther had stared at herself in the mirror wondering if Samuel would find her attractive when he returned and saw her belly swollen with child. She'd imagined his look of total joy as the two of them pondered baby names. Seven months later, Samuel missing in action, she'd been grateful to deliver a daughter, whom she'd named Holly Samantha.

Ach, now was not the time to dwell on the past. The rising sun cast lavender fingers swirling across the cloud-covered sky. A rooster crowed.

Esther was plenty warm from her brisk hike. Up ahead stood the Fishers' farm: their spacious three-story white house with its wrap-around porch, the semi-gambrel–roofed barn, numerous outbuildings, three silos, and a windmill.

She stopped short when she spotted wires running from a street pole to the barn. Was Samuel's father, Jeremiah, using electricity to milk like the Englisch or had a non-Amish family bought the place? As far as Esther knew, Old Order Amish still didn't own telephones, unless they partnered with a non-Amishman and set up a business in a separate shop next to the house or barn. Esther couldn't imagine anyone wishing to go into business with Samuel's father. Yet, old man Fisher couldn't run a huge farm by himself.

In the past, with the help of Samuel and his cousins and neighbors, Jeremiah Fisher tended fields of tobacco, corn, alfalfa, and other crops, not to mention raising hogs, sheep, goats, and milking his herd. And horses, she reminded herself, recalling Samuel's pinto his father purchased for him. How Samuel loved Splashy.

Esther heard a guttural growl cutting the air like a serrated knife, then saw a German shepherd mix standing in her path. She stood for a moment, her heart pounding, and tried to breathe steadily. What if someone caught her prowling around at this hour? Should she turn tail and flee? No, she'd played the coward too long. She would at least determine if a new family had purchased the farm. Even if Samuel's parents still lived there, she presumed they wouldn't recognize her.

She extended her hand, palm up. "Good boy?" Its hackles raised and its head lowered, the dog stalked over to her and finally wagged its tail, thank the Lord.

Lights burned in the kitchen but Esther couldn't knock on the door at this time of day. She stealthed around the side of the house toward the barn to peer in a window and noticed a sliding door open a few feet. Her nostrils caught the hint of a woodstove fire.

Sunlight cast burnished gold on the barn's white surface, seeming to enlarge the majestic structure. Esther's opportunity to peer inside the barn without being seen was waning quickly.

With the dog sniffing her ankles—she still didn't trust the animal—she peeked in the door and saw an elderly bearded gent and three men, aged around twenty. All four wore straw hats, black pants, and heavy jackets. The young men were busy milking two dozen or so Holsteins in stanchions using modern equipment, powered by a gas-run generator—like Isaac's operation.

The cows swished their tails. The air smelled of warm milk and hay. A cat followed by five kittens circled the men, begging for a squirt.

The youngest man turned his face to speak to the bearded gentle-man sitting on a chair. Esther noticed the young man was of Asian descent, but dressed Plain—cleanly shaven, his straight black hair cut like the others: long bangs skimming his eyebrows—which made not a whit of sense. Had the world turned on its head? Had the Fishers adopted an Asian even though their son died in Vietnam? Growing up, she'd heard of Amish families adopting children—a baby from Indiana birthed by an unwed mother and an infant from Iowa. In Seattle, Esther knew a couple who'd adopted two darling girls from China, but she couldn't imagine an Amish couple submitting to the governmental red tape involved, let alone traveling to Asia to pick up a child.

The dog woofed and all four men looked toward the barn door at Esther.

Certainly the Fishers had moved away, she told herself, giving her the courage to enter. Unanticipated disappointment flooded her as she realized strangers inhabited Samuel's childhood home. Although, on closer inspection, two of the younger men resembled Samuel: the same wavy auburn hair.

"I can't believe my eyes." The elderly man got to his feet and shuf-fled over to her. "Can that be you, Esther?" The man's voice sounded crusty but enthusiastic. "Don't stand out in the cold. *Kumm rei.*"

She assessed his chalky-white beard and his heavily lidded brown eyes. Perhaps if Samuel had lived, he might have eventually looked like this man.

The younger men, their eyes groggy, swiveled on their stools and smiled at Esther. A cow craned its neck and bellowed, its tail flipping. The men spun back to continue their task.

"I don't understand." Esther wished she could retreat into the dawn like a mote of dust.

"Don't ya recognize me?" the man said. "I'm Samuel's father, Jeremiah. Gut seein' ya again, Esther."

He was happy to see her? Impossible. Clearly the man had gone senile.

CHAPTER TWENTY-FIVE

I wandered downstairs at six thirty and found Isaac sitting in the kitchen talking with Mommy Anna while Greta worked at the stove preparing breakfast. The succulent aromas of oatmeal, eggs, fried potatoes, sausage, bacon, and toast made my mouth water.

Their conversation quieted when I entered the room wearing Nathaniel's daughter's dress and apron.

"We gotta get that dress and your city clothes in the wash," Mommy Anna said, smiling.

"Betcha want your jeans back right quick," Greta said to me as she stirred the oatmeal.

"They're too tight," Isaac said, from the head of the table. "In those revealing clothes, Holly's a bad influence on the children."

"Sorry, where I come from everyone wears jeans. They're not considered immodest." I hugged myself. "I must admit, once I figured out how to attach the straight pins, this outfit is comfy."

"Now all ya need is a Kapp." Isaac gave me a nod.

"Hold on, I'm not ready to cover my hair." Conceal what I considered one of my best attributes with a diminutive white prayer cap? "I'll change into my corduroy pants this afternoon and return these to Nathaniel." Earlier, I'd found the zipper in my spare pants was snagged; I'd detangle it later.

"Old Order Amish in this district don't wear corduroy," Isaac said.

"Seriously? What could be more benign than corduroy?"

"Yah, 'tis true," said Greta. "Our bishop frowns upon it."

Mommy Anna patted the chair next to her. "*Kumm,* sit by me." As I neared the table, she peered through the doorway toward the sitting room. "Have ya seen Esther?"

Uncle Isaac tapped his fork's handle. "What's keepin' her?"

"I don't know." Greta lifted a pan of biscuits from the oven. "I have yet to see her today."

I didn't blame my uncle for being impatient. Mommy Anna had mentioned he rose each morning at four thirty to milk the cows. After breakfast, he slopped the hogs and his older children fed the chickens before school.

"I'll get her." I took the stairs two at a time. I knocked, then opened her door. Her bed lay messy, the covers strewn off to the side—not her usual routine. At home, she made her bed right away. I poked my head in the other upstairs rooms, then checked the Daadi Haus's first and second floors.

I dashed back to the kitchen. The abundant breakfast lay on the table and the children were seated.

"I searched the house from top to bottom and can't find her," I said. "Where could she be? Now that I think about it, her raincoat's not by the front door."

"My woolen jacket I lent her yesterday is right here," Greta said.

"'Tis too cold a morning for a lightweight raincoat," Mommy Anna said. "Must have dipped to freezing last night. I can feel it in my bones."

I settled on the empty chair between her and one of the younger children. I should have been blissful, feeling the warmth of my grandmother's arm against mine, but my stomach twisted, stealing my appetite.

Isaac said, "Let's not allow the food to get cold." He bowed his head and gave his throaty signal to commence a silent prayer.

I was getting the hang of their prayers. After all, at home I sometimes prayed in my head, talking to God as I drove my car—asking him to keep me safe on the highway or even supply a primo parking place, which seemed trivial to me now.

"Breakfast looks fabulous," I told Greta, who was serving Isaac first.

"She prepared the whole meal by herself," Mommy Anna said. "I overslept for the first time since I can remember. 'Tis so quiet in the Daadi Haus. Why, if it weren't for a bird chirpin' outside my window, I might still be there."

"*Des gut,*" Greta said. "You've earned your rest." She spooned eggs on my grandma's plate, then offered me some. "Eat yourself full," she said.

"I doubt I can until I know Mom's whereabouts."

I could tell by Mommy Anna's creased brow, she was also concerned about my mother. "Where could our Essie be?" she said.

"Makin' Mamm worry is a *greislich* thing to do," Isaac said, and munched into a strip of bacon.

I got this itchy feeling something was wrong. At home, Mom often took the bus, but never walked by herself. "She must be burning off calories," I said, wanting to reassure Mommy Anna.

"Workin' is all ya need to stay healthy," Isaac said. "Those fancy Englischers think they're so smart, vegetating in front of televisions and computers, then payin' money to join what they call a health club."

I couldn't shake off my uneasiness. "It's odd no one heard Mom leave the house."

"Must be what she wanted." Isaac speared a sausage with his fork. "Could be she skipped town again."

"Aw, Isaac." Mommy Anna said. "You mustn't say that." She grasped my hand. "Your mother wouldn't take off without sayin' good-bye, would she?"

"I don't think so. Her purse and knitting bag are in her room. She wouldn't leave without them."

"I wouldn't put anything past her." Isaac sliced into his sausage. "She could be makin' her way to the train station. Or catching a bus."

"Not without her purse," I said, feeling Mommy Anna's fingers tightening around my hand.

"Maybe she's visiting Beth." Mommy Anna sounded lackluster.

"This early in the mornin'?" Greta said.

From what I could tell, Beth was the last person Mom would visit, any time of day, but I wouldn't voice my thoughts.

A sense of urgency slithered over me. I glanced out the window at the brightening sky, pastel-colored mist to the east, but brooding clouds lurking in the west. I recalled Mom's horrified expression when I announced I wanted to meet my dad's parents. I couldn't imagine her paying them a call before breakfast. But nothing about my mother seemed normal anymore. She was a pendulum swinging from one extreme to another.

"I'd better look for her," I said, rising to my feet. "Do you know where my father grew up?"

"The Fishers' farm?" Isaac clanked his fork on his plate. "She wouldn't go there."

"I'm bettin' 'tis the last place you'd find her," Mommy Anna said, but I insisted she give me directions. Her hand shook as she wrote them on a slip of paper, using landmarks to guide me. "'Tis large," she said. "Ya can't miss it."

I stashed the directions and my wallet in my apron pocket, stuffed my arms into my jacket, and hopped into the rental car. Mommy Anna was right about the temperature. The ground sparkled with ice crystals. Shivering, I flipped the car's heater to high.

After a five-minute ride, I neared the grandest farm on the road, as Mommy Anna had described it. I noticed a mailbox with a set of numbers, although it meant nothing to me since she hadn't given me an address. I took a left down the driveway. At the end stood a three-story house, several silos, and a barn twice the size of my family's. I contemplated the differences between a boat and a yacht. This place was definitely a yacht. Meaning my grandparents were rich. Yet my mother had never asked them for financial support while raising me. We'd scrimped and saved. Dori had given me her daughter's old dress for prom night; Mom altered the outdated garment, but it never fit. My shoes came from discount stores and Mom cut my hair until my midteens, when I started earning my own money.

Growing up, I was the only kid on the block with no dad or grandparents. But now that I had my Mommy Anna, did I really want to meet my dad's relatives? I recalled Mom's saying they loathed her. Had they transferred their hostility to me? Maybe Mom had pleaded with them for financial assistance, but they'd refused.

My foot rammed down on the brake pedal and the car jerked to a halt. I recalled Mommy Anna's trembling hand when she wrote the directions. I wondered if she'd made a mistake or if I'd misread them. I'd suggested using the car's GPS system, but Mommy Anna said she didn't know Dad's parents' address. Maybe she was *ferhoodled*, as she'd described herself. Befuddled, I guessed is what she meant. Or was she anxious because she knew the Fishers abhorred us?

I wished I hadn't raced out the door. I should have asked someone to accompany me for moral support. Zach came to mind; he'd know who lived where. As a veterinary doctor, he'd probably visited half the farms in the county.

Dusty heat blasted out the car's vents, making me sneeze. I turned the fan down, but goose bumps erupted on my legs. Fields and trees came into view as sunlight penetrated the fog, brightening the sky the color of cotton candy.

Turning off the headlamps, I reasoned with myself. I didn't know for sure Mom was on her way here; I was acting on a hunch. At this moment she might be scarfing down breakfast with Mommy Anna, Greta, and the kids. Mom might have been in the barn admiring the horses or wandered over to Nathaniel's and was watching him milk his cows. I frowned as I imagined them together.

I was gripping the steering wheel so tightly my knuckles ached. My imagination was spinning like a hamster on a treadmill. I expelled the thoughts from my mind. Now that I was here, I'd proceed as planned. What did I have to lose? I'd experienced a lifetime of disappointments and was still in one piece.

I watched a hawk dive down to a field, then lift up carrying its prey. Poor little critter. I envisioned my arrival through Dad's parents' eyes, if the Fishers lived here. Should I find my grandparents, would my presence cause them agony as they relived their son's death? They might shush me away and seal the door like a coffin lid. Or would our shared sadness build a common ground? I had to find out before my mother arrived and said or did something to widen the gap.

I'd dawdled enough. I steered the car into the extensive driveway lined by a white fence. To one side lay a field of pumpkins, hundreds of orange globes. On the other side there looked to be harvested corn.

I pulled up to the front of the house, its porch broad. Green shades covered the windows, which I took to mean this three-story clapboard structure was an Amish home. No other automobiles or garage. No electrical wires stretched to the house, but a line hung from the pole on the road to the barn.

I got out and left the keys in the ignition, not worrying about a thief stealing the car—my hunch was I was the only person around here who knew how to drive. Since I'd arrived in Lancaster County, I'd learned most of the household action took place around back or in the kitchen. If anyone were up, they'd most likely be in one of those two places. Wishing I'd worn a warmer jacket, I closed the car door and strolled toward the side of the house.

A dog woofed, then a gigantic mongrel the size of a rottweiler with long wiry hair charged at me from the direction I was headed.

Ordinarily, I had an affinity with dogs, but this snarling mutt was off-leash—a menacing animal defending its property.

I drew in my breath evenly and slowly to appear confident, when in fact my heart was beating triple-speed. I back-stepped, my hand groping to feel the metal of the car door's handle.

"Go away." My thigh finally bumped into the car's fender. The dog snarled, his canine teeth bared like a shark's. I knew Mom; she'd never cross this beast's path. She wasn't anywhere within miles. What a dunce I was for coming.

The front door opened abruptly. "Who's there?" A woman about Mommy Anna's age advanced onto the porch. Clad in an ankle-length pewter-gray dress and black apron, she appeared my height and wore wire-rimmed glasses and a scowl.

"I heard your car," she said, as if I were trespassing. This crotchety old lady could not be my dad's mother. I refused to be related to her.

"Sorry to disturb you," I said. "I was looking for someone." The fleabag stood poised, its rear legs planted, ready to lunge at me. "Would you please call your dog?" I asked.

"Wolfie," she said. The dog lowered its tail, trotted to the front porch, and sat at her side, facing me.

"Thank you," I said. "He scared me half to death."

"Our Wolfie is a gut judge of character." Her high-pitched voice revealed suspicion. "No one comes at this hour except the milk truck."

"Sorry, I guess I'm at the wrong house." And was glad of it.

"Yah, you must be. And you're makin' me ruin the breakfast."

A younger woman about Greta's age strolled out onto the porch. She also wore a traditional heart-shaped prayer cap, but her periwinkle blue dress and dark apron hung to midcalf. "If the young lady's lost, can we help her?"

I didn't want their two cents' worth if it meant confronting the dog. "That's okay." I cracked the car door. "My grandmother gave me directions."

"We know all our neighbors, ain't so, Mamma?" The younger woman's gaze took in my dress and apron, then came to rest on my shoulder-length hair. I hadn't washed my face, not that she was wearing makeup, either.

The delicate strings of her cap fluttered in the breeze. "Give me their name and I'll point ya in the right direction," she said.

"The Fishers." Ready to make my getaway, I opened the car door.

"Why, that's my last name, since I married my husband. But there are plenty of Fishers in these parts."

The older woman scrutinized me like I was a mutant. This biddy didn't look like she'd approve of anything I wore. "What do you want with them?" she said, her words strained. Her cap strings were knotted severely under her pointed chin.

"Mamma, is it our business?" The younger woman—her daughter or daughter-in-law?—wandered down the steps. Her butterscotch-colored hair peeked from under her prayer cap. "*Gude Mariye*, I'm Rachel," she said.

I put out my hand to shake hers. "Hi, I'm Holly Fisher."

The old woman on the porch covered her mouth with the back of her hand.

"Glad ta meetcha." Rachel's handshake was gracious but firm, I guessed from years of kneading dough. She eyed my car and smiled. "Seems we're distant kin. Most of the Fishers around here don't drive." She tilted her head toward the woman at the front door. "I'm married to her son. But like I said, we're not the only Fishers in the district. Could ya give me their first names?"

A raindrop splatted against the top of my head. "I don't know. My mother never told me." Intentionally? How many secrets was Mom keeping?

Another droplet landed on my shoulder.

"You're welcome to come in while we sort this out." Rachel spoke sotto voce. "Ya pay no attention to my husband's Mudder. She'll warm up to you once she gets to know you."

I closed the car door and followed her up the steps, but the old woman barred our way. "Who's your father?" she demanded.

While growing up, that question bombarded me countless times at open houses, parent-teacher meetings, you name it. But I had rarely admitted the truth. "I never met him."

"And you're lookin' for him?" Rachel said.

"No, he died before I was born."

She let out a lengthy sigh, full of compassion. "Sorry ta hear that."

"Your mother." The older woman still hadn't introduced herself. She reminded me of a Halloween witch; all she needed was a broom and a black hat. "What's her name?"

I crossed my arms and stared into her eyes through her thick-lensed glasses. "Esther Fisher. Anna and Levi Gingerich's daughter." My words seemed to bullet into her, the way she recoiled.

"You'd better come in," she said, stepping aside.

An angry squall ruffled the hem of my dress and the clouds opened up, spewing down raindrops pinging against the car's roof.

I hesitated as I weighed my options. Why enter a house where I was obviously unwelcome? The surly old woman and her dog still looked ready to tackle me.

"Come along," Rachel said, her hand on my arm. "We have a good breakfast waitin' for us."

I followed her into the house. The dog growled, but remained on the porch.

CHAPTER TWENTY-SIX

Esther sat on a wooden bench in the barn with Samuel's father at her side for twenty minutes and watched the three young men milk the cows, what her Samuel might be doing if he were still alive.

Jeremiah must have been contemplating the same notion because he said, "No one could milk faster by hand or with more skill than our Samuel—ain't so?"

"Yes, 'tis true." Decades ago she'd perched right here, admiring Samuel's brawny arms and shoulders, all the while envisioning their upcoming adventure to California. She recalled the evening they left—the scene spooled through her mind with clarity. "Wear Your Love Like Heaven," she'd sung, a Donovan hit she'd heard on a juke-box in New Holland. That tune, and others like it, persuaded her to discard *das alt Gebrauch*—the old ways.

Was she blaming her wicked escapade on a once-popular singer or the Vietnam era? A lifetime of excuses instead of taking responsibility.

Her chance to speak to Samuel's father in private would end any moment. She hoped the three young men couldn't hear her.

"Jeremiah, I'm sorry." Her voice came out like a wisp of smoke, curling up to the rafters. She wasn't sure he'd heard her. "Truly, I am." After avoiding these words for decades, Esther couldn't believe she was wading into this dreaded conversation.

She paused to ask God for courage, then prodded herself to continue. "I regret my reckless actions more than you can know." Her elbows on her knees, her forehead fell forward into her hands.

"I expect ya do." Jeremiah stroked his beard; it covered his chest. "*Du bischt lezt*—you were wrong. But there's no need to apologize. We hold no ill feelings."

"But Samuel's mother—"

"When my wife found he was gone, she ... well—she went crazy. *Wiedich*. She hopped in the buggy and drove straight to the bishop and brought him back with her."

Esther couldn't force herself to look Jeremiah in the eye. "If she held me responsible, she was right. I was a terrible influence on Samuel. You two must hate me."

"*Fer was?* Esther, ya know that's not our custom. We're instructed to forgive others as God forgives us. The bishop preached many a time that no transgression is too big for God's pardon if we repent and live according to his will. And our Samuel wasn't yet baptized."

Esther took Jeremiah's statement to mean Samuel wasn't restrained by the rules of the Ordnung. Neither Samuel nor she had been baptized, thankfully, or the two of them would have been shunned. Not that being put under the Bann would have changed her life much. She had in effect exiled herself.

She listened to the three young men chatting in Deitsch as they worked. Minutes later, they dumped their final buckets of creamy liquid into the silver refrigerated vat against the wall nearest the road, then commenced to muck out the stalls.

She straightened her back and stabbed her hands into her coat pockets. "There isn't a day I don't miss him," she said, when she thought the young men were out of earshot.

"We miss him too, Esther."

She was determined to come clean, as the Bible said in Isaiah, to change her sins from scarlet to as white as snow. "I wasn't honest with your son. I promised Samuel we'd return home within the month. And I lied about leaving my parents a note."

"One lie brings the next one with it." Jeremiah quoted a proverb Dat often recited when he caught her fabricating the truth. "But what's done 'tis done." Jeremiah added a log to the potbelly stove and stood near it, his hands out to catch the warmth. "For the longest time, my wife couldn't accept our Samuel had passed away. She wrote every military hospital and mental institution."

A tear threatened the corner of Esther's eye, but she willed it away. She had no right to cry. "So did I. Several men fit his description." Each time, disappointment thrust Esther into the pit of depression.

"Our hope is we'll see Samuel again in heaven," Jeremiah said.

"I'm counting on it." Esther's minister back home had assured her Samuel was with the Lord, but no need to get into a theological debate with Jeremiah. She came this morning to smooth the path for Holly, should she show up. Which reminded her: She didn't want to be here when and if her daughter arrived.

"I best be getting back." She felt drained, a sponge squeezed dry. She appraised the vast interior of the barn and the hayloft, several handsome standardbreds and ten mules. In the old days, Samuel's father preferred mules to draft horses because they tolerated the heat and ate less. Jeremiah had a keen eye for horses—their confirmation, gait, and temperament. If he'd lived, Samuel would have attended many an auction with his father.

"I missed my dat's funeral." As if kneeling in a confessional, Esther anticipated each admission of guilt would lighten her burden, but her heart felt as heavy as a rock at the bottom of a well.

"Yah, I know." He massaged his calloused hands together. "The night your dat died he was on his way to a meeting with the bishop, preachers, and me to talk about you and Samuel."

"I wish Dat had put his foot down and locked me in the chicken coop. Anything to keep us from leaving."

The Ordnung's decrees didn't sound stifling to her anymore. She recalled a ballad Janis Joplin had sung about freedom being a word for nothing left to lose. In truth, Esther had everything to lose.

"Young folks must experience the world before committing themselves to a lifetime in the church," Jeremiah said. "Although both of your mothers would have liked to lop your running-around years off early."

"If they'd had their way, Samuel would still be alive." Holly would have been brought up Amish, be wed, and have a family of her own. At her age now, Holly's chance of marrying and bearing children was slim-to-none.

"As I tell my wife, 'tis water under the bridge."

Esther pictured Mill Creek, flowing smooth as silk, drying into an arid riverbed, void of fish and vegetation. If she were in Jeremiah's place, she didn't think she could ever let go of her outrage.

"Ich bedank mich" was all she could get out her cottony mouth.

"Come join us for breakfast," Jeremiah said. "My wife will be glad ta see ya."

Samuel's mother had always been *batzich*—haughty—although she'd hidden her animosity when Samuel was in the room, and on preaching Sundays she'd emulated the picture of humility. Two-faced is what she'd been. But who was Esther to make accusations?

"Thanks for your kind invitation, but I'd better go." Esther's right leg ached from her grueling hike. "My mamm will be worried about me." Relishing the smell of the feed and livestock, she inhaled one last lungful of air. She doubted she'd ever enter this peaceful oasis again.

"Don't go 'till ya meet my grandsons," Jeremiah said, snagging Esther's attention. He aimed his finger at the oldest, coming their way carrying a shovel. She guessed he was twenty.

"That's our son Matthew's boy, Seth," Jeremiah said.

Jeremiah had another son? Esther's mouth gaped open. She must have misunderstood him or was losing her hearing.

The tousled-haired man, his bangs skimming his eyebrows, said, "Hullo."

Esther turned to Jeremiah. "Did I hear you right?" she asked. "You had more children?"

"I figured you knew. My wife was pregnant with Matthew when you and Samuel left. She never mentioned her condition to anyone but me. She was, and still is, mighty superstitious and was afraid of another miscarriage."

"I'm ever so glad," Esther said, awash with astonishment, followed by gratitude. "An answer to prayer, I'm sure."

"Yah. The good Lord smiled upon us. Two years later, he gave us a daughter, Naomi. She and her husband and six children live not far from here." He pointed to a young man, opening the barn's side door to let the cows out. "That's Leo, one of my daughter's sons," Jeremiah said. "He stops by twice a day to help with the milking."

Leo opened a side door. "*Kumm,* Bossie, Firefly," he said, and the herd filed outside.

Jeremiah glanced up to the hayloft at the last young man with almond-shaped eyes and black hair as straight as straw. "That's our Aaron, tossing down hay to line the milking stalls. He's seventeen, but works as hard as any grown man."

"Your son married an Asian woman?" The words sprang out of Esther's mouth before she could filter them. Many Asians populated Seattle, but here in Lancaster County?

"My nephew and his wife became Mennonites," Jeremiah said. "They adopted Aaron months before my nephew's wife died. Aaron came to live with my daughter and her husband, and calls me Daadi, just like my other grandchildren. I couldn't love Aaron more. 'Tis a long story I'd be happy to share over breakfast."

The dog barked as a large vehicle pulled up to the barn and came to a stop, its engine running. A whirring motor kicked in. "'Tis the milk truck collecting from our cooling vat," Jeremiah said.

"I might ask the driver to give me a lift if he's headed in the right direction." Esther placed a hand on Jeremiah's forearm. "Should my daughter, Holly, show up, please promise to treat her with kindness."

"Of course we will. We've been longin' to meet her. I sent ya letters."

"You have our address?"

"My wife said she gave my letters to your mother to send."

"Are you certain? We never received them. Not one." Had Samuel's mother intercepted them?

"All the more reason to come in the house, won't ya?" he said. "My wife and I live in the Daadi Haus, but we gather each morning for breakfast."

Esther's stomach grumbled with hunger and she thirsted for a cup of coffee, but she'd wait until she got home.

"A question before I leave," she said. "I noticed wires running to the barn." She gazed at the large metal container. "The milk cooler— is it powered by electricity?"

"Nee, an alternator and a car battery cool the milk. The electrical and telephone wires run to the shop next door, where our son Matthew and his partner make furniture. Since it's separate from the barn, the bishop gave him permission to keep a fax machine and telephone."

At that moment a man wearing a straw hat strolled into the barn. He was the spitting image of her beloved Samuel, but wore a beard.

The backs of her knees weakened as she studied his eyes, his familiar smile. If she didn't know better, she'd think Samuel had returned from Vietnam—that he'd come home.

White noise filled her ears.

The room spun, her vision blurred, and she collapsed against Jeremiah. She felt him grab her around the waist and lower her to the floor.

"*Was is letz, Esther?*"—What's wrong? "*Kumm schnell!*"—Come quick!—Jeremiah said to the man.

CHAPTER TWENTY-SEVEN

Through coke-bottle glasses, Beatrice glared at me from across her kitchen. Beads of perspiration dotted her forehead and shriveled face. I saw nothing to like about her.

Why had she allowed me in? From the moment we met, it seemed this irritable woman hoped to antagonize me into retreating to the rental car. If it weren't for Rachel's invitation, I wouldn't have agreed to stay for breakfast, although delectable aromas of cinnamon, yeast, and melting butter filled my nostrils.

"*Wu is dei Kapp?*" Beatrice said to me, then turned to the stove to pour pancake batter onto a cast-iron skillet atop a gas burner.

"Do you mean: Where is my cap?" My hand moved to my head and I raked renegade strands away from my face. Of course—my borrowed dress and apron had confused her. "I'm not really Amish," I said.

She glowered over her shoulder, the corners of her mouth stabbing down. "A *Dummkopf* can see that, what with your automobile and your accent." Using rapid movements, she lifted the lid off a pot of oatmeal.

"Please, Mamma," Rachel said. "Holly can't help it. She's obviously not from these parts."

I tried to ignore Beatrice's harsh words and see my haphazard attire through her eyes. Judging from her cement-gray hair and severe part, she probably hadn't gone without a prayer cap since childhood.

"I'm from Seattle." I removed my jacket. "I didn't think I spoke with an accent."

"That shows what little you know." Beatrice flipped strips of sizzling bacon with a fork.

Rachel extended a hand to take my jacket. "May I?" She positioned it on a peg near the back door. "Did I hear ya right? You're from Seattle?"

"Yes, visiting my grandmother, Anna Gingerich." I scanned the orderly kitchen, much like Mommy Anna's, but with a larger refrigerator, a double sink, and a sizable counter; several loaves of bread sat cooling on its surface. In the center of the room stood a rectangular table covered with a green-and-white checkered oilcloth, ten chairs around its perimeter.

Rachel clapped twice. "In that case, ya could be my husband's niece."

I gathered my courage and directed my questions at Beatrice, who stood stirring the pancake batter with a long-handled wooden spoon. "Ma'am," I said, nearing her. "Are you my dad's mother? His name was Samuel Fisher."

Her right arm jerked and she dropped the spoon, splattering batter on the linoleum floor. She bent down, grabbed the spoon, and threw it in the sink, while Rachel rushed over to mop up the mess with a towel.

"I have no answers for ya, because I don't know," Beatrice said, her pencil-thin lips barely moving.

"But ya could be, don'tcha think?" Rachel rinsed and laid the soiled towel on the counter next to the sink. "You and Jeremiah had a son named Samuel—ain't?"

Beatrice flushed water over the spoon and shook it dry. "Yah," she finally said. "We named our boy after my *Grossdaadi* on my mamma's side. But my sister called her second son Samuel too. And our neighbors two farms over—"

The kitchen door shimmied open, rattling its single pane. "Beatrice!" An aged bearded man poked his head into the room. "'Tis Esther. She's come back."

My mother was here?

The old man called to someone outside. "Matthew, is she able to make it inside?"

"Yah, we're comin'." The timbre of the other man's voice told me he was younger than Mom and a local.

The elderly gentleman hung his hat, moist with rain, on a peg next to my jacket. Noticing me, his eyebrows lifted. "Hullo, I'm Jeremiah Fisher," he said, panting. "I didn't know we had company comin' for breakfast."

"She showed up uninvited," Beatrice said. "Drivin' a car."

I heard multiple footsteps on the back stairs. A moment later, a bearded man in his midforties, one arm supporting Mom, steered her inside. Looking bedraggled—her hair and shoulders damp—she trudged into the kitchen with her gaze lowered, not acknowledging me or Beatrice.

"You remember Esther, don't ya?" Jeremiah said to Beatrice. Her husband? I pitied the man married to that mean-spirited woman.

"How could I forget her?" Beatrice narrowed her eyes at Mom, creasing a line between them. "She hasn't aged well." Beatrice shook her small head. "And dressed Englisch. No surprise there."

Jeremiah said, "Esther's feelin' *grenklich*." I took that word to mean ill.

She wasn't the only one. A headache expanded from my temples across my forehead. Questions wormed their way through my brain: Why was Mom here, and why wasn't she defending herself from Beatrice's diatribe? Mom reminded me of the robin that flew into our picture window at the Amish Shoppe and lay dazed, barely breathing for an hour.

If Mom wouldn't defend herself, I would. Beatrice was begging for a confrontation I couldn't resist.

"How dare you speak to my mother that way?" I stepped over to Mom. "Are you all right?" I asked. Her listless face echoed her pale beige blouse and her lips were chapped.

She rubbed her upper arms. "Yes, fine."

"You don't look okay. Did you walk all the way here?"

She nodded, her lower lip quivering. She must be exhausted from the strenuous trek. She might have had a heart attack or a stroke.

"How did you slip past me?" I said. "You must have left Mommy Anna's on foot before sunup. That stupid dog stopped me from entering the barnyard."

"He ain't stupid," Beatrice said. "Our Wolfie protects us from unwanted intruders."

"That's no way to speak to guests," the younger man said. "I'm Matthew," he told me, removing his hat. "Jeremiah and Beatrice's son."

Rachel guided Mom to the table. "Please have a seat." Rachel pulled out a chair for her. "What happened? Do ya need a doctor?"

"No, just light-headed." Mom sat down with a thud. "For a moment I thought—Well, I'm too embarrassed to tell you what I was thinking."

"She mistook Matthew for his older brother, Samuel," Jeremiah said, and Mom buried her face in her hands. "That's not so outlandish." He tilted his head at Matthew, standing near the back door hanging his jacket, then unlacing his boots. "Except for the difference in age, the two boys could have been twins."

"That's what my father would have looked like?" I gulped as I took in Matthew's features, his even white teeth, his nut-brown eyes, the same color as mine, and his wavy rusty-brown hair. He was a handsome man, even with his beard and suspenders. In this farmhouse kitchen they suited him.

"I can see the resemblance to Mom's photo of my dad," I said.

Beatrice's scrimpy eyebrows deepened her frown lines. "Esther owns a photograph of our Samuel? Picture taking is against the Ordnung."

"I'm glad she has Dad's photograph," I said. "Proof he existed. You have no idea what it was like to grow up without a father."

"You have no idea what it's like to lose your son!"

Her words felt like a slap on my face. I recalled our minister in Seattle teaching from the book of Matthew: If a person wanted to see clearly he must eliminate the plank from his own eye before attempting to remove the speck of sawdust from another's. I realized I was being sanctimonious, writing off a woman whose son was sent to war even though Mom said he was a pacifist, as were

Beatrice and Jeremiah. No wonder Beatrice bore malice toward Mom and me.

Rachel slid onto the seat next to my mother. "I'm Matthew's wife. Are ya his long-lost sister-in-law?"

"I think so." Mom studied Matthew intensely as he drew near the table and joined them. He smiled at her, but she turned to me, her eyes searching mine.

I sat across from her. "Don't ask me, Mother. You're the one with all the answers."

Her glistening eyes blinked. "I'm as shocked as you are, Holly." She reached across the table to take my hand, but I leaned back, out of her grasp. "I didn't know your father's parents had more children," she said to me. "My mamm never said a word."

"Don't blame your circumstances on my grandma." I recalled the shoebox filled with letters—my outrage when Mom first displayed them. My whole life would have been different if she'd allowed me to read them as they arrived. This kitchen wouldn't be foreign. In fact, Beatrice might love me if she'd met me as a child. Aunt Rachel could have been like a sister.

Jeremiah sat beside me. His face showed eighty-plus years. His upper lip was cleanly shaven, but I bet he hadn't trimmed his beard since forever. "I'm Samuel's father. 'Tis true, our Samuel married your mother."

"Who's ta say they were legally married?" Beatrice's voice sounded as brittle as ice chips.

"Samuel wrote and told us," Jeremiah said. "He wouldn't have lied." He spoke to me gently. "Holly, if you're Samuel's daughter, you're our granddaughter."

Beatrice charged over to him, her skirt and apron flapping. "Are ya buyin' into Esther's hogwash?" she said. "That woman bewitched our son."

I felt like vaulting out the door and diving into the car. But I needed to know the truth. Feeling my throat tighten around my voice box, I forced out the words. "Then it's true, you're my dad's parents?"

"Who's ta say who your father was?" Beatrice crossed her arms, tucking her hands under her armpits. "Your mother could have entertained many a man while our Samuel was overseas. She lived in a hippie commune. Ya know that? All sorts of goings on."

Mom shot to her feet. "I swear before God, Samuel was my only love. I never—"

"How dare ya swear before the Almighty?" Spittle flew from Beatrice's mouth. "You never bent at the knees before the congregation and were baptized. If you had been, you'd be under *die Meiding*—the shunning."

"I have our marriage certificate," Mom said. "I'll send you a copy."

"Proves nothing." Beatrice sniffed the air, then her head whipped around. Smoke billowed from the fry pan. "Ya made me burn the breakfast!" She bolted over to the stove and dumped the pan's charred contents into the garbage bin, then swung her torso around to face Mom. "What do you want, Esther? To move in with us?"

"Hold on there." Jeremiah rapped his knuckles on the table. "Let's not start makin' assumptions."

"Your father's bedroom is still vacant, exactly as he left it," Matthew said to me. "Should you two wish to stay."

"Guests use it every once in a while," Rachel said. "Would ya like to see it? Some of Samuel's clothes are still in the closet."

Beatrice widened her stance. "Over my dead body."

Jeremiah said, "Wife, I thought we were past this bitterness. We agreed to forgive Esther years ago."

"I thought I had. But seeing her in the flesh makes me think we've invited Satan into our home."

CHAPTER TWENTY-EIGHT

Beatrice's words—intentional knife wounds—assaulted Esther, what she'd expected and why minutes ago had no intention of entering the house. But then she'd fainted, her legs giving way and her vision diminishing into one tiny dot.

She recalled Jeremiah's arms catching her, then someone else—a younger man—assisting her up the steps.

At the Fishers' kitchen table, her vision still blurry, Esther wanted to plug her ears and make her escape, but might as well have been tethered to her chair. Anyway, she reasoned, if she jettisoned out the back door she'd come face-to-face with Wolfie standing sentry outside. Esther wasn't afraid of dogs, but this animal might pick up on Beatrice's hostility and turn aggressive. And Esther shouldn't desert Holly, who looked as forlorn as Esther felt. Protecting her daughter had been Esther's goal in coming here in the first place.

Had Holly received a smidgeon of welcome from Beatrice upon her arrival? Unlikely. Holly's fairytale happily-ever-after ending was falling flat, like Esther's last sweet potato soufflé attempt.

Esther's gaze came back to rest on Matthew. Now that she focused on her beloved Samuel's double, she was fascinated by the similarities and couldn't help staring. She decided both men had taken after their father in appearance and temperament. Until her death, sitting in the same room with Matthew was the closest she'd ever be to Samuel.

Speaking to Beatrice, Jeremiah's voice interrupted Esther's crippling thoughts.

"Ain't ya being a bit harsh?" He gave his wife a stern look, demanding silence. "Can we put this dispute aside until after we eat?"

"Yah, I'm starvin'," Matthew said. "The boys are done with their chores." He directed his words to Holly. "Our nephew Leo, my sister Naomi's son, headed home, but Seth and Aaron should be in any minute."

Rachel served him coffee. "Clarissa's still in bed." She set the sugar bowl next to his cup and he stirred in two teaspoons, the way Samuel had.

Rachel told Esther, "Our youngest daughter, age twenty, is still in her Rumspringa. She stays out late and sleeps in, all lazy and smart-mouthed, when she should be finding an Amish beau and gettin' married."

"After four years of her shenanigans, I'm about to toss her out on her own if she don't shape up," Matthew said. He consumed half his brew in a single gulp.

"Yous should have done that last year," Beatrice said, her words ragged. "She needs to be in baptism classes, not kicking up a ruckus with her fancy Englisch friends."

"I hear tell she owns a car, if you can imagine that," Jeremiah said, shaking his head.

"We think she hides it somewhere." Rachel set plates around the table. "She works part-time at Bird-in-Hand Family Restaurant to afford the gasoline."

Esther was tempted to offer to counsel Clarissa, to warn her not to get baptized until she was 100 percent sure she was satisfied with the Amish life, and also share with her the heartache of severing ties with her family. But she didn't dare open her mouth. Esther felt like a wounded pheasant, huddling in the field, hoping a hunter would pass her by unnoticed. She was still stunned to find Jeremiah and Beatrice had other grandchildren. The fact their nephew, and then their daughter, had adopted an Asian child struck her as impossible. She was consumed with curiosity. How could Beatrice spurn Holly, her own flesh-and-blood granddaughter, but feel unconditional love toward Aaron?

"Rachel," Beatrice said, her cheeks carving hollows, "we mustn't air our dirty laundry in front of strangers."

"Esther and Holly ain't strangers," Jeremiah said. "They're family whether ya like it or not."

"*Himmel!*" Beatrice turned down the burners but left the food on the stove. She pointed at Esther as if she were an inanimate object. "I will not sit at a meal with that woman. Have one of the boys hitch up the buggy, won'tcha, Matthew? I'll fetch the bishop. He'll have something to say to Esther about comin' clean and confessing her sins."

"My mother's brother Isaac is a preacher," Holly said.

Esther's scalp tightened. "Whose side are you on, daughter?"

"Mom, I thought you'd be proud of him."

Isaac was the last person Esther wanted to see. As a minister, he might jump on Beatrice's bandwagon.

"Your mother's brother Isaac has little jurisdiction over us," Beatrice said, with what sounded like pride, a trait uncharacteristic for Amish. But Beatrice had never been a typical submissive Amish wife. "We're in a different district now. Our population doubled, so we split in half, twice. Our bishop will know how to handle this situation. He's mighty strict."

"Silence," Jeremiah said. "I'm the head of this household. I'll decide if and when anyone's fetchin' the bishop."

Esther was glad she and her naïve daughter wouldn't come under the scrutiny of the Fishers' bishop, what with Holly's dress and apron, coupled with her unkempt hair. Not to mention Esther's own vulnerabilities.

Her thoughts flung her back in time like a barbed hook cast into a murky lake. She recalled the evening she and Samuel ran away— decades ago, but the night seemed like yesterday. With Samuel waiting below her bedroom window, she'd scrambled into her Englisch thrift-shop clothes. A week prior, her preacher had taught from the Bible: "Be not conformed to this world: but be ye transformed by the renew-ing of your mind, that ye may prove what is that good, and acceptable, and perfect, will of God"—in German. But Esther had ignored the preacher's instruction as if she were a temporary visitor all along.

An hour later, a truck driver steering a semi heading west had picked up Samuel and her. "Where you headed?" he'd asked.

"As far as you're going," Esther had answered, feeling like a firehouse-red cardinal taking flight. As she spoke to the driver, Samuel glanced out the back window.

Beatrice directed her words at Esther. "Matthew's daughter Clarissa reminds me of another young woman I once knew."

Esther wanted to shut off her mind, but she couldn't help her memory from spinning in on itself and landing on the fall of Saigon in 1975, her ears hearing the whirling chopper blades slashing the air, mingled with the pleas of refugees. She'd watched the terrifying footage on the TV news; the images remained imprinted in her memory.

Why had Samuel disappeared, when every other living GI in his unit returned to the States? In the chaos of the escaping refugees and military personnel had an enemy combatant snuck up behind her beloved and hidden his lifeless body, or did Samuel panic, lose his sense of direction, wander into the dense forest, and step on a land mine?

"Come on, Mom." Holly stood, patting her skirt and apron, bringing Esther back to the skirmish at hand. "We'd better go so the Fishers can eat their breakfast. Maybe I could swing back later by myself, if that's okay."

"I'm hoping ya do," Rachel said.

Beatrice cut Esther a look of reproach and Esther got to her feet. She felt lopsided and wondered if her legs would support her.

Jeremiah said, "Tomorrow, on Sunday—'tis not a preaching Sunday—the rest of the family and our neighbors will stop by. You're invited." He clasped Holly in a tight embrace, the hug Esther longed to receive from her father-in-law. She felt jealousy rising though she knew she should be happy for her daughter.

"We'll be expecting ta see ya," Jeremiah told Holly, who leaned her head on his shoulder, leaving a moist spot on his shirt.

Beatrice spun around, grabbed a damp rag, and wiped the stove's surface so hard Esther thought she might scrub off the enamel.

"Beatrice will calm down by then," he said in Holly's ear. "I'll throw salt over my left shoulder, what she claims prevents quarrels."

"I don't blame her for being upset." Holly blinked several times. "We should have contacted you first instead of propelling ourselves over with no warning." She frowned at Esther. "Mom, the car's out front. Can you make it?"

"Yes, like I told you, I'm perfectly fine. I came because I thought you might show up. I hoped to pave the way—"

"With splinters of broken glass?" Holly sounded as grouchy as Beatrice, right when Esther needed her daughter's support.

Holly turned to Matthew. "Do any of you see much of Mommy Anna and her family?" she asked.

"Now and again," he said. "At barn raisings and weddings. The such."

Beatrice flung the rag in the sink. "And funerals." Her voice sliced the air.

"Is my father buried nearby?" Holly asked.

"Just a marker, since his body was never recovered." Jeremiah let out a sigh, his chest seeming to cave in.

"I'd like to see it," Holly told him.

"Sure, on another day I'll show ya."

Esther suspected the Fishers had a family plot somewhere on their hundred-plus acres. Not that Samuel resided in the ground—wherever that might be. He was in heaven with the Lord.

Her thoughts jumbled together like the ball of yarn one of her customer's children had plucked out of his mother's bag and kicked across the floor. After the conclusion of the war—the mad scramble to evacuate Vietnam—the military claimed it conducted a thorough search to locate all POWs and remains of MIA soldiers. But her Samuel never surfaced and was declared dead. Visiting the makeshift graveside might put Esther's doubts and turmoil to rest, finally.

Jeremiah held Holly's jacket out and she pushed her fists into the sleeves. "Guess you know four of my mother's brothers are in Montana, scoping out property," she said.

"Yah, I hear tell."

"As you probably know, their neighbor Nathaniel King is buyin' Anna's farm," Matthew said.

"You've got to be kidding." Holly's voice rose to falsetto. "All this talk about moving to Montana and no one said a thing."

"Nathaniel told me himself," Matthew said.

"Did I hear ya right?" Esther's mind reeling, she stood, her legs wobbly as a one-legged stool. "He never mentioned it to me."

"He wouldn't tell you of all people," Holly said.

The floor seemed to undulate beneath Esther's feet. Why would Nathaniel ask for her hand in marriage, yet never share his plans to buy her family's property?

CHAPTER TWENTY-NINE

My foot slammed down on the accelerator pedal harder than I intended. The tires spit up dirt and rocks. Mom and I jerked along the Fishers' driveway—not the farewell departure I'd planned.

I slowed the car and waved out the window, hoping my first good impression hadn't dissolved. Rachel had just reinvited Mom and me to return to the Fishers' on Sunday for visiting and fellowship with relatives and friends. "Plenty ta eat," she assured us. Then she asked us to participate in a quilting frolic several days later, which I supposed was like a quilting bee. But my mother had the audacity to turn down the invitation, saying she had her hands full looking after her mother. But she wasn't busy.

"Why be so rude?" I asked, all the while hoping my rowdy driving hadn't caused Rachel to rethink her invitations. She and Daadi Jeremiah had walked us through their sitting room and front hallway to the porch. I was glad Beatrice and Matthew remained in the kitchen. Beatrice might have hurled another insult and my mother could have retaliated.

Mom clipped on her safety belt. "See, I was telling the truth when I said your father's parents want nothing to do with me." She wiped her forehead, then the back of her neck.

"Jeremiah was as nice as can be." I glanced in the rearview mirror and saw him and Rachel waving good-bye.

"But you heard Beatrice compare me to the devil. She doesn't want me near them."

Wolfie chased the car, nipping at the tires until we reached the main road. He let out a howl, his tail raised, then turned and trotted back to the house. If anything was satanic, it was that dog.

"Take a right on Centerville Road," Mom said. "Then after we cross Mill Creek, turn onto Zeltenreich."

I followed her instructions, glad I'd entered Beth's address in the car's GPS in case Mom and I got lost. I had to face the facts: Mom's logic and actions were helter-skelter.

"Beatrice was caught off guard," I said. "I don't blame her, the way we materialized, stirring up the past, bringing with us heart-breaking memories." I couldn't say I harbored warm fuzzy feelings for Beatrice, but I'd call her my grandma whether she believed her son Samuel was my father or not.

While sitting at the kitchen table, I'd examined my uncle Matthew's features. The strong bridge of his nose, his eyes, and his full lips assured me half my DNA came from my father, Samuel Fisher. The way Mom gawked at Matthew, like Dad resurrected from the grave, confirmed my opinion. I wanted to question the Fishers at length, to delve into every detail of my father's childhood, the family my mother had hidden from me. An act of cruelty, as far as I was concerned.

"Mom, I'm not going to allow you to take the coward's way out. Even if you don't come back Sunday, please go to the quilting frolic with me. I'll feel like a fish out of water." I envisioned my bed's quilt in Seattle: burgundy birds perched on wreaths of tulips applied to an off-white background—six stitches per inch—each sewn by my mother's hand.

"It's you they wish to see, daughter."

"But you're the quilter in our family. I'll bet you could teach them a thing or two."

"The Amish women, particularly Beatrice, wouldn't look kindly if it appeared I was showing off."

"I wish you'd taught me how to quilt," I said. One of my many regrets.

"I tried, but you refused after the second lesson."

She was right; I wouldn't quilt or knit, beyond fashioning a simple scarf. Why had I been so headstrong? A grain of friction always rubbed between us; too bad our abrasive relationship never produced a pearl.

"You should have forced me." I pictured the quilts we sold at the Amish Shoppe—meticulous hand stitching, bold geometric shapes, brilliant colors juxtaposed. Ever since we'd arrived in Lancaster County, I'd wondered why the Amish women wore subdued hues—the opposite of their quilts. In Seattle, I wouldn't think twice about coupling my fuchsia turtleneck with navy or forest-green slacks.

I glanced at my mother, her face sunken, and saw her lifeless hands in her lap. I noticed a thickening at the top of her spine, causing her shoulders and head to bend forward.

"Mom, you haven't knitted since we arrived." Another oddity for her. I was used to seeing her hands in motion—as if of their own volition—my entire life. When I was young, she'd knitted in the dentist's waiting room, in front of the TV, and as a passenger in my car or on the bus. Her hands were always occupied like they had minds of their own. And she took great care selecting yarn, as if on a treasure hunt.

"My needles were confiscated at the airport."

"So you claim. I didn't actually see the guard impound them."

"Now you don't believe one thing I say?"

"In any case, you could borrow a pair from Mommy Anna or Greta, if they knit, or I'll drive you to a store. Greta said there's a fabric and yarn shop named Nancy's Notions and Clothing in Intercourse." I smiled at the town's quaint name, which had taken on a new meaning since the nineteenth century.

"I'm not in the mood." She chewed her thumbnail.

"That's like my saying I'm not in the mood for your snicker-doodles." I waited, but she didn't smile. "How could I manage at a quilting frolic without your help?" I asked in all sincerity. "Won't the women be speaking Pennsylvania Dutch?"

"They'll speak English for you, and I wouldn't be surprised if some of their Mennonite cousins or neighbors came."

"But what do I know about quilting?"

"There will be plenty of women to help you get started." A smile finally raised the corner of her mouth. "I remember my mother's mother, *Grossmudder* Emma Mae, teaching me the Ninepatch, a simple pattern, stacking the quilting squares ..." Her voice trailed off. She gazed out the windshield at the plowed fields—fertile earth the color of coffee beans—all part of the Fishers' property. It might have been partly ours if she hadn't run away from home like an idiot.

"Other than cows, what does Daadi Jeremiah raise?" I asked, as we passed a herd grazing in a field. The clouds were parting and the sunshine turning the pasture chartreuse.

"When I left, his mainstay was tobacco," Mom said. "I noticed his tobacco barn is still standing."

"The Amish smoke cigarettes?"

"Rarely, but they're good businessmen. And tending the leaves gives the men work during the winter."

I'd smoked as a teen and in college battled to quit the habit. "I hope he's changed his crops. I should have asked. I will. On Sunday. I'm coming back."

"I wouldn't dress like you are today. Please put on your normal clothes."

"I wish I'd brought a skirt. The zipper on my slacks is jammed."

"I'll help you fix it."

"I hope you can, because I agree with Isaac. My jeans are too tight for this group of women. If you'd warned me ahead of time I would have brought looser fitting clothing. My cords are baggy, but their bishop disapproves of corduroy." I wanted to fit in, to be one of the family more than anything. "I wonder—I could launder these and don a prayer cap." Would my unruly hair submit to being parted down the middle and fastened into a bun? "No makeup, but I didn't bother with it today. Do you think I'd be accepted?"

"I'm warning ya, Holly, don't go acting foolhardy." She didn't seem to notice we'd crossed Mill Creek again.

"You make the Amish sound like a cult," I said. No way would I fall for her scare tactics. She reminded me of the horror-spoof movie *An American Werewolf in London* that my girlfriends and I rented on Halloween night years ago. "Stay on the road. Keep clear of the moors," the driver had warned. Thinking of the movie still gave me the willies.

"Were your parents and brothers hypnotized to stay against their will?" I allowed derision to rule my voice.

"No. They were happy, for the most part."

I slowed and turned onto Zeltenreich Road. "Then come with me to the frolic and get reacquainted with old friends and relatives." With one hand I stroked my apron's fabric. "What will you do with yourself if you don't?" I wondered if she held an ulterior motive.

"Don't ya worry 'bout me, I'll keep busy," she said. "Mamm, Isaac, and Greta might be entertaining friends and relatives themselves on Sunday," she said. "If you go to the Fishers' you'll miss seeing your aunts and their children."

"No I won't. Not if I stay here until they move to Montana. Who knows, maybe I can get them to change their minds about leaving."

"Why on earth would you want to do that?"

"So Mommy Anna won't have to move."

I couldn't keep Matthew's comment about Nathaniel's buying the Gingerich farm from pestering my thoughts. Could Mommy Anna afford to rent the Daadi Haus from Nathaniel and remain living there if he didn't have other plans? If Mommy Anna stayed in the area, I could stick around and take care of her.

At least I thought I could. Just days ago I was desperate for a job in the stock market and considered myself a citified woman, through and through. In the past, I'd joked I never wished to be more than a ten-minute drive from a Nordstrom store. If I was honest with myself, would I go stir-crazy out here in the country? I still hadn't checked out nearby New Holland, but heard the population was a mere five thousand—not exactly a booming metropolis. The townships of Bird-in-Hand and Intercourse were dots on the map I had yet to see. Something to look forward to next week.

After crossing Peters Road, I took a left onto Hollander Road, heading north. My vision took in postcard-perfect farms—many Amish, I could tell by the missing electrical wires and cars—pastures, fields of drying corn Mom had mentioned would soon be harvested for cow fodder, and a distant forested hillside to the east, the trees clinging to vivacious flashes of ruby-red and mustard-colored leaves.

I considered the Plain people, surrounded by the Lord's bounteous gifts. Could I be happy living here? Did I even know what happiness was? I imagined my grief when Mommy Anna passed away. I was more determined than ever to keep my grandmother in my life as long as possible.

"When I drop you off, I'm heading over to Beth's to use my computer," I said. "I'd better let Mommy Anna know where we are so she doesn't worry about us." I reached for my cell phone, nestled at the bottom of my apron's pocket, but then remembered my grandma didn't own a phone. "How can the Amish manage without telephones?"

"They write letters. And they have their phone shanties and Mennonite neighbors."

"Thank goodness for Mennonites like Beth," I said, but Mom didn't nod in agreement. "Why don't you like her? Don't deny it."

Straightening her collar, she ignored my remark.

Rolling at fifteen miles an hour, I passed a buggy driven by a bearded man. I thought of my deceased grandfather, my mother's father, Daadi Levi, perishing in a hideous collision with a car. I assumed the horse had died too. My grandfather never would have been on the road that night if my mother and father hadn't run away. I should inquire about my Daadi Levi Gingerich while Mommy Anna was still around to be the family genealogist.

"Why didn't I think of it earlier?" I said. "I know Uncle Isaac disapproves, but I'm going to ask Beth to help me make a doctor's appointment for Mommy Anna. First, I'll get online and google her symptoms to see what comes up."

"How are you going to pay for an office visit? What if the doctor wants to put Mamm on medications? I'd better warn ya, she'll most likely refuse if Isaac tells her to."

"I'll cross those hurdles when I come to them. Why are you painting such a bleak picture?" With a delivery truck on my rear bumper, I sped up again. Gee, the cars drove quickly for such a narrow road. "Don't you want Mommy Anna to get better?"

"Yes, but I don't like seein' ya disappointed, truly I don't."

As the truck accelerated to pass me, I brought out my cell phone. "I'll call Beth to see if it's too early for a visit."

"It's against the law to drive while using a cell phone."

"Don't make me laugh. It's a felony to intercept the US mail the way you did my whole life."

"If Jeremiah's telling the truth and he tried to contact you, one of your grandmothers never forwarded the letters," Mom said. "But don't believe everything he or Beatrice say."

"You have some nerve wagging fingers, you and your shoebox. Like it or not, Beatrice and Jeremiah Fisher are my grandparents. On Sunday, I may bring Beatrice chocolate-covered cherries to sweeten her up."

"She could see a gift as a bribe."

It felt like Mom was forcing me to swallow cod liver oil. "Why must you morph my ideas into negatives?"

I knew for my own sake I should let bygones be bygones. Last month our pastor quoted from the book of Ephesians: "And be kind to one another, tenderhearted, forgiving one another, even as God in Christ forgave you." My remembering scripture was a near miracle; I often daydreamed during sermons and had never taken the time to memorize Bible passages. At church, I'd been assured I was saved by God's mercy, so I figured I was off the hook.

I rarely prayed outside of church, but on a lark I said out loud, "Okay, God, if you're listening, please bless the rest of our visit here, which for me might be a very long time."

"You're stayin'?" Mom swiveled in her seat, her hand coming to rest on my arm. "Ach, you don't mean that, do ya?"

"I honestly don't know."

CHAPTER THIRTY

Sunlight angling over the tops of cornstalks the color of broom bristles made Esther squint, giving her an excuse to close her eyes. She had never experienced a more exhausting morning and was ready for a nap. But when they got to their home-away-from-home she'd have some explaining to do—why she'd slunk out without telling anyone and how her plan to arrive at the Fishers' before Holly had gone awry. Turned into a verbal brawl is more like it. If she never saw Beatrice Fisher again it would be too soon.

Puh! Beatrice had given birth to two more children but Mamm never mentioned them in her letters. Mamm knew Matthew was the exact likeness of her Samuel. Why had she withheld the information? Esther might have returned earlier had she known.

Sitting in the passenger seat, Esther imagined her brother Isaac's speculations over her whereabouts. "*Wu is sie?*"—Where is she?—he was no doubt asking Mamm. "Hiding down in the cellar like she did as a girl when she didn't want to help clean up after supper? Traipsing back to her fancy city life in Seattle?"

And now Esther must return to face the music, as Dori might say. Truth be known, other than Sunday Singing nights—opportunities for young men and women to pair up—Esther had heard little music as a child, except birds chirping or the congregation droning the hymns from the *Ausbund* in German, some fifteen or twenty minutes long. The "Loblied" was always the second hymn, followed by an introductory sermon and the silent prayers of the People, then the second sermon.

Later, living in San Francisco, singing along with Samuel and his newly acquired secondhand guitar, for the first time she'd lifted her voice and found she was a soprano who could carry a tune. She'd felt exhilarated, her confidence energized. She discovered a knack for memorizing songs she'd heard only once. Then a young woman in the commune taught her to read music and lent her a book of popular hits.

"Your voice is better than Carly Simon's," Samuel had told her one day. "You could be a soloist, easy."

"Are ya sure this singin' is okay?" she'd asked him. The confining teachings of the Ordnung clung to her like ivy leaching the sap out of an elm tree. According to her folks' bishop and preachers, if she didn't obey the Ordnung, God would never allow her into paradise. Like a chunk of coal, when she died he'd hurl her straight into the inferno of hell.

"Yah, 'tis fine," Samuel said. Later that day, he'd opened a borrowed Bible with ease, like relaxing with an old friend, and read from Psalm 33:3: "Sing unto him a new song; play skilfully with a loud noise."

"The Lord encourages singin' and musical instruments?" Never having read more than short passages, Esther had been flabbergasted, then delighted when he nodded.

"I can give you dozens of references to singing, and playing harps, flutes, and tambourines."

Holly hummed as she drove, apparently oblivious to Esther's reliving her past, not so hard to do when Esther recognized familiar farms and the grove of trees she and Samuel used to meet under.

"I bet Beth's up," Holly said. "I'll call her now. She's so cordial. I know she'll invite us for breakfast if she has her electricity back on. I like that woman."

More than you like me, Esther thought. She hoped when they returned to Seattle, Holly would forget about Beth.

Glancing at her cell phone, one hand lazing on the steering wheel, Holly tapped in Beth's telephone number, a reckless stunt. Esther supposed she should learn to drive so she wouldn't have to depend on Holly. Or was it too late for this old mare? Esther wondered if she could still handle a horse and buggy. Sure, how could she forget the feel of the leather reins?—even though she'd declared it an antiquated form of transportation when she and Samuel moved to California. "You'd never find a buggy on the Golden Gate Bridge," she'd said decades ago, and both of them had laughed.

As the rental car jostled along, Esther recalled that Hollander Road curved to the right before it jutted north again, only minutes from home. She glanced out the windshield and noticed a camel-colored cow crossing the road in front of them.

"Watch out!" Esther yelled.

Holly screamed and dropped the phone. She slammed on the brakes, grabbed hold of the steering wheel and rotated it, overcompensating. The tires squealed as the sedan fishtailed and grazed the bovine's hindquarters.

Esther braced herself for a gruesome collision.

The car plowed off the road into a ditch. Grasses and weeds leaped up to engulf the front fenders and hood. With a metallic crash, the automobile thudded against something hard enough to stop them dead in their tracks. Esther's head whipped forward. The airbag exploded, pummeling her face and chest, ramming her against the seat, and shutting off the world into a dark bubble of silence, except for a hissing from under the engine.

A sob gurgled from Holly's mouth. "Did I hit a tree? Did I hurt the cow? Oh, no, I wrecked the rental car. What's that weird noise?"

"Turn off the key," Esther said, remembering advice she'd gleaned from watching an old TV show.

With a shaking hand, Holly managed to reach the key and cut the engine.

Sandwiched between the seat and the airbag, Esther felt claustrophobic and helpless. The scene shot her back in time; she recalled her father's pinning her shoulders against the wall with his mammoth hands and rebuking her for attending a Sunday Singing at a neighbor's barn at age fifteen, months before her sixteenth birthday, when the events became acceptable. Not that Samuel and she ever stuck around for more than a few minutes.

"Did I kill the cow?" Holly said. "I'm afraid to look."

The words "Judge not and ye shall not be judged" curbed Esther's tongue and kept her from chastising her daughter for her lackadaisical driving habits. Using a cell phone! Paying no attention to the road! Thank the good Lord, Holly hadn't run over a child on a scooter.

"Don't say a thing, Mom." Speaking into the deflating airbag, Holly sounded submerged in a fish tank. "I feel bad enough."

"Are you all right?"

"I guess. Nothing's broken, I don't think." Holly drooped against her seat like a wilting tulip. "Dearest heavenly Father, please don't let the cow be dead."

Esther was gratified to hear her daughter pleading to the Almighty. At home, during predinner prayer time, she doubted Holly did more then anticipate supper, waiting for Esther to hurry up and finish saying grace before the food grew cold.

The airbag deflated, releasing its hold. "Can you get your door open?" Holly asked.

Esther took her question to signify Holly was afraid to get out and survey the damage.

"You want me to lead the way?" Feeling her right shoulder bruised, Esther took a physical inventory, wiggling her hands and ankles, and decided she was in one piece. She unlatched her safety belt, wrestled with the handle, and shoved her shoulder against the door, urging it open. Not that she wanted to see a wounded cow writhing in agony.

She wriggled out the partially opened door. Her feet sank into several inches of gushy mud, but dirty shoes were the least of her problems. She pushed aside a bush and knee-high grass and trudged onto the road.

A tan-colored cow with patches of white stood nearby, its rear leg lifted. It bellowed as Esther approached.

Esther ventured closer and saw the bumper had skinned the bovine's hip and leg—shaved off the hair. But her hide was intact and no sign of blood. Esther prayed the car hadn't broken a bone or inflicted internal injuries.

The cow lowered its head and let out a plaintive moan.

"*Gude Mariye,*" Esther said. "'Tis okay, girl." She hoped.

Esther called to Holly, who was picking her way out of the undergrowth. Her daughter's cheeks were blotched red from the airbag's slap and she tottered on unsteady legs. A bramble hung from her skirt, encircling her ankle like a snake.

"It's a beautiful Guernsey," Esther said.

"Who cares what kind of cow it is?"

Esther heard uncalled-for irritation grating Holly's voice. "Why are you taking your anger out on me?" Esther grappled to control her temper. After this horrendous morning, she felt like a rubber band stretched taut, beyond its capacity, ready to snap. Maybe she'd been too lax as a parent—a wet noodle—because now she had a full-grown brat on her hands.

"It appears you hit a fence post, rammed it right over," Esther said. Holly should be grateful the car missed smashing into a substantial sycamore, only feet to the left.

"At least I didn't kill the poor cow," Holly said. She held up her cell phone. "I found this on the floor."

"We'd better call a vet."

"Before 9-1-1?"

"If she belongs to an Amish farmer, I doubt he wants the police involved. Lucky for you."

"I'll try Zach." A moment later Holly spoke into her cell phone. "Sorry to disturb you, Beth." Holly gaped at the cow, then the automobile. "It's Holly. I hit a cow with my rental car. I didn't mean to—I don't know Zach's telephone number. Would you please call him and ask him to meet us, if he's available? I'd better let my mother explain where we are."

She handed the phone to Esther—shoved it at her, really.

Esther was reluctant to beg for Beth's assistance, but there was no way around it. "I'm sorry to disturb you at this hour," she began.

"It's okay." Beth yawned. "Where are you?"

Esther gave her the location. In their teens, Samuel had pulled his courting buggy off to the side of the road near this spot for periods of cuddling and smooching many times. If only Esther had been content with her life, she and Holly would never be in this predicament. Of course, if Beth had lured Samuel away with her saccharine flirtation and talk of knowing God in a personal way, there would have been no Holly at all.

As a Mennonite, Beth had memorized scripture and prayed to God, openly touting his glorious nature for all the world to hear—like they were best friends. Yet Mamm invited Beth to the farmhouse often. Esther wondered if Mamm had debated with Beth about her beliefs.

When Esther moved to Seattle and attended Dori and Jim's church—quite a shock with its hymn books and Bible pew racks, arched ceiling like an upside-down boat's hull, and ornate stained glass windows—she'd come to worship in the same manner. Through reading God's Word and attending Bible studies, she'd finally accepted he was concerned with every facet of her life.

Beth's voice interrupted her thoughts. "If Zach can't find you, he'll call. I have Holly's number on my caller ID. Is she okay?"

"Yah, just shaken."

Beth hung up without saying good-bye or asking about Esther's health. She probably hoped Esther would drop dead.

"Beth's calling Zach." Esther handed the phone to Holly.

The cow bent its neck to examine its injured leg.

"I can't believe I was so careless," Holly said, her voice thick.

Esther wanted to agree with her, but pressed her lips together.

"What if they have to put the cow to sleep?" Holly said.

Irritated as she was, Esther couldn't stop herself from trying to soothe Holly. "Let's not go rushing to conclusions. *Alles ist ganz gut*—all will be well."

"I hope you're right." Holly wanted Esther to be right? A first since leaving Seattle.

As they waited, Zach called to report he'd just finished tending a mule a couple miles away.

In spite of her clashing emotions, Esther's heart went out to Holly, who'd always adored animals. As a girl, she'd been inconsolable when her dog died; Esther should have given her daughter another puppy right away. One of Esther's customers owned a litter of ten-week-old Yorkshire terriers and had offered to trade a pup for a quilt.

Ach, Esther made so many mistakes raisin' her girl. When Holly was a youngster, Esther should have remarried to give her daughter a father figure. Dori and Jim knew a single widower, an orthodontist, and had set up a blind date one evening at their house, although Dori claimed she'd simply invited two friends at random over to dinner. Esther found Michael a nice enough fellow. She might have eased into more than a platonic friendship if she'd spent time with him, like sinking into a hot tub and growing accustomed to the heat. But she'd declined his invitation for a movie the next weekend, and meeting for lunch at the Sunflour Bakery Café the next month. Eventually he gave up asking—a relief for Esther.

"I didn't expect to see Zach again so soon," Holly said, glancing up and down the road. "Does he strike you as being stuck on himself?"

"You mean conceited? No, just the opposite. Why must you find fault with every man you meet?"

"I don't. For instance, I like Nathaniel King just fine."

"I can give you ten reasons why Nathaniel's wrong for you." Esther wouldn't mention her personal incentive—not that she would accept his unconvincing marriage proposal since she'd found he'd been deceiving her with his covert land purchase. How could she trust him again?

Minutes later, Zach's pickup zoomed down the road and came to an abrupt halt. He jumped out and rushed over to inspect the restless animal.

Zach ran his fingertips down the cow's side. "What have we here?"

She lowered her head and began munching grass at the side of the road, bless her heart. He thoroughly but gently examined the cow's rear quarters.

"We got lucky," he said. "The wound is superficial."

"But she's limping." Holly's hand moved to her neck. "Are you sure nothing's broken?"

"In my humble opinion she's fine." His voice sounded confident, maybe a ploy to calm Holly's nerves. He strode to his pickup and returned with disinfectant and ointment.

Esther was tempted to describe her daughter's negligent driving, but knew better than to mention how she'd struck the cow and then careened into the ditch. If using a cell phone while driving were against the law in Pennsylvania, as it was in the Northwest, Holly might be given a citation, her license revoked, and her insurance rates skyrocket.

"I think I recognize this cow, and she's wearing an ear clip," Zach said. "We'll need to get hold of the owner and ask him to come fetch her."

Eyeing the car and bent fencepost, he tipped his head toward acres of pastureland, and a barn and house standing in the distance. "My best guess is she belongs to the Swartzendrubers' dairy farm. They keep a good size herd of Guernsey—forty head. They don't own a phone, so I'll drive over there. I'll be right back."

"And leave us with the cow?" Holly said. "What if she gets worse? What if she runs away?"

He smiled, his expression amused but sympathetic.

Esther heard a clip-clop-clopping on the road and noticed a horse and buggy trotting their way with several cars tailgating it. As the gray covered buggy pulled off the road behind Zach's truck, the automobiles sped past.

The bearded buggy driver leaned out the window. "Anything I can do ta help ya, Doc?"

"You know John Swartzendruber from that farm over yonder?" Zach asked.

"Yah, he's my *Onkel.*"

"Would you mind heading over there and telling your uncle one of his cows has been injured? Nothing serious."

"You might mention the driver has auto insurance," Holly said.

The man shook his head. "No need."

"Thank you, ever so much." Esther had forgotten how charitable and accommodating the Amish were, and had always been, now that she thought about it. If they were in Seattle, names and numbers would be exchanged and a policeman called to the scene.

As the horse and buggy cantered down the road to the Swartzendrubers' farm, Zach's attention turned to the rental car, its rear bumper and hatch in view. Steamy vapor billowed from the ditch, erupting from under the hood.

"What happened?" Zach asked. "Someone run you off the road?"

"No." Holly's eyes went glassy. "It was all my fault. I wasn't paying attention."

Esther could see his taking in Holly's muddied socks and shoes, and the blackberry still dragging from the hem of her dress.

"I can ask neighbors to pull the car out of the ditch with a team of draft horses or call a tow truck," he said.

Her chin dipped. "I should inform the car rental agency too."

He stepped over to her and draped an arm around Holly's back. She leaned against him, not what Esther expected after Holly's remarks about him. Maybe Holly would grow fond of him if she spent more time here. But what about the suitor Holly knew from church in Seattle? Although Holly claimed they were merely friends, he'd be a preferable choice, for sure.

Holly rubbed her eyes, then turned to watch the cow. "She looks better now, don't you think, Mom?"

"Yes. But don't ask me. Zach's the expert."

As Holly used her phone to call the car rental agency and Zach spoke to their recommended towing company in New Holland on his, Esther's thoughts zigzagged like a mouse in a maze. If Zach and capricious Holly grew closer, Beth and Holly would too. It seemed as though Esther and Beth already shared Mamm, which vexed Esther to no end. At least Beth had kept her distance since Esther and Holly's arrival. But that respite might not last.

"Where were you and your mother just now so early in the morning?" Zach asked Holly as they both put away their phones.

"At my father's parents'." She sniffed and dabbed the corners of her eyes with her sleeves. "A dream come true meeting my grandparents, Jeremiah and Beatrice Fisher."

"Matthew Fisher's your father?"

"No. Samuel, their older son, who died before I was born."

"I didn't know they had a boy other than Matthew." He ran a hand along his jawline. So Beth had not filled him in on Esther's duplicitous past.

Zach extracted his keys from his pocket. "I could drive you back to their house."

"No!" Esther said. "We're headed to my mamm's, if it wouldn't be too much trouble."

"Happy to oblige. We'll wait for John Swartzendruber and the tow truck, then I'll take you."

Using one foot to hold it down, Holly tugged the blackberry branch off her dress; its thorns fought her and pricked her thumb, but she didn't complain. "Once I get cleaned up, I was planning to visit your mother to use my computer. You think it'll be all right to drop in on her again?"

"Absolutely. Her electricity's back on. I'll call and give her the heads-up. And let my answering service know where I am. I usually go to the office until noon on Saturdays, but my phone continues to ring all day."

Esther could feel the skin on her feet wrinkling from her soggy socks; she'd be happy to soak them in warm water. Or should she dash into clean clothing and accompany Holly? Who knew what Beth might divulge about Esther's past? Like transparent drops of arsenic, Beth would surely poison her daughter against her.

CHAPTER THIRTY-ONE

I watched two of John Swartzendruber's teenage sons guide the limping cow up a plank into an open wagon hitched to a draft horse. The Guernsey's udders hung heavy with milk. To think, I almost killed that lovely doe-eyed animal!

"Please, God, let her be all right," I whispered.

After my chaotic morning, I wondered if God was listening or ever had. How could he possibly keep track of everyone's requests? I imagined, years ago, Mom's begging for Dad's return from Vietnam. The Almighty hadn't protected my father, yet Mom said she'd held tightly to her faith. And Mommy Anna? She said she never gave up on Mom's returning to Lancaster County. Would my grandma die the week after she reached Montana? Was it up to me to make sure she stayed here since God wouldn't intercede?

My faith used to flow like Mill Creek, bending, then straightening, lulled to tranquility by the force of gravity. But over the last few years my commitment to God had faded. Without him, what held my world together? Family. Making the whole Amish lifestyle seem right and nurturing. But I reminded myself their ways centered on obeying God.

I heard a man's voice, then Zach introduced Mom and me to John Swartzendruber—a man in his fifties, bearded, and wearing a straw hat.

"I'm so sorry," I told him. I hoped Mom wouldn't elaborate or open her mouth again for the rest of the day. Not after our visit with the Fishers.

"I have no idea how Lulu got out," John Swartzendruber said to Zach. "Lots of shenanigans going on this last month." He hooked his thumbs in his suspenders. "If ya ask me, kids in their Rumspringa are overstepping their boundaries."

When he used the term Rumspringa, Mom looked away. I'd have to ask Mommy Anna about this running-around period. Did parents turn a blind eye when their children became sixteen, allowing them to break all rules?

While I was in high school, Mom had hounded me with restrictions, which I guessed kept me out of trouble when it came to boys. Who wanted to date a girl who had to be home by ten thirty? My thoughts returned to Beatrice and her hostility toward Mom and me this morning. Maybe the Fishers had the story backwards—maybe my father had been the one with wanderlust.

No, this morning my mother wore guilt like a scarlet letter across her chest.

"You could be right, John," Zach said. "But it wouldn't hurt to check your fence."

John Swartzendruber removed his hat for a moment and wiped sweat from his brow. "Don't need to. I know that fence like the back of my hand. And my cows spend the night under cover next to the barn."

Zach assured John he wouldn't accept his usual veterinary fee. "I'll stop by to check on Lulu later this afternoon. Need help getting that post replaced?"

"Nee, my sons will fix it once that car's out of the way. These city folk …"

Soon after the Swartzendrubers' wagon departed, a tow truck barreled down the road from the other direction and halted near Zach's pickup. A cleanly shaved late-twenties man in overalls got out and gave Zach a hearty handshake. A border collie sat in the passenger seat.

"Thanks for coming so quickly, Gregg." Zach reached through the open window to stroke the dog under the chin.

"Anything for you, Doc. If it weren't for your house call a couple years back, our Gabby here wouldn't have made it. Nor her pups."

"And my mother wouldn't have her beloved Missy."

"Missy couldn't have a better home." Gregg's glance sized up the rental car.

Did Zach know every man, woman, and animal in the county? I didn't know why his popularity bugged me. But it did, like he was a puffed-up superhero. I bet women swooned all over him. And to think only an hour ago I'd leaned against him like a damsel in distress. Had tears actually blurred my vision? I'd never cried in public. I mean, never.

Backing his tow truck toward the ditch and reeling out a hook, Gregg got busy hauling the car. A fencepost and boulder at the bottom of the ditch had dented the hood, and the front bumper splayed off to the side, dislocated, gathering twigs and grass.

"Why didn't I purchase the extra insurance offered at the airport?" I said to myself, but Mom overheard me.

"Too late to lose sleep over it now," she said.

If she were trying to make me feel better, her tactic wasn't working. "Your mother should have named you Pollyanna," I said. Everything about Mom rankled me, like yellow jackets swarming around my ears. "I hope my regular insurance covers the damage. The two-hundred-dollar deductible will empty my account. Do you even know what deductible means?"

"Of course I do. I own a business with fire and theft insurance, don't I? And I've asked you over and over not to use the phone while driving."

I glanced at Zach and felt blood rising up my neck. "This is my first car accident, I swear."

"I believe you." He raised his hands as if under arrest.

Wishing I'd wake up from this nightmare, I said, "At least the cow's okay. Isn't she? I've never hurt an animal in my life."

He let out a slow breath. "She'll be fine. And I'll swing by John Swartzendruber's to check her over again." Zach gave me a half smile. Pondering the cow's welfare, I wasn't convinced Lulu was all right.

Mom brushed a dried leaf off her slacks. "Holly, aren't you going to thank Zach for his generosity?" Must she embarrass me again?

"I was about to, Mother." I turned to Zach and saw he was wearing faded jeans and a wrinkled shirt. His hair looked windblown, as if he'd combed it with his fingers. Had he even had his morning coffee? From the look of his stubbled chin, I doubted he'd done more than splash his face with water. "Thank you very much, Zach," I said. "You've been more than kind."

"Glad to help."

"Let's not keep this busy man waiting any longer," Mom said.

I took her comment to mean I was a slowpoke, producing one blunder after another. All true. I had no one to blame but myself for stranding us by the side of the road. What was wrong with me? Wasn't I the sophisticated woman who'd dreamed of working in the world of high finance using the left side of my brain, not traipsing around the county at sunup, carousing into ditches? I thought of my former boss, Mel, and wondered if the market had rebounded. I should call him.

"Shall we take off?" Zach said. "Gregg can handle this."

Zach's hand at my elbow, he escorted me to his pickup. Did I look like I was going to keel over? I glanced down at my grimy shoes, dress, and apron. I should have taken the time to fix my zipper and worn my slacks and a long-sleeved sweater this morning. What had drawn me to the dress and apron again? Probably the desire for community that ran through me like an underground stream.

"Can we all fit in?" Mom asked Zach as we neared his pickup.

"Yes, it's got a wide bench seat, plenty of room." Zach opened the passenger door and motioned for me to get in. Trying to clean my feet, I swiped the side of my shoes on the ground, but the bulk of mud remained, already drying. I grabbed a stick and flicked some off, then gave up.

With Zach's assistance, I climbed into the cab. I should have asked Mom to sit in the middle, but she would have insisted I get in first. I wasn't up for another squabble.

"Put on your safety belt," she told me and waited to hear it click before fastening her own.

Once Zach ignited the engine, he asked, "Are you two sure nothing's sprained or broken? Want me to run you by the ER?"

"Nothing's broken," I said. "How about you, Mom?"

"Just shaken." She rubbed her forearms as if trying to get her circulation moving.

In truth, my left arm from shoulder to fingers felt achy. Not that I'd admit it. The last place I wanted to go was a hospital.

In the pickup, my legs swung to the right, against Mom's. Her shoes and socks looked in worse shape than mine. Fortunately Zach's floor mats were already littered with dirt and bits of straw.

Cruising onto the road, we sat in silence, the transmission mounting, then ebbing, the shock absorbers bouncing over a pothole.

"May I take you to breakfast?" Zach asked us. "My treat."

"Sure, I'm famished," I said.

"No," Mom said. "I left the house without a word this mornin'. Mamm could be fretting up a storm."

"Then I'll take you right home." Apparently in no hurry, Zach followed a horse-driven wagon laden with baled hay.

"Thank you ever so much for your kind offer," Mom said to him. "Mamm probably has a pot of Kaffi brewing and some fresh sticky buns should ya like to come in."

My chuckle came out like a snort. "Mother, you're sounding more and more like a local."

"Well, you're lookin' like one," she shot back, a gust of hostility blasting the side of my face. At least she wasn't harping about my accident or the cow. I felt sick enough about it. In Seattle, she often tossed out unsubtle remarks about my driving, like: "Are we in a hurry, dear?" or "Seems like everyone else is driving slower." If she didn't appreciate my chauffeuring her, she'd had every opportunity to learn to drive. I'd even offered to teach her. "I enjoy the bus" was her answer. But carting grocery bags home on the bus was a burden, so I usually stepped in to save the day. Or Dori offered to help by picking up milk and eggs. Mom paid her back with fresh Amish Friendship Bread, so Dori insisted she got the better end of the bargain.

Why was I analyzing my mother, who would never change her ways and was kind enough to let me live with her? We'd spent too much time together, I decided, looking forward to a break—with Beth and my computer.

Minutes later, Zach steered his pickup around the side of Mommy Anna's house.

"Thank you for the ride," Mom said. She opened the door and slid to the ground. I followed her, my skirt getting caught in the seat belt. Zach helped me untangle myself, no doubt getting a good look at my grubby legs up to the knees. As if I hadn't embarrassed myself enough for one day.

Mom and I straggled into the barnyard to find Isaac and Nathaniel face-to-face, standing closer than usual. Grasping a legal-size manila envelope, Isaac ignored our arrival. I figured my uncle, up milking since dawn, was tired and thoroughly annoyed with Mom. Couldn't blame him there. But Nathaniel pushed his hat back and sent Mom an engaging smile. He hardly noticed me!

Trodding up the back steps, Mom and I left our shoes and socks in the utility room and scrubbed our hands. While Mom padded into the kitchen, I wiped dried mud off my legs with a damp towel. Through the door, I heard Isaac say, "Now listen here, Nathaniel. Who do ya think you are?"

I was tempted to dawdle and eavesdrop, but saw Mommy Anna ahead waiting for Mom and me. My grandma's face looked haggard—most likely she was agitated, seeing the men at odds and wondering where Mom had been hiding herself.

As I entered the kitchen, the temperature rose a welcoming twenty degrees. Three lattice-covered pies with crimped edges sat on the counter. A cloud of fruity ambrosia filled my nostrils; the air radiated with the scent of apples, cinnamon, and butter.

"There you are," Mommy Anna said. "What can I get yous ta eat? Pie made of apples from our orchard?"

I'd always wanted a grandma to spoil me rotten. "Dessert for breakfast sounds divine. After the morning I've had, I may pour a heaping tablespoon of sugar over the top."

"Never can be too sweet—like you." I appreciated that she hadn't questioned me about my day and why we hadn't returned in the rental car. She knew I'd headed to the Fishers' but—unlike Mom—would let me unravel my experience in due time.

Mommy Anna sliced me a generous wedge of pie and positioned it on a plate, off to one side. "Any cheese?"

"Yes, please. But I can get it myself."

"Nee, darling girl, I will." Mommy Anna brought a tube of sausage out of the refrigerator and set it on the counter.

Mom and I stared at the sausage, then at each other in silent surprise.

"Sure you didn't mean ta get cheese?" Mom returned it to the refrigerator and substituted it with a block of cheddar. She handed me the cheese on a cutting board. "I think I'll fry myself an egg," she said.

"That ain't much of a breakfast." Mommy Anna massaged her temples.

"To make you happy, I'll eat it with toast." Mom placed a pan on the stove top and turned on the burner.

Mommy Anna's mouth lifted into a smile. "Holly, I'm already soaking your jeans. Ya ready for me to launder the dress and apron?"

"Would you mind? I could help."

"I'll give you a lesson."

"Are you sure you feel up to it?"

She rubbed her temples again, pushing her prayer cap back to expose a balding scalp. "Just a headache. I get them every so often." She tucked loose wisps of hair back under her cap and straightened it. The strings came untied; she left them dangling. "Monday is usually laundry day, but we'll make an exception in your case. Let's see, what day is it? Wednesday? No, 'tis Thursday. The last week in April."

"It's Saturday, mid-October," Mom said. "Are you okay?"

"I've felt better. And sometimes my head gets muddled."

Not knowing the day of the week was one thing, but did Mommy Anna really think it was April? What did she expect to find in Montana? Thawing snow and spring flowers? I wanted to blame her confusion on her early rising.

I sliced into the cheddar. "No matter what time of year, you're the best grandma in the world as far as I'm concerned."

"Better than Beatrice Fisher?" She steadied herself against the counter. "She can be a *schtinker*, but she ain't that bad once you get to know her. We're in different districts now—I can't say I mind one bit. And pretty soon we'll be livin' on the other side of the country. Near Seattle. If you don't come with us, you can visit often."

"I might just do that, but I love it here." For fear of disappointing her, I didn't reveal how far Seattle lay from Montana—the Cascades, Eastern Washington, Idaho, and the Rocky Mountains would separate us. "I'd rather visit you in Lancaster County."

Mom craned her neck to get a better view out the window. Of Nathaniel? If I didn't know better, I'd swear she had a crush on him that couldn't be reciprocal. Not only was she a couple years his senior, she owned a house and a business in Seattle. And she was my mother!

I toddled up behind her and saw Isaac remove a map and photos from the envelope. Isaac opened the map and showed it to Zach. I was itching to ask Mommy Anna if Nathaniel had made an offer on her property, but maybe she didn't know of the sales transaction.

Nathaniel's face turned our way, his gaze catching Mom's. No doubt about it, a disturbing current of tension ran between the two of them. Had Nathaniel already told Mom details of my family's move to Montana and left me out of the loop?

My family. I liked the sound of those two words. Should I go with them? At least help through the first winter?

As Mom and I stared out the window at the men, Mommy Anna added a slab of butter to Mom's fry pan, sending up a burst of sizzling smoke.

"That's way too much," Mom said.

Mommy Anna added another hunk. Then she moved to the refrigerator and brought out four brown eggs, broke and whisked them into a bowl, and set the swirled mixture on the counter next to the stove.

"Is that for me?" Mom frowned. "I said I wanted one fried egg."

"One egg won't tide you over until the noon meal. Unless Beatrice fed ya."

"Only coffee," I said. "And it wasn't half as good as yours."

"Denki," Mommy Anna said. "Better eat yourself full. There's plenty to be done this morning."

"I'll be glad to help later," Mom said. "First, I'd like to visit the cemetery to see Dat's grave. And Samuel's, too, if I can figure a way."

"Ya know, Samuel's body was never found," Mommy Anna said.

Grief, followed by anger, seemed to transform Mom's face into an old woman's. "Don't you think I know that fact better than anyone?" She switched off the burner. "But the Fishers said they had erected something. And I want to see it!"

I was struck by the enormity of Mom's sorrow. She still loved my father. She couldn't possibly be interested in Nathaniel. But why turn her anger on my grandma?

"So do I," I said. "Even though Dad's in heaven now." I sat and swallowed a mouthful of the best apple pie I'd ever tasted.

"My Levi was committed to God and followed the Ordnung," Mommy Anna said. "I look forward to seein' him again. Now, I don't know about Samuel."

"He's in heaven!" Mom stamped her foot like a girl. "I suppose you think I'm not going to heaven either, because I'm not baptized Amish. You should listen to your Mennonite neighbors more."

"Like Beth?" Mommy Anna tilted her head.

My mother grimaced, then gawked out the window again. I couldn't shake a creepy feeling she was more than fond of Nathaniel. I bet she hadn't seen Lizzie, his cute housekeeper.

"You think my dad's marker is on the Fisher property?" I asked Mommy Anna.

"Most likely."

"How about Nathaniel's wife?" Mom said. "Is she buried close by?"

Mommy Anna sucked in her lower lip. "As far as I know she ain't buried nowhere. She disappeared some fifteen years ago."

"She ran away from home?" I asked.

Her hand wobbling, Mommy Anna topped off my coffee. "I can't imagine she would, what with Kinner ta look after and a fine husband like Nathaniel. Anyways, she'd made a lifetime commitment to the church. Divorce is strictly *verboten*—forbidden." Mommy Anna returned the coffee urn, but kept hold of the handle. "No one knows. She was visitin' cousins in Tuscarawas County in Ohio. She left no farewell note."

"Could she have been struck by a car?" I said, still shaken by my irresponsible driving. "A hit-and-run accident?" I set my fork on my plate. "Could someone have kidnapped her?"

"She was stayin' with family. 'Tis highly unlikely anyone intentionally harmed her. Although ya might have heard of past violence toward the Amish."

"Yes, I read about the murders of the children in a schoolhouse." I'd been astonished the Amish community had readily extended their forgiveness. But the topic was too grisly to contemplate over apple pie. "Still, it makes you wonder. Nathaniel's wife was never located?"

"Not in all these many years. Nathaniel didn't ask for police assistance, but they swarmed both counties and sent bulletins 'cross the state, and found no hide nor hair of her." She slumped onto the bench at the table, her arms forward. "It must have been God's will. It's generally thought she committed suicide by drowning. Her sweater and shoes were found on the banks of the Tuscarawas River. She was a shy woman and known to suffer from depression."

"That's why Nathaniel never remarried?" I said.

"Not yet, anyways."

"Nathaniel's poor daughters, growing up without a parent." I felt a familiar yearning—an emptiness gaping as wide and deep as the Grand Canyon, yet to be filled.

Mommy Anna reached around Mom to turn the stove top back on. "Nathaniel went near insane lookin' for her. But I believe through God's mercy he and his daughters finally found peace."

I half-stood and glanced out the kitchen window. "Those men look anything but peaceful." I could tell by the rigid set of Isaac's shoulders as he refolded the map.

"Wonder what they're talking about," Mom muttered.

When I sat for another bite of pie, I saw Mommy Anna bringing additional eggs from the refrigerator. "Good morning, Holly," she said. "Yous two got up late. What can I fix ya?"

CHAPTER THIRTY-TWO

Esther's exhaustion ran bone deep. She watched Mamm remove another half dozen eggs from the refrigerator and set them in a bowl. Now what? Mamm was planning to scramble more eggs? She'd forgotten the day of the week, the month, and now she was confused about this morning's events.

Leaving the bowl on the counter by the sink, Mamm opened the window a few inches, enough for Esther to better hear the men's garbled voices outside. Nathaniel spoke Esther's name. They were talking about her? What on earth?

"Our Isaac needs me in the barn," Mamm said. "'Tis time for milkin'."

"No, Mamm." Esther felt heat radiating from the fry pan atop the stove. "He did that hours ago." She turned the burner off again.

"We saw the herd in the pasture when we got home," Holly said, then shoveled in more pie. Where were her table manners?

"I s'pose you're right." Through the window, Mamm glanced up at the midmorning sky—a canopy of clouds parting to expose a swath of azure blue. "But they might have forgotten Spicy."

Esther recalled the mostly white Holstein the family had owned when Esther was in her teens. "Didn't Spicy die of old age by now? She must have. Unless you named another cow in her honor."

Mamm squinted. "I guess our Spicy did pass away, now that you mention it. I forget things."

Was Mamm dwindling like water-deprived peas on a vine? How could Esther have been so blind? She could no longer deny her mother's mental and physical faculties were declining. Signs of Alzheimer's? Did the disease run in the family? Later, Esther would have to come to terms with her pride and venture with Holly to Beth's house to read over her daughter's shoulder on the computer, hunting for clues and an expert physician. Ask if others had suffered from the same symptoms.

Esther heard Isaac say, "You had no right—" Then he rotated to the barn and his words blurred together. Inundated with curiosity, Esther inclined her ear to the window but couldn't make out the end of his sentence.

"That ain't a good enough reason," Nathaniel said a moment later.

"You getting enough to eat?" Mamm asked Esther over her shoulder. "You should put more meat on those bones. Might be cold in Montana."

"I won't be there." Turning to evaluate her mother's facial expression, Esther scalded the side of her hand on the pan. "Ow!" She felt like lashing out in frustration, but steeled her face from showing her pain, as she always did. She turned off the stove again.

"Are you sure you should go to Montana?" Holly asked Mamm. "When I was eight, our friends Dori and Jim drove me to Glacier National Park." She licked her fork clean. "It was beautiful, but would you be happy living there?"

"Sure. And you'll come with us too, Holly Berry. We'll finally be a whole family."

Mamm had designated Holly a nickname? When Esther had called her Holly Berry in the past, her daughter insisted she never repeat it. But Holly's face brimmed with happiness—until Mamm knocked Esther's coffee cup off the counter with the back of her hand, splattering brown fluid across the floor.

"I'll get it." Esther rushed over with a sponge to mop up the spill. She wondered if Mamm's transformation from health to infirmity had taken decades, like a battery draining of its juice. She couldn't have known, having only read the letters, Mamm's efficient cursive handwriting masking illness—especially since Esther wasn't looking for clues. No, Esther was stretching the truth: Mamm had complained of aches and pains, what Esther thought were conniving ploys to lure her here.

Well, she should have come!

Esther's handwriting had always been sloppy in comparison, always hurried. When she thought about it, she was akin to Isaac's hogs—slovenly. The worst daughter in the world. And maybe Esther was losing her mental faculties too.

Holly leaped up to help dry the floor with a towel. "With your dizziness, I agree with Mom. I can't see you traveling across the country to set up house, even with your sons and daughters-in-law and all their children to help you."

"It would be better if you and your Mudder were there," Mamm said.

Esther tossed the sponge in the sink. "Mamm, are ya sure you want to leave your church district and friends? Leave this house where your relations have lived for over one hundred years?"

"Better than splitting up my family."

"The way I did," Esther said. "And no good came of it."

Mamm rummaged around for a fork and finally located one in the drawer where the cutlery had always been stored. "Truly, ya did, Esther. You ripped this family in half." She handed Esther the fork and a napkin. "But no need fussing now that we're all back together."

Questions cavorted through Esther's mind like pirouetting swallows. "Is Nathaniel really buying the farm?"

"Yah. When he caught wind of our leaving, Nathaniel made a generous offer to purchase our property."

"He's buying this house? Everything?" Holly said.

"Yah. 'Tis all decided."

"Why didn't you mention it in a letter?" Esther said.

"Then you never would have come to visit. Ain't so?"

"I would have," Holly said. "Years ago. No matter where you were."

They were ganging up on Esther like a couple of vultures. Esther rinsed her coffee cup, refilled it, and gulped too quickly, the liquid hitting the back of her throat. She coughed.

"The men don't look like they're gettin' along," Mamm said, standing at the window again.

Esther cleared her voice. "There may be much you don't understand about Nathaniel," she said, and Holly shot her a quizzical look.

"And you do?"

Esther's thoughts somersaulted back to last night. Nathaniel hadn't hinted his wife committed suicide, a tragedy that now bothered Esther greatly. When her Samuel didn't return from Vietnam, Esther had considered ending her life. If it weren't for her baby Holly, she might have jumped off Seattle's Aurora Bridge—without sending a farewell note to Mamm. Ach, Esther had been self-centered and knew she still was. She couldn't blame her actions on her mother's controlling attitude anymore.

"You want me to stick around until your family leaves for Montana?" Holly asked Mamm. "I could help them pack."

"Yah, stay," she said, "then come with us. Be the children's schoolteacher."

"But I don't have a teaching license. I'm not certified."

"No matter, if you've graduated from the eighth grade."

Holly's face grew animated, her eyes alert. "I could really be a teacher? I'd love that."

"Since when?" Esther hadn't seen her daughter so excited in years, but she assumed only Old Order Mennonite or Amish women could teach. And Esther wouldn't like having her only child living in Montana in a community without a home phone or Internet connection.

"While you were in college, I tried talking you into getting your teaching degree," Esther said, her voice gritty, "but you'd have no part of it."

"I was young. Hey, Mom, a girl can change her mind, can't she? You always told me the sky's the limit."

"But teach in a one-room schoolhouse in the backwoods of Montana?"

"I could give it a try. I don't have money to spend, anyway. And if I dress Amish-style—"

"You'd wear a prayer cap and give up driving a car?" Esther said, incredulous. She couldn't imagine Holly's intrigue would last once she found out teachers were single women. Or had Holly given up on finding a husband?

Through the window, Esther watched Nathaniel straighten his straw hat. Had a compromise been reached between him and Isaac? No shake of hands and Isaac's expression was as severe as ever. Her youngest brother had been a funny, outgoing boy when Esther ran off. Isaac's dour mood was probably Esther's fault. She owed him sympathy and an apology. But not today.

She supposed her brothers' plan to move had been set in motion six months ago. They'd probably contacted an Amish settlement in Montana that recommended acreage. Her brothers had inspected and found the land suitable.

Nathaniel glanced up at Esther. She tried to recede into the shadow, but he noticed her and tipped his hat. Should she wave or pay no attention? The longer she knew him, the less she could decipher her feelings.

"I'll be right back." Holly wandered through the front room and out onto the porch. Esther heard Holly's words rising and falling, what must be a cell phone call.

"Come, have a seat, Essie," Mamm said, and patted a chair. "You're sweet on Nathaniel, ain't ya?"

"I'm hungry is what I am." Esther decided to cook Mamm's bowl of eggs, a maneuver to change the subject. And make her mother happy. She owed Mamm that much.

Moments later, Holly strolled back into the kitchen. "Mommy Anna, I'll be big as a horse by the time I leave, but how about another slice of pie?"

Seeing Mamm grinning at Holly filled Esther with a mixture of happiness and remorse. Why had she cloistered her daughter to herself? Why had she held on to Holly so tightly? Worse than Mamm and Dat ever did. Did Esther have such scarce confidence in her daughter that she feared she'd lose her? Holly must have hundreds of relatives in Lancaster County. Was Esther afraid she herself would revert to the Plain people and Holly would follow? What was so terrible about that scenario? Holly was single, without a love life, without family—except an inadequate mother.

In the Bible, the apostle Paul stated he was the worst of sinners. Esther was sure she'd surpassed him.

A petrifying scene unfolded in her mind. She imagined herself kneeling before the congregation next preaching Sunday, in a little bit more than a week, asking God and the community—the bishop, preachers, deacon, her mother—every member of the district, to forgive her. Would she finally feel absolved of her sins?

Her Seattle pastor—a trustworthy man—had assured her that the blood of Jesus paid her debt in full, but Esther felt as blameworthy as ever. When speaking privately with Esther, he'd encouraged her to visit her mother before Mamm passed away.

Maybe she should plunge into the abyss, move to Montana, and spend the rest of her days caring for Mamm and finally forge a relationship with her brothers, who were strangers to her. Then would she break through her prison bars?

"I'll get cleaned up," Holly said, impeding Esther's flighty thoughts. "Zach's driving me to Beth's house so I can use my computer."

"Did you make arrangements for another rental car?" Esther asked. She couldn't imagine her daughter without a set of wheels.

"Not yet. Maybe later." Holly gave Mamm a hug. "Thank you for the scrumptious pie. Even better than Mom's. Not that she'd let me eat dessert for breakfast."

Esther noticed her eggs were overcooked, and left them in the pan. "I need to use the phone shanty to call Dori and see how the shop's running without me."

After she spoke to Nathaniel.

Esther waited for Holly to climb the stairs to the second floor, then she scooted out the kitchen door. She found a pair of men's work boots in the utility room and slid her feet into them. She wondered which of her brothers the boots belonged to and felt an aching in her heart to be reunited with them. Without photographs, she couldn't imagine what they looked like as adults.

Realistically, Esther couldn't take a prolonged vacation from the Amish Shoppe, especially not with Christmas approaching—the most hectic and profitable season. Although Dori had assured her she was enjoying every moment working at the store, Esther still wasn't sure she wanted a partner. Or had she grown weary of her independence?

She hastened outside without tying the bootlaces. The cool air urged her to move faster. Scanning the barnyard, she heard fragments of Isaac and Zach's conversation floating from the barn. What would become of the animals when Isaac settled out West? Maybe he would send his top breeders, and Nathaniel would buy the rest of Isaac and Mamm's livestock as part of the sale of the Gingerich farm. Still, Esther found the thought of Isaac's abandoning the only home he'd ever known and the animals that toiled for him without complaint infuriating. Did he no longer love Lancaster's rich limestone soil, what their dat had described as the most fertile on earth?

As she stooped to tie the laces, she reminded herself she'd abandoned the farm too. Worse: She'd deserted her family.

Exiting the barnyard, she intended to confront Nathaniel about his property deal. She cringed to think he was intentionally cheating her family, but why else would he ask her to marry him and fail to mention the land purchase?

She rounded the side of the house to the road and spotted Nathaniel striding home. In spite of her battling emotions and doubts, she admired his workingman's shoulders and his freely swinging arms. She tried to resist the feeling; he was like a magnet drawing her, a helpless scrap of steel.

She noticed the phone shanty off to her right. She'd told Holly she was going to call Dori, and she should. Was it too early in Seattle? No, but Esther placed her priorities in order—she'd tackle the hardest job first. She passed by the phone. If Holly asked, she'd say someone else was using it. No she wouldn't. No more lies. Not after a lifetime of fabrications. She asked God for the strength to keep honest with Holly. With everyone, including herself.

She clambered, the boots several sizes too big, to catch up with Nathaniel, but couldn't. His pace was long and purposeful. He didn't stop until he circled his house and reached his back steps, where he stomped his feet to loosen caked mud.

By then she was panting. "Nathaniel! Wait up."

His eyebrows rose. "Esther. *Willkumm.*"

She felt a blush of embarrassment for chasing after him.

"It wonders me ta see you here." He removed his hat and raked a hand through his flattened hair. "Have ya come with your answer? To make this old-timer happy?"

Was he toying with her? Trying to make himself look meek, when in fact he held all the cards?

"You're not old," she said, catching her breath and hoping to sound nonchalant. "You're younger than I am."

"Not by much, as I recall. When you get to be our age, who's countin' anymore?"

"You're still young enough to start another family."

The back door blew open and a bouncy young woman strode outside, her creaseless apron and dress swishing above trim ankles. "There you are, Nate. Glad you're back." Her blonde hair was parted down the center and nary a rogue curl peeked out from behind her pressed prayer cap. Her blue eyes sparkled as her gaze enfolded Nathaniel. Holly's junior by eight to ten years, the young woman's creamy-white skin seemed as smooth as Esther's favorite porcelain teacup.

"I was gonna run home while the banana bread's in the oven, but didn't want to leave the house." She caught sight of Esther and the young woman's rosebud mouth transformed into a contrived smile, her lips covering her teeth. "Gut mornin'," she said, her voice losing its enthusiasm. "I didn't realize we had company."

"Esther, I'd like ya to meet Lizzie," Nathaniel said.

Esther assumed Nathaniel would introduce Lizzie as his daughter or niece, but upon second thought, no daughter or niece ever gazed at her father or uncle with such appreciation. The twentysomething, well into marrying age in these parts, was infatuated, Esther thought—in love with Nathaniel. Surely he must know.

"Hello." Esther attempted to muster a smile. She hadn't bothered to peek in a mirror before leaving the house. She'd never felt so dowdy and obsolete.

"Nice ta meetcha." Lizzie inspected Esther's slacks and clunky boots. "I'll be right back before the bread's done." Then she flitted out of the barnyard and onto a lane, what must be a shortcut to her parents' farm.

"I see you have an admirer," Esther said, her mouth dry.

"She comes once a day to help clean and cook. She's like a daughter to me."

"She's—she's young enough to be your daughter." Esther felt a prickle of envy, making no sense. Why would she care whom Nathaniel married? Didn't she suspect his proposal was a scam? Some in the community might think Nathaniel's accumulation of land was a sign of greediness—but a marriage might satisfy the bishop and muffle wagging tongues.

The aroma of banana bread wafted through the screen door and Nathaniel sniffed the air. "Yah, she's like a daughter," he said with fondness in his voice. He glanced across the barnyard as if waiting for Lizzie to return.

"I imagine she'd like to be more than a housekeeper." Esther figured fair-haired Lizzie had many suitors since she'd turned sixteen, but was saving herself for Nathaniel. "Perhaps your wife?"

He chortled. "Get hitched to an old coot like me?"

"Sure, why not?" She glanced around Nathaniel's estate, taking in the size of his barn, outbuildings, silos, and house. Neat as a pin, Dori might say. Esther admired his attention to orderly detail, but kept her thoughts on the subject looming ahead. "Don't you want more children? How can you run your farm without Kinner?"

"Don't worry about that. There are plenty of young men lookin' for work in these parts. You probably don't know how much has changed since you left. There's not enough land for every man and his family to farm, so a whole lot are workin' for others or starting their own businesses. Some get bussed to construction sites with lunch pails, which the bishop don't like one bit."

"My dat would have hated working anywhere but the farm," Esther said, trying to visualize Amishmen laboring in factories. "Farming is all he ever knew or wanted. How can the Amish way of life continue without the man of the house at home teaching his children how to farm? Not to mention the women. Must they work outside the home too?"

"Some single women do, like Lizzie. A few wives operate their own businesses, apart from their husbands. That's why your brothers are buying farmland where they can expand for generations. They don't want their children learning an industrial trade when they could be plowing and sowing, raising livestock, and keeping the family and faith strong. It was a tough decision. Isaac and your brothers prayed long and hard, consulted the bishop, and asked God for direction."

"I didn't know their reasons or that making a living in these parts was so challenging."

"The local economy ain't that bad, what with the tourists. A couple years back, a friend leased out his farm. He opened a business building diesel engines and installing them in used electrical appliances for the People. When his company grew too big and prosperous, with ten employees, he sold it to an Englischer for a tidy profit. Then my friend and his family up and moved to Indiana where he bought several farms for his children, with money left over."

"You've done well for yourself, too, Nathaniel."

"My organic produce is popular all over the state. 'Tis the Lord's doing." He tugged his beard. "I have more than I need, for sure."

"Then why are you gobbling up my mamm and Isaac's property?"

"Hold on." Nathaniel set his hat back on his head, pushing long bangs over his eyebrows. "Ya make me sound like a swindler. I made an above-market-rate offer on Anna's farm. She and Isaac accepted."

"What were you and Isaac arguing about?"

"Nothing to do with money, that much I can promise."

"In any case, you're a wealthy man, Nathaniel. What we call an eligible bachelor in Seattle."

"If you're referring to my expanding farm, my bishop says 'tis essential not to become proud. My financial success is a gift from God. But in other ways I ain't so successful. I've been a lonely man for many a year."

"I bet Lizzie would like to give you companionship," Esther said. "She ogles you like you're a movie star." Lizzie was probably prohibited from attending the movies unless still in her Rumspringa and could do as she pleased. Who knew what favors she'd granted to Nathaniel. No, Esther couldn't stand to let herself visualize him with another woman. Yet she had no right.

He positioned his hat at a jaunty slant, enough to tell Esther he was amused. "Lizzie's my daughter Tina's best friend, her husband's younger sister," he said.

"Then you're already related, but not by blood. An easy transition to matrimony, when you think about it."

He let out a belly laugh. "I have plenty of friends and relatives. What I need is a wife."

He took Esther's hand and she felt a tingling rush of warmth cascade through her arm and chest, like back in the days of her youth. With Samuel. Nathaniel could never replace her beloved Samuel any more than she could replace his former wife. Still, Esther had been desperately lonely.

Her fingers wrapped around his. She couldn't control them. She stared at their hands, entwined—his almost twice the size of hers—and savored the feel of his calloused skin.

She stared up into his face, drank in his rugged features. The two stood motionless, like the hickory trees growing behind his barn.

She shuddered inside as a hurricane of forewarnings brewed through her mind like the stormiest winter's wind. She hardly knew Nathaniel aside from childhood. She lived in Seattle. She was too old to remarry. She owned the Amish Shoppe and had planned to live out her days running it.

She wouldn't allow impetuous actions to steer her life as they had in the past.

"What am I doing?" she said, and let go of his hand. Hers fell against her thigh like a lifeless appendage, but his remained outstretched.

"We're not equally yoked," she said. "You know 'tis true. No bishop would marry us. Even should I decide to bend at the knees and be baptized, I would still love the Lord Jesus above all and continue to study his Word."

"As it should be. We'll make it work, my dearest Esther. *Ich liebe ich*. I love you."

Esther remembered the Dionne Warwick song "The Look of Love." Did she see "the look" in Nathaniel's eyes? He'd seemed to gaze into Esther's very soul the other night and again right now, but maybe his intensity was a sham. There was too much she didn't know about him.

She felt dizzy, teetering on the edge of a cliff, contemplating giving up her previous world and falling into Nathaniel's waiting arms. Would he catch her?

"*Ich auch*—me too—I love you, too, Nathaniel," sailed out of her mouth. Her other hand flew up to cover her lips. What had she just said? Words she swore she'd never repeat to a man other than Samuel.

Nathaniel found her hand and kissed her fingertips. "Gut, we can announce our plans tomorrow on nonpreaching Sunday. We'll tell your daughter, your mamm, and Isaac."

"Hold on. I didn't say I'd marry you."

His grin widened. "But you haven't said no, either."

"Holly won't be happy."

"Why not?" Nathaniel stroked Esther's cheek with tenderness. "She can't expect her father to come back from the grave any more than I expect my former wife to return." He leaned down and gave her a brief kiss.

She pined for more, to be enwrapped in his powerful arms. But she stepped back a few feet.

"Nathaniel, you and I need to talk. I'm a master at sweeping the dust under the carpet. But not this time."

CHAPTER THIRTY-THREE

"I've come to a monumental decision," I told Beth as I opened my laptop. Dressed in my slacks—after battling the zipper—and a turtleneck, I perched on the love seat in her living room while she sat on the carpeted floor mending a small rag rug, looping stitches over unraveled threads.

Beth pushed the needle through the thick fabric and gave it a tug. "I hope this means you'll be sticking around."

Missy lay against Beth's leg, the dog's ribs further expanded with her litter of pups. I reached out to stroke Missy's belly and felt movement, making me want to own a puppy. Or to feel a child growing within me? No, too late, I told myself. Give up on that fantasy.

I opened my laptop and logged in. "I'm not leaving until I solve the riddle of Mommy Anna's poor health. I'm baffled the family hasn't made her physical and mental welfare their main concern. I watched her bumbling around the kitchen today, getting out egg after egg, but no one's mentioned her memory lapses."

"They've tried their best, taking her to physicians and using home remedies. Isaac let me escort Anna to my naturopathic doctor, who tested her for everything she could think of, including Lyme disease. But each lab result returned negative." She punched her needle into a pincushion—a miniature stuffed quilt. "I wish I could give you better news."

"So Uncle Isaac will drag Mommy Anna across the country where she'll die in pain or wander off and get lost?"

"Maybe the fresh air and altitude will agree with her." I figured Beth's words were meant as encouragement, but her gaze remained downcast.

"Surely you've noticed my grandmother's memory is coming unglued," I said.

"Yes, it's muddled, and yes, I'll miss her terribly. I've been keeping my distance to give you and your mother more time, but I usually visit Anna every day."

"Is there no way to stop her from leaving?" I asked. "Besides the stress of the trip, in a new environment she'll be disoriented and more likely to fall. I'll bet there isn't a decent hospital in the area if she breaks a hip."

"We don't know that." Her smooth face gave the impression of serenity, but she fumbled with a needle, tangling the thread. "Montana isn't a third-world nation," she said.

"True." I scanned my messages. Ever since we'd been here, I'd forgotten to keep tabs on the stock market, my usual ritual.

"Any news from home?" Beth asked.

"Nope. A dozen spam and two emails from Larry, a guy I know. He wants me to come home right away or says he'll jump on the next plane and visit me here."

"Sounds serious." Beth sat taller. With her blonde hair and elegant posture, she was a beautiful woman. Unlike Mom, who didn't wear makeup and never changed her hairdo. Although, when I thought about it, Mom fit right in around here. And her skin was naturally smooth.

"Has he popped the question?" Beth asked.

"No, no—we've never even been out on an official date. I'm surprised by his persistence. My guess is Larry's chasing after me because I'm so far away."

"Don't discount yourself, Holly. I wager many a man would find you irresistible."

I wondered: Was I still pretty, or had I turned bland? Today, I was wearing makeup, but might feel more comfortable with a freshly scrubbed face, clad in the Amish dress and apron. Before I'd left the house, I told Mommy Anna I'd help her wash them and my jeans.

I crossed my ankles. "Larry really is a nice, supportive guy, but the last thing I need is another distraction. Which reminds me, I should call Hertz. I can pick up another car, but I'm too nervous to get behind the wheel after my accident. I never thought I'd be afraid to drive." I longed for the slowpoke pace of a buggy ride. "Here's a thought: Larry could rent a car and chauffer me around."

"My Zach and I can do that. Just say the word."

"After waiting for me to get cleaned up and then drive me over here, Zach is probably sick of the sight of me."

"No, he's not." Beth tickled Missy behind her ears and the dog closed her eyes. "I shouldn't be telling you this, but I think my son's sweet on you."

Had I heard her right? I glanced up from my computer screen and tried to catch her expression, but saw only her profile as she rethreaded her needle.

"He was a lifesaver with the cow," I said. "And then the tow-truck driver. No wisecracks or lectures about my carelessness, which I certainly deserved." Perhaps as a veterinarian Zach was trained to encourage distressed pet owners, not to mention local farmers, who depended on their livestock to plow fields and feed families. Or maybe Zach was born with a naturally calm temperament like his mother's. Not such a bad trait.

As always, when I suspected a man was interested in me—not that I thought Zach found me dazzling—I was both flattered and alarmed. Head for the hills, I'd think. He'll lie and cheat on me like my former fiancé. Or worse, he'll disappear like my father. Even though Dad adored Mom and would have loved me, he'd left us stranded. Illogical childish thinking, I knew—because he didn't choose to die. But deep inside an undercurrent of loss saturated my veins.

"I doubt Zach was being anything more than kind to my mother and me," I said. Now was my chance to do a little sleuthing of my own. "I wonder how he's managed to stay single for so long. He's successful and outgoing." On the outside, I reminded myself. Who lived inside that handsome exterior?

"People could wonder the same thing about you. You're a beautiful young woman."

"Ugh, I'm hardly young."

"Then finding a husband should be a top priority, if you'll forgive me for being so forward."

"Maybe I don't want a husband." I forced a chuckle to hide my falsehood, because I did want a soul mate, a man I could trust.

"Most women wish to get married," she said. "It sure is nice having my Roger around again. He got home last night, but is off running errands. I think you'll like him. How about joining us for dinner tonight?"

"Okay, thanks, I'd like to meet him, but need to check with Mommy Anna first." My hunch was Beth's meal would include Zach at the table. Was she playing matchmaker? I should be flattered, but a feeling of apprehension grabbed hold of me. Zach couldn't possibly be interested.

"Today I want to focus on my grandma's health." I got on Google and entered her symptoms. I came across several conditions and diseases I'd never heard of before. "Do you know if she's seen an endocrinologist?"

Beth stabbed the needle back into the pincushion. "I don't think so. I should warn you, at this point Anna may refuse to go to another doctor. And Isaac may forbid it."

"He already has, but I'm not going to let him stop me from helping Mommy Anna. If the endocrinologist idea comes up empty, I could escort her to Montana and get a chance to meet my other uncles. I hear they'll need a schoolteacher."

"Who should be Amish."

"So I hear. Would my being baptized Amish be so terrible?" I'd been mulling the radical idea over in my mind—like picking up an agate at the beach and slipping it in my pocket, fingering its smoothness. "Aren't your Mennonite beliefs almost the same?"

"In many ways, yes. In fact, my grandparents on my mother's side were Amish, but they switched to the Mennonite church for a long list of reasons. As my parents recalled the story, the uproar nearly fractured our family."

"Like mine. Thanks to my mother." I was speaking boldly, so why not continue? "What is it about you and Mom? You carry an obvious grudge against each other."

Beth tossed her pincushion on the coffee table, but it skidded off, plopping on the floor. "When we were young, I didn't make it easy for your mother to like me." She folded the rag rug in half and reached for the pincushion. "I had a miserable crush on your father and Esther didn't appreciate my attentions one bit. I interpreted her leaving as a ploy to keep Samuel and me apart."

I pictured striking and gregarious Beth as a young teen enticing my father away from Mom. "You were in love with Dad?" I felt like the cow I hit on the road.

"Puppy love is more like it. Infatuation." She set the pincushion on the coffee table. "In college, I met Roger, my perfect match, and married him. I wasn't meant to lead the Amish life. Not that I don't love and respect my Amish friends and relatives dearly." She stroked Missy's throat. "When Esther and Samuel ran off, and then Anna's husband, Levi, died, Anna grew so distraught she could barely function."

Beth got to her feet and sat on the easy chair, her elbows resting on her knees. "When Anna finally heard from Esther and obtained her mailing address, she begged your mother to come home. And Samuel's father, Jeremiah, also wrote, warning Samuel he'd lose his conscientious objector draft exemption unless he returned right away or went to live in another Amish farming community."

"What do you mean?"

"I assumed you knew. He would be drafted into the Vietnam War."

"My dad could have been exempt if he'd stayed here?" I envisioned his faceless body among the throng of over fifty thousand American soldiers killed in Vietnam. "He was missing in action," I said, although she must already know.

"Yes, MIA. His body never recovered, finally pronounced dead."

The uncertainty of Dad's death still clawed at my heart. "Why would he have been exempt?"

"He was a pacifist, instructed from childhood to turn the other cheek—to never retaliate, as are all Amish and most Mennonites. In the fifties, Congress passed laws exempting Amish and other conscientious objectors from active duty due to their religious beliefs, but required them to perform civilian work contributing to the country's health and safety for two consecutive years, such as working in hospitals. Then—I think in 1969—Amishmen were allowed to perform farm labor instead of other duties."

"Mom never told me." My hands balled into fists, my fingernails jabbing into my palms. "It's her fault he died. She made him leave this safe haven and live in San Francisco."

"That's how I saw it. Your grandfather's and then Samuel's death, and Anna's despair spurred my anger." She unclipped her hair; it drooped forward. "I thought I was past my resentment and was surprised what came surging to the surface when I saw Esther the other night. I was being judgmental."

"I don't blame you. I'm relieved Mommy Anna let us in the house. But she welcomed us."

"Your mother didn't mean to intentionally hurt anyone. She was so young."

"And selfish." The reality of Mom's transgressions broiled in my mind like a witch's caldron. "She still is. For instance, she came on to Nathaniel the moment she saw I might have a connection with him."

The corners of Beth's mouth curved up. "Nathaniel's a good man, but he's too old for you. Are you sure he isn't more like a father figure?"

"A surrogate dad?" Was I that desperate? "You could be right." My throat tightened around my words. Daddy never held me in his arms. When would the pain of not knowing him fade away? I'd asked God to lift my sorrow, but the void lingered like a black hole.

I felt stinging at the backs of my eyes. "That doesn't change the facts," I said, trying to compose myself. "My mother lied to me. Did you know she told me Mommy Anna was dead? I have every right to hold my mother accountable."

"Has she asked for forgiveness?"

"Last week I didn't know I had anything to forgive."

Beth set the hair clip aside, tugged her flaxen strands back, and braided them. "Sorry if I sound preachy, but withholding mercy is a sin. Truthfully, even if she hadn't asked you, we are admonished by God to forgive others as he forgives us."

I knew she was right, but my outrage took on an invigorating life of its own. Our pastor at church had spoken of unforgiveness: a chain around our necks holding us down, anchoring us to the past, and keeping us from fulfilling God's commandment to love one another.

"Mom told me my grandmother passed away before I was born and that all our relatives moved to places unknown. Can you imagine anything so cruel?"

"I'm sorry, Holly." Beth's features turned somber. Missy gazed up at her as if she could understand her mistress's distress.

"I should mention, I wrote Esther," Beth said. "In hindsight, I shouldn't have, knowing how she disliked me. But I stuck my nose where it didn't belong and my lack of compassion probably made matters worse." She reached over her shoulder and tugged her braid. "I wrote again after Samuel's death and heard you were born, offering my condolences and also congratulations, and mentioning that since she'd turned her back on the Ordnung and her Amish heritage, she might as well accept the army's death benefits offered to widows. She was living Englisch. Why not take advantage of the army's help raising you?"

"Are you talking about money?" My voice squawked like a parakeet's.

"Yes. I think ten thousand dollars."

"And she refused it?"

"The Ordnung forbids Amish from buying or accepting insurance benefits."

"But she wasn't living Amish." Incredulity rose in my throat like bile.

"I assume Esther was doing what she thought was right. I'm sure your parents' bishop would have agreed. Anna, too."

The words *all Mom's fault!* screamed through my brain.

"When I was a kid, we were dirt poor. Growing up, I wore frumpy dresses Mom sewed for me. Worse than hand-me-downs. When old enough, I took the bus to the Goodwill and found used clothing I liked ten times more."

Beth sat forward, clasped her hands. "I was wrong to bring up this subject. I should learn to keep my mouth shut."

"I'm glad you told me. I deserve to know the truth. She deprived us of what was rightfully ours." I planned to confront Mom on her deceitfulness, but didn't want Beth feeling guilt-ridden.

Missy let out a yawning whine as she got to her feet and laid her muzzle on Beth's knee.

Then it occurred to me Beth might be mistaken. As much as I liked her, she could be unreliable for all I knew. How old was she when Mom and Dad left? Could I count on a young teen's recollections? After all, Beth had romantic inclinations toward my father. Had her deep-seated animosity for Mom sprouted into a thorny bramble, piercing the truth?

Tomorrow was a nonpreaching Sunday. According to Mommy Anna and Greta, relatives and neighbors from all over the county would stop by to socialize. I'd invite my dad's parents, Beatrice and Jeremiah Fisher, too—ask them to come early before their own guests arrived. Possibly they knew more about my father's death and might verify why Mom refused the money.

CHAPTER THIRTY-FOUR

Nathaniel's marriage proposal and kiss blinked in Esther's mind like a firefly trapped in a jar as she swept the utility room and lined up Isaac's spare boots.

She was thankful Mamm hadn't inquired about her giddiness—or had she guessed? When Esther was a girl, Anna could practically read her thoughts. But each time Esther had confided in her mother, Mamm would tell Dat everything, then he'd tighten his grip, an incentive for Esther to gain distance from both parents.

Ach, at seven in the morning on the Lord's Day, why did Esther's mind keep returning to the past like a homing pigeon?

The piquant fragrances of cloves and cinnamon wafted into the utility room from the kitchen. Following her nose, Esther joined Mamm and Greta, who stood baking a plethora of pies and cookies for today's visitors. Never had she expected to act as her mother's kitchen helper again, but Esther settled into the routine, peeling apples and chopping nuts.

"Did ya know Holly spent the night at Beth's?" Mamm asked Esther.

"I saw her bed wasn't slept in." First a dinner invitation and then an overnight? What was Beth up to? "I hope Holly had the decency to let you know."

"Yah, Zach drove her by. They also stopped at the Fishers'." With Greta's assistance, Mamm set two pumpkin pies into the oven. "Seems Holly invited Beatrice and Jeremiah to come by today."

"*Himmel*, what for?"

"'Tis time we entertained them. A fine-gut idea, really." Mamm's elbow playfully tapped Esther's. "I'd better make sure the house is lookin' just right before Beatrice arrives."

Esther imagined Beatrice's disapproving eyes surveying Anna's home, tainted by Esther's presence. She hoped the house would be jam-packed with sisters-in-law, nieces and nephews, cousins she hadn't seen in many a year, and neighbors. She could avoid Beatrice altogether.

"I'll scrub the floor and *redd* up the kitchen when we're finished baking," Esther said. Nothing took her mind off its quandaries like hard work.

Greta left the room to usher her children upstairs, and the moment for Esther to explain Nathaniel's astonishing offer surfaced. Esther had wanted to mention Nathaniel's plan at dinner last night, but Isaac was so enthusiastic as he described Montana to Greta and his family, Esther hadn't wanted to burst his inflated bubble. Her brother wasn't about to change his mind concerning leaving Lancaster, anyway, nor were her other brothers planning to return. With the help of neighbors, their wives and children would pack up and follow before the end of November.

"In Rexford, the bishop doesn't stand for the frivolous conveniences that are tearing this county in half," Isaac had stated over dinner. "No squabbling over cell phones, battery-run laptop computers, or hay balers." The brothers would refurbish several barns and houses, removing the electrical wiring and reroofing. Esther knew better than to comment.

Standing at the stove, Mamm cracked the oven door and stole a glance. "I bet Beatrice can't bake a better pumpkin pie."

"'Tis bound to be *appeditlich*"—delicious.

"Ich bedank mich." Mamm's mouth stretched into a grin. "Looks like the apple crisp is near done. I should have asked Holly to bring along vanilla ice cream when she comes home."

"That would surprise Beatrice." But Esther couldn't imagine Beatrice's complimenting her mamm. "The Fishers might not show up, what with family and friends stopping by their house today." Esther hoped upon hope they wouldn't.

"Their son Matthew and his wife can do the entertainin'. It'll all work out, you'll see."

Esther remembered the wires running into Jeremiah's barn. "Seems Jeremiah's son and his partner have a small business, separate from the barn and house," she told Mamm. "They build miniature rocking chairs and dollhouses for Englisch children. They might have an electric freezer in their shop, out of their bishop's eyesight, and a stockpile of ice cream."

"Yah, I heard tell the Fishers are a right successful family, not that they brag about it or nothin'. But word gets out."

"As is Nathaniel. Successful, that is."

"True, and a gut humble man if ever there was one."

"He told me something important yesterday." She certainly wouldn't reveal their declaration of love for each other. It was the Plain way to keep courting a secret.

Esther still couldn't imagine herself remaining here even though Dori had promised to visit and insisted Esther would maintain control over the Amish Shoppe. "Jim built a website so customers can order via the Internet from all over the world," Dori had reported on the phone last night.

Mamm braced herself against the counter.

"Are ya feeling dizzy again?" Esther patted the hickory rocker in the corner near the fireplace. "Have a seat and put your feet up."

"No time for dallying. Not with company comin'. I'm thinkin' we'll have a full house." She wiped her hands on her apron. "What's that you're tryin' to tell me?"

Esther grabbed a lungful of air. "Yesterday, Nathaniel swore to me that you, Holly, and I may continue living here for as long as we choose. The rest of our lives, if we like."

Mamm's lips parted. Her hand raised to cover her mouth.

"Did ya hear me?" Esther asked. "He and Isaac finally settled the details. Nathaniel purchased our farmland, but the carriage house, horse stable, and barn remains in your name until you don't want it." And in Esther's name too, but she wouldn't mention that fact yet.

"You're not teasing me, Essie?"

Esther shook her head.

"That Nathaniel would be so kind. I don't know what to make of it."

"You could stay here, Mamm. You wouldn't have to move to Montana."

"Live in this very house?" She massaged the small of her back. "An *alt maedel*—by myself?"

"What if I told you I might stick around?"

"Ya don't mean it." Her eyes searched Esther's.

"I'm considering it with all my heart." Could she and her mamm coexist once Holly returned to Seattle? So many unanswered questions.

"Then I'm between a rock and a hard place. Don't know what to say." Mamm pulled her Kapp strings loose. "I 'spose I could follow the rest of the family in the spring." She sank into the rocking chair. "I'll pray long and hard on it." She closed her eyes and set the chair in motion with her feet.

While Mamm rested, Esther scrubbed the counters and stove top. She brought out dishes, cups, and glasses from the cupboard, and brewed coffee. In what seemed like minutes, she heard the first buggy arrive, then several more, transporting her sisters-in-law and their children. Entering through the back door, they carried baskets of food emitting the tantalizing redolence of peach cobbler, whoopie pies, and peanut butter cookies. Several youngsters woke Mamm with hugs and kisses on her cheeks. She gathered them into her arms. The smaller children clambered onto her lap, prattling in Deitsch. Esther found herself understanding most of their conversations. And wishing she had grandchildren of her own.

Esther's sisters-in-law reintroduced themselves to Esther, whose brain was so addled she'd forgotten two of their names. Except for Mary Ann, the lanky brunette with a parrot-like nose.

"It wonders me to see you here," Mary Ann said, giving Esther a rigorous looking over. "I thought you'd have hightailed it back to your fancy city life by now."

"Yes, I'm still here." Esther forced a smile.

A sandy-haired woman approached Esther. "Remember me? I'm Francine."

"Yes, hello." Esther was glad to see her pretty face.

Francine set her wiggling toddlers on the floor. "And this here is Martha and Julie."

"Nice ta see ya." Esther recalled Martha's golden hair and petite frame, and Julie's plump cheeks and rotund girth.

Several Plain-dressed people Esther's age or older flocked into the house. Each gave her a smile. "Must be neighbors or distant relatives," she said. "They look familiar."

"I bet ya got one hundred cousins in these parts, for sure," Julie said, her hands resting on her belly. "Plus folks you knew as a child."

"All wondering what became of you." Mary Ann aimed her index finger at Esther. "You're lucky you were never baptized, then put under *die Meiding*."

"I agree." Esther was determined to squiggle out of Mary Ann's snare. "May I serve you Kaffi? I brewed a fresh pot."

"I'd rather drink lemonade," Mary Ann said. "I can help myself."

As Esther cut pie and offered cookies to the children, Isaac spoke to his older nephews, in their late teens but not yet wed—she could tell by their cleanly shaven chins. The young men agreed to direct buggy traffic and bring the horses into the barn for water and feed. The boys seemed honored to be given the responsibility, unlike most teenagers Esther knew in Seattle. Her neighbors' sons were good kids, but instead of attending church and appreciating family time on Sundays, their parents whisked them off to soccer practice, then coerced them into doing massive piles of homework, as she had done with Holly. In high school, Holly had been studious, but never settled on a passion, other than hours on the phone with her girlfriends. In college, she'd earned a BA from the School of Business at the University of Washington, learning the skills Esther figured she'd picked up on her own in what Dori called the school of hard knocks.

Holly sashayed into the kitchen wearing a calf-length skirt she must have borrowed from Beth and a sweater vest over a collared shirt. Esther could tell by Holly's demeanor—her movements jerky and brows lowered—she was *gretzich*. Cranky.

Upstairs last night, Esther had noticed Nathaniel's daughters' Amish dress and apron, laundered and ironed, hanging in Holly's room, where Mamm had slept until recently. A heart-shaped prayer cap lay like a white dove on the dresser. Had Mamm intentionally left the door open hoping to entice Esther to enter?

In fact, Esther had been tempted to shed her Englisch clothes and try on the dress, apron, and Kapp. A test run, she'd thought, to see how she felt and looked. But she'd resisted.

"Anna, hello." Beth followed Holly into the kitchen, hurried over to Esther's mamm, and kissed her cheek.

"Ach, 'tis gut ta see ya, Beth," Mamm said, making Esther wince. Beth wore her hair fashioned into a French roll, a calf-length small-floral-print dress, and no watch or jewelry other than her wedding band—Esther guessed to ingratiate herself with Mamm and her friends.

Esther's sisters-in-law gathered round to chat with Holly and Beth, hugging them both.

"Glad you're still here," Martha said to Holly. "How ya doin', Beth?"

"Just fine, thank you."

Esther assumed Beth's stature in the community soared because she was Zach's mother and Mamm's dear friend. Mamm had mentioned Beth was often invited to work and quilting frolics. Her fingers were nimble, according to Mamm. No doubt more skilled than Esther's.

She heard tromping up the back steps and through the utility room, and saw a man wearing black trousers with a black vest over a white shirt, and a wide-brimmed hat. With an air of dignity and authority, he scanned the kitchen until his gaze latched onto Esther. He walked toward her with a stilted gait, as if one leg or hip had been injured in the past. As he neared Esther, the women, even Mary Ann, who stood almost as tall as he did, lowered their gaze, stopped their chatter, and receded to the perimeter of the room.

"Are ya Anna's daughter?" the man asked Esther, his voice gravelly.

Now what? "Yes, I'm Esther Fisher." She studied his somewhat familiar-looking face, a latticework of fine lines above a graying untrimmed beard hanging near to his waist.

"Hello, I'm Bishop Troyer." He removed his hat, held it at his side.

"*Willkumm*, Bishop." Isaac moved over to them and took the bishop's hat. "Esther, do ya remember Bishop Benjamin Troyer from when we were kids? Well, I suppose he wasn't a bishop when you left, 'tis been so many years."

Always a reminder of her dicey past. If she stayed here, she would be a marked woman, a target of scandal, no way around it.

As she recalled, Benjamin Troyer had been ten or twelve years her senior and recently married when she and Samuel left.

"Nice to see you again." She laced her fingers together, trying to remember if it were proper for a wanton woman to shake a bishop's hand. The Ordnung carried with it countless rules, but according to Mamm, many had been modified.

Bishop Troyer's shaved upper lip barely moved when he spoke. "What brought ya back home?" he asked Esther.

She had no clear-cut answer to give him. No logical defense. "My daughter, Holly, wanted to meet my mother," she said, but shame smacked her like a slap on the face. "No, Bishop, that's not true. Fact is, Mamm begged me to come see her."

"And about time ya did," Isaac said. "Just when we're leavin'." He stepped to the back door to hang up the bishop's hat and greet arriving guests.

The bishop moved closer to Esther and said, "'Tis never too late to return to the fold." His piercing gaze reminded her of Dat when he'd caught her barefooted and sunning herself on a summer's day instead of weeding the garden.

"In the book of Luke, ya know the story of the shepherd with one hundred sheep?" the bishop said to her as if the room had emptied, when in fact another family was standing only feet away selecting cookies. "He leaves them to go lookin' for the one lamb that wanders from the fold." The bishop briefly placed a hand on Esther's shoulder and his features softened. "There will be great rejoicing should ya return," he said.

She was so gratified by his statement, she couldn't stop her eyes from glazing over with a veneer of moisture. The fact that the Almighty would leave his flock to come looking for one lost lamb filled her with wonder.

The words to the hymn "Great Is Thy Faithfulness" threaded their way through her inner ear. She'd sung the hymn many times at church, but the lyrics hit her anew: "Thou changest not, Thy compassions they fail not; As Thou hast been Thou forever wilt be."

Then uncertainty shadowed the room, dimming her sight. Why would God give a nickel for a woman who'd abandoned her parents and brothers, and repeatedly lied to her daughter? Nattering anxieties crisscrossed Esther's mind. Was Bishop Troyer using a biblical parable to manipulate her? Had Mamm or Isaac told him about Esther and engineered this meeting? Had Nathaniel already asked the bishop's permission to marry her and inquired about her getting baptized? Had the bishop refused?

Well, she wouldn't ask with people milling nearby. Bishop Troyer tipped his head at several and Esther said, "May I fetch you something to eat and drink?"

He patted his flat stomach. Judging from his lean frame, Esther assumed he was a farmer. "Sounds gut," he said.

Mary Ann strutted up next to him balancing a plate heaped with food. "Bishop, I brought ya your favorite cookies and a nice wedge of pumpkin pie with extra whipped cream."

Taking the plate from her, he said, "What will I do without you?"

"Well, ya won't be able to depend on Esther, that's for sure."

Esther bet Mary Ann wished she'd married a man chosen by God, which would have given her more status. Esther imagined her poor sisters-in-law and her brothers living in Montana with this prickly woman. Yet she knew she had no right to be indignant. She'd treated the family shabbily and deserved any verbal darts hurled her way.

"I'll be right back with Kaffi for ya, Bishop," Mary Ann said. "Just the way ya like it."

Esther glanced around the room she'd grown up in. Where was Nathaniel? Surely he wouldn't miss visiting Mamm unless he were avoiding Esther. She wouldn't blame him, but her heart would surely be broken. She'd awakened this morning contemplating marrying Nathaniel and living together. First thing, should they wed, she'd remove most traces of his former wife. No, she had no right being jealous or acting spiteful toward a woman she'd never even met. She recalled her precious photo of Samuel. She'd give it to Holly; that's what she'd do.

"*Wie geht's*, Jeremiah," the bishop said as Samuel's father entered the house dressed in his Sunday best. Beatrice's hands impelled the small of her husband's back until she gained space to squeeze past him.

"Gut ta see ya, Bishop Troyer," she said before Jeremiah could get out a word.

Esther felt like bolting into the front room, but Jeremiah and Beatrice had already spotted her. Beatrice's features grew sharp and her face white, like her hair was fastened too tightly under her prayer cap.

Esther sensed a change in her breathing, as if standing at a high altitude—atop Mount Everest—the air too thin.

"Welcome," she managed to say, glad the bishop was standing close by to act as a buffer. She hoped Beatrice wouldn't mention Esther and Holly's early morning visit or how their dog, Wolfie, had pegged them as intruders.

Holly ambled over to them, and hugged Jeremiah and Beatrice. Jeremiah clasped her in his arms, but Beatrice's hands hung at her sides.

Holly turned to the bishop and shook the man's large hand. "Hi there, I'm Esther's daughter," Holly said. "Jeremiah and Beatrice Fisher's granddaughter."

"This is Bishop Troyer," Esther said, wishing she'd informed Holly about his stature in the community.

"Hi there," Holly said, as if he were any old neighbor. "Do you know my grandparents, the Fishers?"

"Yes, my whole life. And they lived in my district before we split."

Holly turned to Jeremiah and Beatrice. "Thank you both for coming. There's so much I want to ask you. Please stick around so we can talk. Okay?"

"What's so all-fired important?" Beatrice glanced at Esther with a look of disdain, then her gaze drilled into Holly.

"I want to hear the whole story." Holly raised her volume to include anyone in earshot. "How and why my father, Samuel Fisher, left home and got drafted. Was my dad really a pacifist? A bona fide conscientious objector?"

"Yah, 'tis true of all of us," said the bishop. "Most Mennonites, too."

Was he referring to Beth? Esther wondered. Beth was turning Holly against her own mother out of spite, the epitome of aggression as far as Esther was concerned.

"I recently learned my mother refused money provided by the military to widows upon their husbands' death." Holly glared at Esther, who felt the blood draining from her face. She would have taken the same course of action again, as she'd been taught by her parents and the Ordnung, that relying on insurance was not relying on God and the community. Not that she had much community in Seattle—her own fault for not joining a small group at church or a Bible study. And she'd paid into unemployment, workers' compensation, and Social Security, benefits she never planned to collect, on principle.

"Holly, let's discuss our personal affairs at another time," Esther said.

Holly narrowed her eyes, furrowing her brows. "I'm not letting you snake out of this conversation, Mother. I'll never forgive you for making me grow up poor because you enjoyed being miserable."

"Ya wouldn't have needed to worry about money if you'd lived here," Isaac said. "The People would have cared for you."

"They would?" Holly said.

"Yah, 'tis true," the bishop said.

"We would have taken you in," Jeremiah said.

Beatrice crossed her arms. Esther feared what might spew past her teeth. She hoped Beatrice was clueless about the lump sum or monthly benefits the army wanted to give Esther—and still might, for all she knew.

She placed her hand on Holly's forearm. "I'd like the chance to explain. In private."

Holly yanked out of her grasp. "I've already waited a lifetime for your phony explanations."

"Ain't no secret she bewitched our son away," Beatrice said. "Esther claims they got married, but I have my doubts."

Assailed by memories of filling out Holly's birth certificate at the hospital—Father: Samuel Fisher, deceased—Esther felt ready to explode. "We got legally married in our friends' small church." Here Esther was standing before a bishop. What must he think of her? She'd have some explaining to do.

"Mom, why wouldn't you accept the money owed to you by the army?" Holly's disruptive voice drew the attention of guests throughout the house, who were wandering into the brimming kitchen. "You made me live like a pauper!"

A combination of anger and regret flooded Esther as she looked upon her daughter's crimson cheeks and white mouth; she was acting like a spoiled child on the verge of a tantrum. Esther felt like reprimanding her, but she locked her knees and held herself still, refusing to put on a show for Beatrice.

"Come on, Holly, that's not true." Esther tried to defuse the commotion by speaking in monotone. "All over the world people are starving and suffering. You've always had food and shelter, and a mother looking after you."

"But no father. I would have given up everything for a dad."

Over Holly's shoulder, Esther saw men, women, and children gawking at them. Friendly banter snuffed and coffee growing cold, a density as impermeable as granite enclosed the room like the walls were caving in. Mamm, hunched in the rocker, worked her lips together. Isaac lowered his chin, his mouth drawn back. Martha's little girl hid behind her mother's skirt. Mary Ann's hands clamped her hips.

Holly spun around and said, "I'm looking for the truth about my father. Did any of you know him?" Several bobbed their heads with what looked to be reluctance.

"He was younger than I was," Bishop Troyer said. "But I remember him well." He probably knew every detail of Esther's departure and agreed with Isaac and Beatrice's assessment: Esther was the crummiest daughter in the world. She wished she could vanish into the wooden floor, melt right into it like a puddle of warm wax. Then she felt a hand on her shoulder.

Nathaniel.

CHAPTER THIRTY-FIVE

The room's temperature spiked as relatives and neighbors drifted closer like a rising tide. I glanced around the crowded kitchen and noticed Nathaniel and Zach had arrived. They were gaping at me, but I didn't care. Neither man knew what it was like growing up in Mom's spiderweb of deceit.

I writhed internally as a lifetime of pent-up emotions and frustrations coiled together, urging me to strike out. Until recently I'd felt sorry for my mother, the lonely widow stuck raising her child on a minimal income. But no longer. I couldn't believe anything she said.

"There's much you don't know about our ways," Bishop Troyer said to me.

He must be a real live bishop by the amount of respect everyone showed him. Even feisty Beatrice, who made Mom look like a wimp. Well, my mother was a wimp. Honesty required backbone and she'd proven herself to be spineless, or she would have told me the truth and returned to face Mommy Anna, her brothers, and Dad's parents decades ago.

Isaac stepped to the bishop's side, the two of them like a castle wall.

But I wouldn't be thwarted.

I folded my arms across my chest. "Uncle Isaac, you haven't forgotten Mom deserted your parents, didn't return for your father's funeral, or set foot in this house, have you?"

He tugged his untrimmed beard. "Not forgotten, no. But I've forgiven her."

"How could you? I never will."

"*Du bischt letz*—you're wrong," the bishop told me.

"Me? What have I done?"

"'Tis no way around it, God commands us to forgive as we ask for his forgiveness," Bishop Troyer said.

"That includes us." Jeremiah directed his words at his wife. "Tell me, Beatrice, that you've truly forgiven Esther," he said. "For the love of the Almighty and for the future of our people."

Beatrice seemed to age before my eyes, the way her features sagged and her shoulders slumped. "I thought I had, honest," she said, "until I saw Esther in our kitchen. It made me so mad I felt like—" Her hand flapped up to cover her mouth.

"Then 'tis time to repent," Bishop Troyer said. "To ask God to forgive you for your sin."

She licked her upper lip and stared at his feet, as though a heated discussion raged inside her head.

"Beatrice, did ya hear the bishop?" Jeremiah asked.

She looked up into her husband's face. "Then I'll have nothin' left of our Samuel," she said, her eyeballs veined and rimmed pink.

I felt my face twisting as tears brewed behind my eyes. I understood where she was coming from. She didn't even own a photo of her son. Had she kept a memento, perhaps childhood clothing, to remember him by? Or had my dad's younger brother, Matthew, worn them, a daily reminder of the son she'd lost?

Beatrice hesitated, then finally shuffled over to Mom, who shrank back against the refrigerator.

"Esther," Beatrice said. "*Es dutt mir leed*—I'm sorry, and I'm askin' ya, please forgive me."

A tear rolled down Mom's cheek. Her hand slid up to stop its descent. "I don't deserve it, Beatrice. Yours or anyone else's."

I felt like agreeing with her, but noticed Mommy Anna's grief-stricken face, her lips sucked in. My tirade had ignited the confrontation and ruined her get-together. On the other hand, this roomful of relatives and neighbors might answer the questions Mom had evaded.

The bishop's voice filled the room like a balm. "None of us deserves forgiveness," he said. "But God sacrificed his Son for our sins. The Lord died to cover them. We must not refuse his gift."

My memory scrolled in on itself. I replayed my life like rewinding a movie, the innumerous transgressions I'd committed without even living within the confines of the Ordnung. Yes, I attended church most Sunday mornings. In the safety of the sanctuary I praised God and sang hymns along with the congregation, but the rest of my week was a spiritual wasteland. I couldn't remember the last time I'd asked God for guidance and then listened for his answer. He wasn't my friend because I barely knew him.

The room lay swathed in silence. I glanced over to Beth, standing beside Mommy Anna's rocker. At supper the evening before, while Beth and her husband thanked our heavenly Father, I'd stared at my dinner plate, my mind raging with vengeful thoughts centering on my mother, when in fact I was as much a sinner as she was. I couldn't begin to recall half the sacrifices Mom had made for me. I'd shown her a pittance of gratitude.

Beatrice reached out her trembling arms to my mother. Mom flinched at Beatrice's touch like she'd received an electric shock. Then Mom stepped into Beatrice's embrace. The two women grasped onto each other, Beatrice sobbing on Mom's shoulder and Mom's face buried against Beatrice's.

"*Alles ist ganz gut*—all will be well," Jeremiah said to the bishop with exuberance. "At last, this feud has ended, praise the Lord."

"Yah, I promise." Beatrice removed her glasses, wiped her face with a Kleenex, and blew her nose. "No amount of fuming will bring our Samuel back."

She spoke to everyone, even the youngsters who'd followed their parents into the kitchen. "Before all of yous, and before God, I ask for forgiveness. I've been harboring bitterness and setting a bad example." She said to the bishop, "Ya want me to come in next Sunday and confess before the congregation?"

"Nee, you've repented, I can see that."

"Yah," she said, and sniffled. "For sure and for certain."

Jeremiah's arm encircled her waist and she leaned into him—I figured their show of affection in public was a rare occurrence.

As I watched Nathaniel offer Mom a cloth handkerchief to dry her eyes, the scene vaulted me back in time, listening to my pastor read from Proverbs, how God hates haughty eyes—a proud look. Over the last week, I'd sent Mom my iciest stares as if I were far superior. And what about Zach, who'd stopped by Beth's last night after supper to chat with his father? I'd exhibited contentiousness ever since meeting him. Had I even thanked him properly for giving up his busy morning to rescue Mom and me, and treat the wounded cow? Yet last night he'd offered me a tour of his veterinary clinic tomorrow. After my display of hostility just now, he'd probably changed his mind. I wouldn't blame him.

As I recalled, the proverb went on to say God hates those who stir up dissension among their brothers. What role had I played to smooth the turbulent waters between my mother and Uncle Isaac? Between Mom and Beth? Nothing. I was a wasp, itching for a fight. Was my anger obvious? Yes.

"Mom, it's my turn to apologize," I said, and every face rotated toward me.

"You have nothing to be sorry for." She dabbed under her eyes and stuck the handkerchief in her pocket. "I'm the one who did wrong, my dearest girl."

"I've been critical," I said. "I've treated you rottenly this whole trip." I'd embarrassed her in front of family, old acquaintances, and the bishop, but instead of chastising me, she hastened over like I was a girl who'd skinned her knee.

"None of that matters," she said.

"Yes, it does. I need to grow up."

She stood before me for a moment, worrying her lower lip. "Holly, can you ever forgive me?" Her voice came out a whimper. "I wouldn't blame you if you said no."

Despite my intentions, I felt conflicted, like vinegar and oil repelling each other. As much as I loved my mother, could I honestly forgive her deceitful behavior: hiding my dearest Mommy Anna, my aunts and uncles, not to mention the details of Dad's death? And the benefits owed to us by the military? Her money, but the cash could have helped pay for my education if nothing more. Not that money would bring Dad back.

Heckling voices infested my mind like relentless mosquitoes, reminding me I was the wronged party, the innocent fatherless girl raised by a two-faced mother. I felt myself wavering, as if balancing on a branch atop the lofty oak tree alongside the house. I recalled myself as a little girl, always feeling different, not good enough.

I looked at Beatrice, her head bent, and Jeremiah, his arm around her shoulder as if propping her up. If they could forgive Mom, so could I. But not on my own.

Please, Lord, help me, I prayed under my breath.

My words seemed captured at the bottom of my throat, but "Mom, I forgive you" came out my mouth, tasting sweeter than Mommy Anna's apple pie.

"You do? Truly?"

I nodded.

"Thank you, dearest daughter."

Seeing her joy, I felt thirty tons lighter, like a lead apron had been lifted from my shoulders. "Now tell me you forgive me, too," I said.

Her frame went rigid and she shook her head in slow motion.

A buzz of conversation cluttered the room. I scanned the kitchen and saw mom's sisters-in-law huddled together. Zach tipped his head to speak to Beth. Mommy Anna interlaced her hands, her thumbs tucked in.

"Mom?" I said. "This goes both ways. Do you hear me?"

She let out a dry, parched cough. "I feel funny—not worthy." She turned to the bishop and finally to Nathaniel, who nodded.

I could see from her cowering expression she wished we were alone. She finally looked right into my eyes with a fervor I'd never before witnessed.

"Yes, I accept your apology," she said. "May this be the first day of a new friendship."

"An honest-to-goodness friendship?" The transformation would require humongous changes on both our sides. "No more lies or even omitting the truth?"

"I promise. Nothing but the truth."

"This is fine and gut," Isaac said with exuberance. He arched his bushy brows. "We can move to Montana as a united family."

"Hold on there, Isaac," Mommy Anna said. With Zach and Beth's assistance, she got to her feet. "There's something I need ta tell ya." She held Beth's hand and Zach supported Mommy's elbow. "I've decided to stay put for the time being."

"Not go to Montana?" Isaac said. "Ya can't mean it."

"I'm as serious as can be." Mommy Anna patted her chest. "I finally have my Esther back—"

"So what? I don't hear her apologizing to ya." He was right; my mother owed Mommy Anna an apology. Could Mom ever make up for my grandmother's years of anguish?

His mouth set in a hard line, Isaac swung his shoulders around to face Nathaniel. "'Tis your doing, ain't so, Nathaniel King?"

"I have no need for this house," Nathaniel said, and stroked his beard. "I'm trying to be helpful."

"You have no right interfering in my family."

Mom positioned herself between the two men. "Please, Isaac, don't go blaming Nathaniel. He's been more than generous to give our mamm a roof over her head."

Isaac's fingers curled into fists. "And who's gonna' look after her? Not my Greta."

"I will," I said, gazing up into my uncle's glowering face, looming a foot higher than mine. "I've got nothing going for me at home. I'll stay right here."

Pack up and move to the other side of the country to live with the Amish? When had my radical decision taken shape and solidified?

Mommy Anna's eyes sparkled, capturing the rectangle of sunlight slanting through the window. Tears of sadness or joy? She was witnessing both the reuniting and the splitting up of her family. She might consider her illness the cause. In a way it was.

"It's not your fault," I told her, stepping to her side and taking her free hand.

Zach's gaze caught mine. We stared at each other and I felt a buzz of attraction. Where did that come from? I had to wonder if he often visited Mommy Anna, or had he arrived today specifically to see me?

Again, I found myself thinking about myself. I should concentrate on my grandma and her needs. I said, "Mommy Anna, I'm going to find out what's wrong with you and make you better if it's the last thing I do."

"Herbal remedies are what she needs," Beatrice said, edging away from her husband and seeming to regain her snarly temperament. "My cousin knows a man—"

"Hush," Jeremiah said, his voice gruff. "Prayer to the Almighty is what Anna needs."

"What's Anna got ta lose by consulting him? His tea, a recipe in his family for generations, is what cured my lumbago."

Bishop Troyer rubbed his eyes, his hand blocking half his face. Why wouldn't he speak up? Perhaps with Beatrice living in a different church district, he had less jurisdiction over her. I wanted him to take charge of the conversation, to put an end to Beatrice's advice. Or would an herbal potion help my grandma? I was desperate enough to look into it.

"We've enough problems without your interference," Isaac said to Beatrice, then moved in on me. "Holly, that includes you. Either move with us to Montana or go back to Seattle."

"No, I refuse to leave my grandma," I said. "And certainly not by herself." I'd need to jet back to Seattle to pack warm clothes for winter and other necessities, then return in a few days.

In the meantime, who would look after Mommy Anna in my absence? Not my mother. Because I'd forgiven Mom didn't mean I trusted her.

CHAPTER THIRTY-SIX

"Isaac, I'm staying here too," Esther said. She would not allow her brother, even a preacher, a man chosen by God, to intimidate her or Holly.

Isaac let out a guffaw. "I'm bettin' you'll both be gone in a month. 'Tis *narrich*. Crazy. No way three women can make it on their own." Several men in the room chuckled and nodded in agreement.

"I'll be taking care of planting the crops and milkin' the cows," Nathaniel said. He shot Esther a grin. "I'll leave the women the chicken coop, provide them with fresh milk, and look after their horse and buggy."

Holly folded her arms across her chest. "Mom, what about the Amish Shoppe?"

Esther couldn't blame her daughter for her doubts—like ravenous crows cawing in Holly's ears. How long would it take to rebuild the bridge between them? If ever.

"I spoke to Dori yesterday," Esther said, feeling as if she were on stage under the cone of a spotlight. "We have an arrangement worked out."

Dori had sounded ecstatic when Esther mentioned she'd met a man. "It's your turn, Esther," Dori had said. "Jim and I can handle everything at this end."

"I'll help Anna," Beth said, garnering everyone's attention. "After all these years, I know her as well as anyone. Zach will lend a hand too, won't you?"

"Sure." Zach smiled in Holly's direction. Were the two flirting with each other right in the middle of a family crisis? Esther felt like demanding his intentions, but feared Holly would ask Esther about Nathaniel, who was moving to her side like a benevolent companion.

Ach, no two ways about it, Esther did love Nathaniel.

Was Samuel watching Esther from heaven? Would he be disappointed or pleased? Surely he'd approve of a righteous man like Nathaniel King.

"None of yous got no business meddling in our family affairs," Isaac said, his voice booming.

"I'm Anna's daughter too." Esther tried to exude self-assurance when in fact she was trembling. "Like it or not, Isaac, I am family."

"Some daughter you've shown yourself to be," her sister-in-law Mary Ann said, her hands akimbo. "Beth's more a daughter to her than you are."

Beth funneled her words to Esther. "Have you told Holly and the bishop everything?" she said.

Esther didn't dare ask what Beth was referring to. Esther wished she'd spilled the whole can of beans when it came to Samuel's death and the army benefits, but she wasn't about to backtrack now.

"Mom, there's more you haven't told me?" Holly said.

Esther felt like an injured squirrel with buzzards circling overhead. Her hands covered her ears, then slid to the base of her throat.

"That's enough, everyone," Nathaniel said. "Leave Esther be."

"And I won't stand by listenin' to you squabble on the Lord's Day," Bishop Troyer said. "You must agree to let bygones be bygones."

"But I deserve honest answers," Holly said. Chin lifted, she strode over to Esther. "I have the right to know every detail."

"Show respect to your mother," Nathaniel said. "That goes for you, too, Isaac."

Esther was so filled with thankfulness she couldn't help herself from widening her mouth into a smile. Yes, she would marry him.

CHAPTER THIRTY-SEVEN

The Boeing 757 touched down on the Philadelphia International Airport tarmac with a bump and a skid. A rough landing, but nothing about the last couple of weeks had been as soft as the satin pillowcase I'd left behind in Seattle.

The bottle blonde in the next seat closed her book. About my age, she wore a plunging magenta V-neck sweater and a black above-the-knee skirt, giving the world a view of her sculpted legs.

She poked her toes into her high heels. "Are you here for work, on holiday, or headed home?" she asked me, the first words she'd spoken since we'd embarked after my layover in Chicago.

"I'm not really sure." Conflicting memories reverberated in my thoughts. I recalled my first night in Lancaster County, Mom and my staying with Beth, then Mom's hesitation to see Mommy Anna the next morning. I still didn't comprehend my mother's motives, why she'd left and never returned when she had two loving parents. Why she'd lied to me.

My fellow passenger shoved the paperback into her sack purse and ran a hand over her pantyhose, a contrast to my wrinkled slacks. "Sounds more intriguing than the book I'm reading." She must have detected trepidation in my voice.

"Sorry if I sounded snippy," I said. "It's been a long day." My retrospections reeled back to the blow-up in the kitchen, to Bishop Troyer's admonishing Beatrice to forgive Mom. The two women embracing each other. Their tears.

"My immediate plans are to visit relatives," I said, noticing I'd dribbled coffee down the front of my blouse—also wrinkled. I wouldn't mention where I was headed; I was too exhausted to answer questions. *Ferhoodled*, Mommy Anna would call me.

I'd been hesitant leaving my grandma for the few days I'd spent in Seattle gathering winter clothes and sending Mom her knitting supplies. "*Da Herr sei mit du*—the Lord be with you," Mommy Anna had said as I climbed into the passenger van headed for the airport several days ago. Mom stood at her side, their arms linked, a sight I never imagined witnessing. Perhaps it was a temporary truce to placate me.

Three days ago, part of me had been tickled to land in Seattle, but my hometown seemed too hectic and the air laden with exhaust fumes. A honking car in the alley woke me in the middle of the night, followed by a siren out on the main street. The next morning, while helping me box up my mother's yarn, needles, and patterns, Dori riddled me with questions about Mom, who'd revealed a pending marriage proposal from a widower. According to Dori, Mom wouldn't return to visit Seattle until late February, when snow blanketed Lancaster County.

A wagonload of uncertainties still lingered in the recesses of my mind, haunting me. Were mysteries hiding under Mommy Anna's rag rugs? What about Jeremiah's letters that never reached Seattle? If my Grandma Beatrice hadn't given them to Mommy Anna, why didn't she confess her lying to the bishop? I had to wonder if one of my grandmothers had her own secret shoebox full of letters just like Mom's. My major concern was: Could I be content living in a rural community populated with men wearing beards, suspenders, and straw hats, their attire mandated by church law? The saying "Clothes don't make a man" looped through my brain. Should I wear a dress and apron fastened together by straight pins? What did I know about country life, about keeping chickens and gathering eggs, not to mention harnessing a horse and driving a buggy?

The jet rolled to the terminal and the hatch opened. I glanced out the window and saw the sun hovering above the horizon. Almost dinnertime, but I hadn't eaten more than a mini bag of pretzels for eight hours.

"Hope your trip goes well," the woman said, giving her coifed hair a fluff.

"Thanks. You, too."

She shimmied her arms into her Chanel-style jacket matching her skirt, a suit I would have coveted if I were still working for Mel. I noticed she was wearing a diamond tennis bracelet, but no wedding band.

I stretched to my feet, clonking my head on the overhead bin, and checked my empty seat, making sure I hadn't forgotten any belongings. In truth, I'd left everything behind: neighbors I'd known my whole life, luxuries like TVs, dishwashers, central heating. And cars. I did a self-inventory. I was a thirty-seven-year-old over-the-hill has-been with zilch in the bank, no job, and no husband or children.

But I'd gained what I longed for most. A family.

Of sorts.

I followed the slow-moving passengers into the terminal, descended to baggage claim, and scanned the area awash with strangers. I searched for Beth, who'd agreed to pick me up and take me to Mommy Anna's. On the drive to the farm I planned to delve into conversation with her. I had an inkling she knew more about my mother's history and my father's death.

Or should I abandon the sketchy past? Let go and let God, a slogan I'd seen on car bumpers that might serve me well. If I was willing to allow a pilot—a complete stranger—to transport me across the country, why didn't I trust God to make all things perfect? Because he never had before.

Soon I'd get to see Mommy Anna again, but my future was like the fog the aircraft had muscled through back at Sea-Tac Airport. How did the pilot know which way to steer the jet?

Amidst the Philadelphia airport's hubbub I felt alone and glum. I decided to take a moment to pray, an uncustomary practice.

Eyes open, I began in my head: Dearest Lord, I'm sorry I haven't been checking in with you …

When I prayed, I often felt weak and powerless because I was giving up control to an entity I couldn't see or touch. Were my prayers like floating ribbons of dissolving smoke?

A blaring sound assaulted my eardrums, startling me, indicating luggage was being discharged onto the metal conveyer belt. I trailed the crowd to its perimeter and noticed Zach across the way. He waved and strode over to me. He wore a sports jacket over a collared shirt and slacks rather than his usual work clothes. He looked better than I'd remembered.

"Hello, stranger." He gave me a one-arm hug, reminding me of the jet's recent landing: awkward and clumsy. I didn't know how to respond. In truth, I'd daydreamed about Zach while I was gone, weighing the possibility of a future relationship.

I gazed up at his handsome features. Part of me wanted to hug him back, but I didn't trust my emotions. Did Zach and I share common ground, or were our paths destined to travel in opposite directions?

"Why are you here?" I said, not the cordial greeting he deserved. Sometimes I sounded as brusque as Grandma Beatrice. "I mean— hello, Zach. I was expecting Beth."

"Hope you don't mind. My mother gave me your flight number." He took my carry-on and slung the strap over his shoulder. "Good to see you," he said.

"Even after I ruined Mommy Anna's party?" I shuddered to think how abominably I'd acted. "I wouldn't blame everyone for wanting to be rid of me. I'm glad I had the foresight to apologize to the bishop."

Zach's eyes focused on my face so intently I wondered if he were the bearer of bad news, but then the corner of his mouth hinted of a smile. "I think you'll find," he said, "you've been forgiven." He turned and glanced at the parade of suitcases straggling past us on the carousel. I pointed at the bulky suitcase Dori had given me and said she didn't want back.

"Could you get that for me?" I asked.

"Would you please grab mine, too?" the svelte blonde who'd sat next to me said, giving Zach a winning smile, her lips glossy mauve. I hadn't paid her much attention until now and realized she was stunning: willowy, with a flawless face that was Miss America material.

"Sure." Zach dragged both suitcases off the carousel. "There you go," he told her.

"Thank you, kind sir." She winked at me, her lashes lavish enough for a Maybelline advertisement. "You said you were visiting family. Are you two related?"

"Good friends," Zach said.

"In that case." She handed him her business card. "If you're ever in Philly, give me a jingle."

"Okay. Thanks." He slipped the card into his breast pocket, then pulled up the handle of her suitcase. "Can you manage okay?"

"Sure, I don't work out five days a week for nothing. What's your name?"

"Zachary Fleming."

If they set up a date right in front of me I was going to scream. "Sorry, we need to be on our way," I told her. "We're expected somewhere." I extended my suitcase's handle and stepped between them. I was tempted to roll its wheels over her shoes' pointy toes.

"Perhaps another time," she said to Zach, her voice as creamy as Mommy Anna's caramel pudding.

Minutes later, Zach maneuvered my suitcase through the garage and stowed it in the back of his pickup. After he paid for parking, we headed to the outskirts of New Holland. My new home? Again, I relived my jangled nerves the night Mom and I first arrived. I felt just as nervous this evening, but in a different way.

"I wondered if you'd return," Zach said, "or if you'd prefer your real life in the big city."

"I don't know what's real, anymore." I fished my hand in my purse to make sure I had my wallet, cell phone, and keys. Not that I needed car keys anymore. "Sleeping in my comfy bed was a treat, as was using my hairdryer." I forced myself to settle into the pickup's bench seat. "Thank you for coming to get me," I said, remembering my manners. And because I was glad to see him, particularly after fending off that determined blonde.

"My pleasure," he said. "My assistant was in this afternoon and my answering service will call if an emergency arises." He brought out his cell phone to glance at the screen, and the blonde's business card fell to the floor. Zach ignored it—maybe for my benefit. Would he scramble to retrieve her telephone number later? I felt protective—and possessive.

I wouldn't mention my dinner date last night with Larry Haarberg, who'd hinted he'd come see me if I didn't return to Seattle on my own. "I thought about you the whole time you were gone," Larry had professed over chicken parmesan at his favorite Italian bistro. "Don't be surprised if I show up at your grandma's doorstep."

I hadn't kissed him good night or even hugged him. I could do a lot worse than Larry, I reminded myself, crossing my ankles. Our friendship might have developed into love, given time. But I could say the same about Zach. Unless he'd only picked me up as a favor to Beth.

"I received a tempting job offer while I was in Seattle," I told Zach. "My former boss offered me a new position. But I turned him down." The dumbest move of my life? "I told him I couldn't because I'd promised to take my grandmother to a quilting bee in a couple days, and he laughed out loud."

Zach glanced my way and chuckled. After witnessing my erratic behavior, he most likely wondered why anyone would hire me to work in the stock market.

"I'm all thumbs and nervous about going to this quilting frolic." I tightened my seat belt, then loosened it. "Are these fingers too old to learn new skills? Am I stuck a city gal for life?"

"You're too young to be stuck."

"I wish. Did you know I'm in my late thirties?" I held my breath—out of fear.

"Yes," he said. "About my age." He flipped on his radio to an oldies station, the volume down low.

"Growing old always looks better on men," I said.

"Hold on, neither of us is over the hill yet."

Amidst a caravan of cars and trucks, we drove past factories and urban sprawl. I relived Mom's and my first night here, learning Mom hadn't contacted Mommy Anna to announce our arrival, panic thrumming in my arteries as I jockeyed through traffic to Beth's home. I'd felt like Alice in Wonderland plummeting into a cavernous hole.

Zach angled us west, choosing back roads instead of the highway. The lowering coral-pink sun, suspended in the sky like a Chinese lantern, drew us to the horizon. The mellow scenery of rolling hills, farms, and pastureland unfolded ahead of us like a panoramic movie screen. I cracked the window and breathed in the rich essence of drying cornhusks. After an hour or so, I saw a horse and buggy

approaching from the opposite direction. My heart filled with elation. Yet I noticed I was gripping the door handle.

I detached my fingers and laid my hands in my lap, but found
myself fiddling with my purse.

Zach slowed us to a crawl when we passed a buggy, a red reflective
triangle on its rear. The driver waved and Zach raised a hand in return.

"Do you know him?" I asked.

"No, just being friendly."

"I like that people are welcoming and considerate here. In the
city, hand gestures are often shows of frustration, to put it nicely."

"For the most part folks are hospitable, although we get millions
of tourists each year. Some of them are rather impatient."

"Like me?"

Zach chuckled.

I initiated chitchat about the Amish Shoppe and its new website.
"Business is better than ever without Mom or me being there." I tried
to sound upbeat when in fact fatigue enveloped me. "Did I tell you
we have a real Amish buggy sitting out on the front porch? I used to
play in it as a child."

"Holly, it almost sounds like you haven't planted both feet here."

"No, I'm still undecided."

"Straddling the fence, as they say. Half in and half out of the
Plain life."

"My laptop is in my carry-on and my cell phone's in my purse. I
don't want to give them up."

"You won't have to unless you're planning to get baptized Amish.
You should check out our Mennonite church. Want to come with
me on Sunday?"

Zach's arms were relaxed, his fingers tapping the steering wheel to a tune by the Byrds, a group long since disbanded, barely audible on the oldies station—a song my Mom sometimes hummed. Had she and Dad sung it in San Francisco? I could only remember the opening line: "To everything, turn, turn ..."

"How about it?" he said. "My parents will be there."

"This Sunday? I'd better wait and see what my grandmother wants." I liked Bishop Troyer, but would I be comfortable reading the Bible in High German and forgoing Bible studies? Not that I was a member of a group now.

Zach kept his vigilant gaze on the road. "While you were gone, both our mothers took your grandmother to a top-notch endocrinologist, someone they think Anna liked."

"I hope you didn't mention it to Isaac." Was I starting down Mom's road of deception by omitting the truth?

"My mother thought you or your mom should fill him in," he said.

"Beth doesn't want to be in the middle of another family tussle?"

"I've got to give it to you, Holly, you know how to liven up a nonpreaching Sunday."

"You mean clear out my grandmother's house like a skunk?"

He smiled. "I've heard an Amish proverb. Goes something like: Swallowing your words before you say them is better than having to eat them afterward."

I pondered his words as we traveled Old Philadelphia Pike 340. The sunset diffused, graying the cab's interior. I glanced over to see Zach's eyes were tired, and I wondered if he was just weary of putting up with me.

Minutes later, Zach took a right onto North Hollander Road. "I think Jeremiah and Beatrice would have taken off anyway," he said. "They were expecting guests at their own home."

"As he left, Jeremiah asked me to walk out to their buggy with them," I said. "He took me aside and mentioned they'd received a letter from one of Dad's army buddies months after my father disappeared. According to this guy, Dad had insisted on giving up his seat on an evacuation helicopter to him—because the guy needed immediate medical attention." I choked up, couldn't speak. I felt like a helpless orphan.

I swallowed down the lump in my throat before it blocked off my air supply. "When the helicopter lifted off, Dad was still alive. After that, no one knows what happened."

"Which makes your father a hero in my eyes," Zach said, slowing the pickup.

"Guess you're right. I never pictured him as a hero. I wonder if there's any way to track down that old army buddy."

"I could help you."

I admired his strong profile. "Okay, that would be great, although I don't want to open old wounds for Mom. Not when she's finally moving on with her life."

"Nathaniel's a fine man." He glanced my way for an instant. "I'm thinking your father must have been too. I wish you could have met him."

"Yeah, me, too." I tried to sound blasé.

"But we all have a heavenly Father."

I don't know why Zach's words stung my very skin like he was ripping a Band-Aid off an unhealed wound. How dare he spout off platitudes, making light of the sorrow I carried with me every day?

Out of nowhere, I was mad enough to smack him.

"What would you know about growing up without a dad?" Indignation soured my voice. "You have a picture-perfect family, a great career, and the respect of everyone in the county."

"Hold on." He kept his gaze on the road, turned the radio off. "I've had my share of disappointments. My parents separated for three years after my younger brother died. And my fiancée dumped me. Twice. Then she married a guy I thought was my closest friend."

I felt like a heel. "Sorry, I didn't know."

"No way you would." His hand reached over to take mine, as if he were lifting a sparrow with a broken wing. I envisioned the injured soldier escaping on the helicopter. My father standing below as the chopper lifted off, its deafening blades beating the air.

Before leaving Seattle, I'd tucked Mom's photo of Dad in the side pocket of my suitcase. My mother had asked me to pack a couple woolen sweaters and several skeins of yarn, but had opted to leave the image behind on her bureau. Forever. But I couldn't bear to part with Dad's photograph.

Why did I lash out when Zach mentioned my having a heavenly Father? Did I hold a grudge against my dad? My whole life, I'd concentrated on the joys I'd missed: Daddy reading me bedtime stories, teaching me to ride a bike, admiring me at graduation. They say kids are resilient, but they're not; they learn to accommodate.

Now was the time to forgive Dad. He hadn't run out on me.

I turned my attention to Zach and felt a rush of warmth venturing up my arm and into my chest. He added a comforting pressure to my hand. My fingers tightened around his. Then he returned his hand to the steering wheel.

As familiar farms and cornfields bloomed into view, I thought about how often my first impressions were wrong. I was sure I wanted to be a big shot in the stock market. But if I'd been employed, I wouldn't have brought Mom here. If I'd delayed the trip a couple months, my grandma would have left Lancaster County, lived in a remote region of Montana, or passed to the next world. If it existed. My uncertainties lingered, but I was determined to overcome them.

"I don't deserve your kindness, considering the snooty way I've treated you," I told Zach. "After I found out I'd been lied to for so long, I didn't trust anyone, but I had no business taking my suspicions out on you."

"Understandable, and why I gave you space. Anyway, you weren't so bad. Rather cute and sassy. Beautiful, in fact. The longer I know you the more I'm intrigued."

"With me?" Now I was intrigued.

With New Holland in the distance, Mommy Anna's farmhouse came into sight. Gas lamps glowed in the windows, welcoming me.

"Your family is expecting you," he said, "but do you mind if we stop for a moment before I drop you off?"

"Is something wrong?" My head snapped around. "Is my grandmother worse? Did the cow die?"

"The cow's fine and Anna's the same—for now, anyway."

"Until I arrive?" Was he about to lecture me on proper etiquette in an Amish household? "I give you my word to be on my best behavior," I said.

"Nothing like that." He steered to the side of the road, put the transmission in park, and let the engine idle. "I want to finish our conversation."

An open buggy with a high-stepping mare rolled past us. A young man and woman sat with their heads tilted together.

"That's a courting buggy," Zach said.

"In other words, love is in the air?"

"Exactly. Next month many Amish couples will marry, some after a short, discreet courtship." Zach unclipped his safety belt. "Let's pretend we're in that buggy. Do you mind?" His right arm on the seatback, he scooted toward me. Feeling secure, I snuggled close to him.

He said, "I've wanted to do this since the first moment I saw you in my mother's living room." He bent his head and with a gentle hand guided my mouth to his. Our lips brushed, then softened with passion. Had I ever relished a kiss more?

No.

When we separated—I hated our embrace to end—we gazed into each other's faces, his eyes echoing the luminous evening sky.

A reality gelled in my heart and mind: Zach was a man I could love.

"Holly, would you be happy living here?" He stroked loose hairs away from my cheek and tucked them behind my ear.

"Forever?" What was Zach really saying? I was afraid to ask.

I pictured Mom's marrying Nathaniel and eventually moving to his farm. "While I was in Seattle I spent hours on Google looking up Mommy Anna's symptoms," I said. "I'm not a doctor, or even a rank amateur, but I may have stumbled upon her illness. At least narrowed the playing field to a couple of diseases that aren't life-threatening if properly treated."

Zach nodded. "I've been researching too. We could compare notes over dinner. Tomorrow night. At a restaurant. Somewhere private. Just the two of us."

"I like that idea." I felt feminine inside—not my usual modus operandi, an independent woman who held men at arm's length.

"Then we could talk about you and me," he said.

"As in, a couple?" Leave it to me to blurt out my thoughts.

"Yes." He brought my fingertips to his lips. "Would you consider my courting you for a few months, followed by a marriage proposal?"

My jaw dropped open. "Are you serious? Just like that? No warning? I'm flattered, of course. But leap into a lifetime commitment?"

On the other hand, I'd spent too much time contemplating what might go wrong in life, spinning my wheels and getting nowhere. It wasn't as if I didn't find Zach attractive. Okay, drop-dead gorgeous, if I was honest. He was hardworking, reliable, and respected his parents. And apparently cared for me more than I ever imagined.

"You should marry someone younger," I said, "who can provide you with a boatload of children." I felt heat rising up my neck, filling my cheeks.

"We could try for a family," he said. "And adoption is always an option."

I couldn't believe we were having this intimate discussion, but adored every moment of it. "It would mean I couldn't move to Montana," I said.

"If you moved, I'd follow."

"You'd do that for me?"

"Genesis 2:24: Therefore a man shall leave his father and mother and be joined to his wife, and they shall become one flesh."

"Wow, you can quote the Bible. I'm impressed." I made a vow to start memorizing scripture.

Zach laughed, his baritone voice filling the car with good humor. As he put the transmission in first gear, his features turned serious. He gave me a sideways glance. "Promise to consider my proposal?" he asked.

"I can't imagine I'll think of much else."

Hey, wait a minute. Move across country in part to spend time with Zach? Had I ever met a man I could trust?

How would I know unless I took a chance?

"Yes, Zach, I could be happy living here."

EPILOGUE

Anna Gingerich stood in the barnyard watching the doors of Beth's minivan close, silencing the chatter of Isaac's family. Her beloved son Isaac sat in the front seat next to Beth. The rising sun cast a peach-colored hue across his face. He wore a sober expression, his gaze taking in the fields he'd plowed, nurtured, and toiled over his whole life.

What a good son he'd been to her. For his sake, she forced the corners of her mouth to angle up into a smile. No use giving Isaac regrets about leaving his mamm behind in Esther and Holly's care. Yes, Isaac had forgiven Esther, but Anna doubted he'd ever understand her. He was what folks called a straight arrow, his unwavering goal to serve God, his family, and his community.

Anna was glad her daughters-in-law and the grandchildren would wait several weeks to follow the men to Montana after packing and sending their belongings. Holly and Esther had promised to assist with the organizing and crating. Anna's primary job would be entertaining the youngest children. More time for her to say farewell to them. She'd miss them something fierce.

Holly and Esther stood on either side of Anna. Both women waved, but Anna couldn't rouse the energy to lift her hand. Her left knee throbbed and her head weighed more than a cast-iron pot.

The van's engine turned over and Beth released the parking brake.

"Bye-bye," Holly called, although Isaac and his family didn't seem to hear. Their attention was fixed on their destination: the Lancaster railway station, to drop off Isaac. An adventure. Well, Anna had survived enough adventures for one lifetime. She was content to remain behind with Esther and Holly, her new incentives to hang on, to keep living.

"I wonder, will I ever see my beloved son again?" she said, then hung her head. She knew the Lord didn't want her spreading her doubts to Esther and Holly. So she quoted Philippians 4:6, "Be anxious for nothing."

Esther pivoted toward Anna. Curving an arm around her, Esther finished the biblical verse. "But in everything by prayer and supplication, with thanksgiving, let your requests be made known to God."

"Yah, I will keep praying," said Anna.

The wheels of the van kicked up gravel as the vehicle stole away. Too quickly, in Anna's mind. It occurred to her that Beth was often in a hurry, but then again, Anna was grateful for the young woman, her stand-in daughter for so many a year. Now Anna had her own flesh-and-blood daughter and granddaughter at her side. A miracle, truly.

Holly turned to Anna and said, "Beth told me your blood tests should come in today. She'll call Dr. Brewster's office on the way home from the station and find out if the results are in."

"I liked Dr. Brewster," Anna said.

The endocrinologist had treated her with respect and taken reams of notes. "Simple blood work might solve this mystery," the doctor had stated after scanning Anna's chart. Anna had thought she sounded like a hypochondriac when listing her complaints, but Dr. Brewster persisted. "I notice your blood pressure's high, Anna. Ever feel dizzy? Is your concentration and memory foggy? Poor sleep? Do the bones in your arms and legs ache? Is your hair thinning?" Esther had accompanied her in the examination room. Anna felt embarrassed having her daughter hear her answer every question with an affirmative.

Anna watched Beth's van disappear from sight. "I'm so old, not worth the trouble," she said to Esther and Holly. But, frankly, she was clinging to life more than ever. She recalled a preacher once mentioning King Hezekiah in the book of Isaiah. The Lord heard King Hezekiah's prayers and saw his tears, and granted him fifteen more years.

Holly turned to Anna and crested her arm around Anna's shoulder. "After all the time I've waited to find you, don't you dare give up," Holly said.

"I'm feelin' hopeful," Esther said, although Anna knew Esther didn't appreciate Beth's involvement.

The three women stood like a triangle, Holly and Esther's arms and hips supporting Anna. Ach, she'd never felt so sad and elated at the same time, like the full moon tugging the ocean in both directions.

Anna glanced up at a sliver of a moon, soon to fade from sight. She'd been living in an eclipse, a shadow, all these many years. But now the sun's radiance would brighten her world in all its glory. God's glory. This reunion was the Creator's plan all along. He'd answered her prayers tenfold. In his time.

"Mamm?" Esther paused, as if pondering her words. Was she going back to Seattle now that Holly was here?

"I'm all ears," Anna said, wishing she could plug them.

Esther's mouth expanded into a grin, reminding Anna of Esther as a girl when she'd cracked an egg and found a double yoke.

"I've decided to take baptism classes next summer and become a church member," Esther said. The last words Anna expected to hear.

Anna's knee pain—she'd been hiding it since sunup—vanished. She stood taller, her arms gaining strength. "I'm glad, Essie. More than I can tell ya. 'Tis the best gift you could give me."

"I thought you were already baptized at Dori's church before I was born," Holly said. "Hey, what's on your agenda? You planning to marry Nathaniel?"

Esther's first two fingers covered her lips, but she couldn't mask her excitement.

"Well?" Holly tugged on Esther's sleeve. "Has he asked you?"

Esther gave her head the smallest nod.

"And you accepted?" Holly said, but Esther didn't answer.

Anna knew better than to ask personal questions about engagements, even of her daughter. "Holly, 'tis the People's way to wait for a couple to announce their intentions. You, on the other hand, may tell us yours. What are your plans with your young man?" She watched Holly's cheeks blush like Anna's favorite cerise-pink chrysanthemums. Why, Anna felt good enough to tidy the garden today.

"Which man might that be?" Holly shrugged one shoulder. "I have a suitor back in Seattle."

Anna chuckled. "*Liewe*—dear girl—I can see it in both your and Zach's eyes. You're smitten with each other."

Last Sunday, Isaac had rigged the buggy and taken his family, Anna, and Esther to church service at a neighbor's, but Holly had chosen to go to Zach's Mennonite house of worship. Not Anna's preference, yet she didn't voice a single complaint.

A smile fanned across Holly's *lieblich*—lovely—face. "I was going to let Zach make the announcement." Holly nabbed a glimpse at Esther, whose eyes widened as if she hadn't a clue what Holly would say next.

Then Holly grinned in Anna's direction. "Mommy Anna, we're courting."

"You're getting engaged to Zach?" Esther said.

"Yup."

"I can't believe it!"

"Mom, aren't you going to congratulate me?"

"Yah, but you caught me off guard. Do you two have a ring and a date?"

"Not yet, but we're going to the jeweler's tomorrow."

She turned to Anna. "We have a favor to ask you, unless your bishop wouldn't like it. We're wondering if in a few months we could hold our wedding reception right here in your house."

"Everything's moving so quickly," Anna said, a flurry of emotions scattering through her mind like snowflakes.

"I assumed you'd be happy for me."

"Well now, I am." Anna maintained her composure and kept her voice light. "Kaffi and a cinnamon roll would taste gut, don't ya think? Let's go inside. We have much to talk about."

Acknowledgments

Thank you, Don Pape, and the entire staff at David C Cook. Thank you, Jamie Chavez, for your inspired editing.

Deepest gratitude for my steadfast and encouraging critique group: Judy Bodmer, Peg Kehle, Kathy Kohler, Thornton Ford, Paul Malm, and Marty Nystrom—each a talented writer.

I greatly appreciate Lancaster County readers and advisors Sam and Susie Lapp, and Norma Gehman. Many thanks to relative Mark Roberts, who shared his childhood years with me, and to his mother, Miriam Roberts, of New Holland, Pennsylvania.

Thanks to the kind and informed staff of the Lancaster Historical Mennonite Society, an incredible resource. And to authors Donald B. Kraybill and Stephen M. Scott. *Ich bedank mich* to Professor Emeritus C. Richard Beam and his wife, Dorothy. Thank you to novelist Suzanne Woods Fisher, who helped me at the drop of a hat.

Enormous gratitude to my literary agent, Sandra Bishop!

... a little more ...

When a delightful concert comes to an end,

the orchestra might offer an encore.

When a fine meal comes to an end,

it's always nice to savor a bit of dessert.

When a great story comes to an end,

we think you may want to linger.

And so, we offer ...

AfterWords—just a little something more after you

have finished a David C Cook novel.

We invite you to stay awhile in the story.

Thanks for reading!

Turn the page for ...

- **Discussion Questions**
- **About the Author**

Discussion Questions for
Leaving Lancaster

1. How would you feel if you discovered a parent or guardian had kept momentous secrets from you—in Holly's case that she has relatives she's longed for but has never met? What were Esther's motivations?

2. What are Holly's emotions when she learns her mother has been lying to her? Has a trusted person lied to you? What was your response?

3. Esther's lifelong goal has been to protect Holly. In what ways has she uplifted and helped Holly? Can you identify with Esther?

4. Esther feels responsible for her former husband Samuel's death. Do you think she is? It's safe to say most of us harbor a hidden secret. What is the worst scenario should your secret be revealed?

5. Holly is a grown woman, but inside, in many ways a child. What messages from her youth does she carry that have kept her from maturing and maintaining a good self-image?

6. How could growing up without a dad cause a young woman to feel insecure and not trust men? How did it affect Holly's belief in God?

7. Are Holly's visions of her deceased father unrealistic? Will visiting his gravesite, traveling to the Vietnam War Memorial, or tracking down his old buddies help her heal her wounds? What are other ways to come to peace with her loss? What does Zach mean when he mentions a heavenly Father?

8. If Holly and Esther were separated, as Esther was from her own mother, Esther feels she'd be losing a part of herself. How will having her sons living in Montana affect Mommy Anna? Keep in mind: The Amish do not use airplanes. How would having a beloved family member or friend move away affect you?

9. It seems both Holly and Esther are jumping into relationships and taking great risks with men they barely know. What are Zach's and Nathaniel's good qualities? Can they be trusted and, if so, why? Do you think after growing up in the city Holly can be content living in the country with a veterinarian? Will their relationship last?

10. Holly's mother, Esther, is planning to take baptism classes and join the Amish church. Do you think Holly should explore the Amish church more thoroughly? Is she making a wise choice attending the Mennonite church with Zach's family?

11. Holly is going to be nearby when Beth's dog, Missy, delivers her litter of pups. As far as we know, Mommy Anna has never kept a dog in the house but might be willing to make an allowance for Holly. What other exceptions are Holly's grandmother making

for her and Esther? When has someone shown you bounteous generosity?

12. How would this story have differed if Mommy Anna, Holly's grandma, had harbored bitter resentment toward Esther and not forgiven her? How would this have affected Holly? Do you cling to resentment toward anyone?

13. In Matthew 18:22, Jesus instructed Peter to forgive seventy times seven. Does this sound unrealistic and impossible? How did you feel when Holly's mother, Esther, and her dad's mother forgave each other? How do you feel when someone forgives you?

14. As kids, Holly's parents were instructed that no violence is justifiable. What are your thoughts on total passivism? Have you ever turned the other cheek in the face of adversity? What was the outcome?

15. What other insights and information did you learn about the Amish through reading this book? Are there any Amish customs or practices you might wish to emulate?

About the Author

Kate Lloyd is a novelist, a mother of two sons, and a passionate observer of human relationships. A native of Baltimore, Kate spends time with family and friends in Lancaster County, Pennsylvania, the inspiration for *Leaving Lancaster*. She is a member of the Lancaster County Mennonite Historical Society. Kate and her husband live in the Pacific Northwest, the setting for Kate's first novel, *A Portrait of Marguerite*. Kate studied painting and sculpture in college. She has worked a variety of jobs, including car salesperson and restaurateur.

Kate loves hearing from readers and can be reached through her website, www.katelloyd.net; on Facebook, www.facebook.com/katelloydbooks; or writing to her at:

Kate Lloyd
PO Box 204, 4616 25th Ave. NE
Seattle, WA 98105

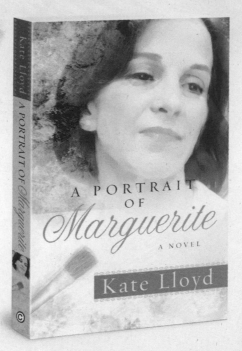